BLOOD LIGHTNING

ALSO BY W. MICHAEL GEAR AND KATHLEEN O'NEAL GEAR

Big Horn Legacy

Dark Inheritance

The Foundation

Fracture Event

Long Ride Home

The Mourning War

Raising Abel

Rebel Hearts Anthology

Sand in the Wind

Thin Moon and Cold Mist

Black Falcon Nation Series

Flight of the Hawk Series

The Moundville Duology

Saga of a Mountain Sage Series

The Wyoming Chronicles

The Anasazi Mysteries

PRAISE FOR THE PEACEMAKER'S TALE SERIES

"Devoted fans expecting another meaty, mystical story thoroughly grounded in historical fact and archaeological evidence will not be disappointed as the stage is set for the final chapter in the fiery Iroquois saga."

— *BOOKLIST*

"Rich in cultural detail. Both longtime fans and newcomers will be satisfied. Another fine entry in an ambitious, long-running series."

— *KIRKUS REVIEWS*

"A timely saga of environmental catastrophe and misguided hubris...Drawing on their backgrounds in archeology, the Gears vividly recreate Paleolithic America in this enchanting and instructive novel."

— *PUBLISHERS WEEKLY*

BLOOD LIGHTNING

THE PEACEMAKER'S TALE
BOOK SIX

W. MICHAEL GEAR
KATHLEEN O'NEAL GEAR

Blood Lightning
Paperback Edition
Copyright © 2024 (As Revised) W. Michael Gear and Kathleen O'Neal Gear

WOLFPACK PUBLISHING
1707 E. Diana Street
Tampa, Florida 33609

wolfpackpublishing.com

All rights reserved. No part of this book may be reproduced by any means without the prior written consent of the publisher, other than brief quotes for reviews.

This book is a work of fiction. Any references to historical events, real people or real places are used fictitiously. Other names, characters, places and events are products of the author's imagination, and any resemblance to actual events, places or persons, living or dead, is entirely coincidental.

Illustrations by Ellisa Mitchel.

Paperback ISBN 978-1-63977-586-6
eBook ISBN 978-1-63977-585-9

To Lynda Walters
English teacher at Tulare Union High School,
California, 1969-1972

She taught an amazing course called "Supernatural Literature," where her students studied the works of writers like H. P. Lovecraft and Edgar Allan Poe. I well remember the outcry it caused in our small community, especially the charges that she was teaching Satanism. Despite pressure to stop, Mrs. Walters had the courage to stand up and continue teaching her students that classic body of literature. I know it wasn't easy.
Thank you, Mrs. Walters. You will never know how much that class meant to me.

Your student, Kathleen O'Neal Gear

NONFICTION INTRODUCTION

The Iroquoian story of the Peacemaker is one of North America's most beautiful epics. There are literally hundreds of recorded versions, often contradictory, and many more versions that are kept alive only by Haudenosaunee *hegeota*, storytellers. These oral historians are the Keepers of the sacred stories. Despite sometimes profound differences, most of the Keepings share two elements: the story opens in a ferocious landscape of war, and three people are struggling to end it: Jigonsaseh, Dekanawida, and Hiyawento. For more information on the grisly nature of the warfare, please see the introduction to *People of the Longhouse*.

Let's talk about "Keepings." What is a Keeping? Keeping takes many forms and is a sacred obligation.

Women were the Keepers of the Three Sisters:

corn, beans, and squash. They were responsible for the agricultural fields, planting, tending, harvesting, and preserving the crops. As part of their Keeping obligations, women controlled food and its distribution. They also decided when to make war and when to make peace. Often, this duty included fighting and leading warriors into battle.

As a fascinating example, in 1687, the French monarchy decided it would steal Seneca lands. King Louis XIV assigned one of his most decorated war heroes, the Marquis de Denonville, to lead the offensive. The marquis believed the best way to accomplish the task was to destroy the Seneca government at the roots. He used a standard European military strategy that had proven very effective in dealing with the wild tribes of Ireland and Scotland. First, he invited the Haudenosaunee leaders—the Grand Council and several clan mothers—to a peace conference, then took them prisoner and shipped them to France as slaves. Fortunately, he was so ignorant of the role of women in Iroquoian society that he unwittingly left the most powerful woman in the nation, the Jigonsaseh, untouched. She made him regret it, for she called up an army of men and women warriors so powerful they virtually destroyed the marquis' forces, and chased the terrified survivors all the way back to Montreal, handing him the most ignominious rout of his life. In 1688, the marquis pleaded for peace and agreed to all of the Jigonsaseh's demands, including dismantling the French fort at Niagara and returning the captives who had survived their brutal slavery—O'Callaghan, 1: 68-69. See also, Mann, *Iroquoian Women*, chapter 3.

Men were the Keepers of the forest. They were generally responsible for the hunt and the execution of warfare. They cleared the fields for the crops, built the longhouses, and constructed palisades and canoes. They hunted, fished, fought, and brought home captives to restore the spiritual strength of the clans. Men were appointed as village chiefs by clan mothers, after which they organized and planned attacks, and served on the national Grand Council, relaying the wishes of their Peoples. They were also responsible for negotiating agreements related to trade, territory, and war.

Men and women also kept their own histories. There were "men's stories," and "women's stories," and they were generally told around separate council fires. This cultural tradition, virtually unknown to the early ethnographers, dictated which versions of the Peacemaker story survived to be passed down through the centuries. Why? Because the first recorders of the Peacemaker epic were almost exclusively European men who'd been born and bred in the Victorian era. Not only were they oblivious to the fact that women kept their own stories, but as outsiders, they may not have been allowed to sit at the Women's Council fires to hear their sacred stories. As a result, nearly every version of the Peacemaker epic that was recorded was a men's story. Most of Jigonsaseh's story has been lost.

There are a few fragments, however. One of our goals in the Peacemaker series of books has been to pull the fragments together and restore Jigonsaseh to her proper place in the epic. From what we can tell, she was the pivotal clan matron responsible for the success of the League. She approved the Peacemaker's mission, and he consulted her on every important decision. One fragment says he refused to begin any meeting until she arrived. Without her support and leadership, it's doubtful that Dekanawida and Hiyawento would have been able to establish a lasting peace. We owe special thanks to Haudenosaunee scholars Pete Jemison and Barbara Mann for their meticulous research on Jigonsaseh.

We know from the oral history that Jigonsaseh used food to create alliances. One story fragment says she fed every passing war party, no matter their nation. She did this to buy goodwill and keep her People safe. It is also probable that she used food to create other types of alliances. The oral history says that Jigonsaseh—at the request of Dekanawida—went to the People of the Flint, the

Mohawk, to convince them to join an alliance to overthrow the evil cannibal sorcerer Atotarho. She also rallied the female leaders of the nations and convinced them of the truth of Dekanawida's vision. She was apparently a formidable politician. She used the clan system as the glue to hold the fragile alliance together long enough for the idea of the League to gain a foothold. As such, she co-founded the League with Dekanawida and Hiyawento.

The few hints we have about her personal history are intriguing. In one version of the epic—Hewitt, 1932—she is Dekanawida's mother. In another, she's his grandmother. In yet another, she doesn't know Dekanawida at all. Rather, she is from a different nation, the People of the Mountain—the Seneca. Dekanawida seeks her counsel early in his life, just as he's beginning his peace initiative. Some stories say she was born among the Wyandot Attiwandaronk, also known as the Neutral Nation. A few versions say she was the direct descendant of Sky Woman, through her daughter, the Lynx. Others say Jigonsaseh was the Lynx.

Regardless of the diversity of elements, one thing is almost certain: She was the head clan matron of the League of the Iroquois. In Chief David Cusick's Keeping—"Sketches of Ancient History of the Six Nations," 1825—the Jigonsaseh in the Peacemaker story was the ninth woman to carry that name.

The other two heroes, Dekanawida and Hiyawento, have been extensively chronicled. An excellent discussion of both characters can be found under "The Second Epoch of Time," in the *Encyclopedia of the Haudenosaunee*, edited by Bruce Johansen and Barbara Mann.

Hiyawento—Ayonwantha—became, by virtually all accounts, Dekanawida's closest friend and adviser. However, story variants picture him as either the right-hand man of the evil genius Atotarho, or Atotarho's greatest political opponent and the victim of the chief's treachery. Sometimes, as in the Johnson's 1881 version, Hiyawento is the Peacemaker. Dekanawida doesn't exist, and Jigonsaseh and Atotarho appear only at the end, and play bit parts.

Nearly every nation claims he was either born among their people, or they adopted him. The tragedy that befell his family, as you will see in *The Broken Land*, is the central feature of Hiyawento's story. Though sometimes his daughters are involved, other times it's his brothers or his wife. His grief drives him to create the "Truth belts," known in modern society as wampum belts. This term, however, is incorrect. *Wampum* is an Algonkian term. The correct Iroquoian term is *otekoa*. Hiyawento's grief was also the source for the creation of the Condolence Ceremony, which is the sacred heart of the League.

The great villain, Atotarho—Tadadaho—in most versions, is depicted as the mad tyrant of the Onondaga, whom many believed to be a cannibal sorcerer. However, in Chief David Cusick's Keeping, Atotarho is the hero of the story. None of the other characters exist.

The Peacemaker's personal history is perhaps the most interesting. His stories are certainly the most divergent. As with Hiyawento, nearly every nation claims he was born among their people, or adopted by them. The earliest versions of Dekanawida's life bear striking resemblances to the life of the Creation Hero, Tarachiawagon. He is shown as a spiritual emissary, a visionary man, who came to the aid of the Iroquois when they were on the verge of destroying themselves. Other versions say he was born of a virgin among the Wyandots north of Lake Ontario. These versions show him being abused by his people, who did not believe in him. When he left them, he paddled across Lake Ontario in a white stone canoe and made peace among the Iroquois. Afterward, he traveled across the ocean and became the person known to Christians as Jesus.

While every major plot element you encounter in these books can be found in written sources, the oral history, or the archaeological record, the profoundly different versions of the story pose unique problems for anyone trying to decipher what actually might have happened. As you read this novel, you will see how we sifted through the different versions, pieced them together, and made sense of them.

No matter which variant you believe, the Peacemaker story is astonishing. In a time of extreme climatic and cultural stress, Dekanawida managed to pull together five warring nations. We think his message of compassion and spiritual unity is as powerful today as it was six hundred years ago. Given current events, perhaps more so.

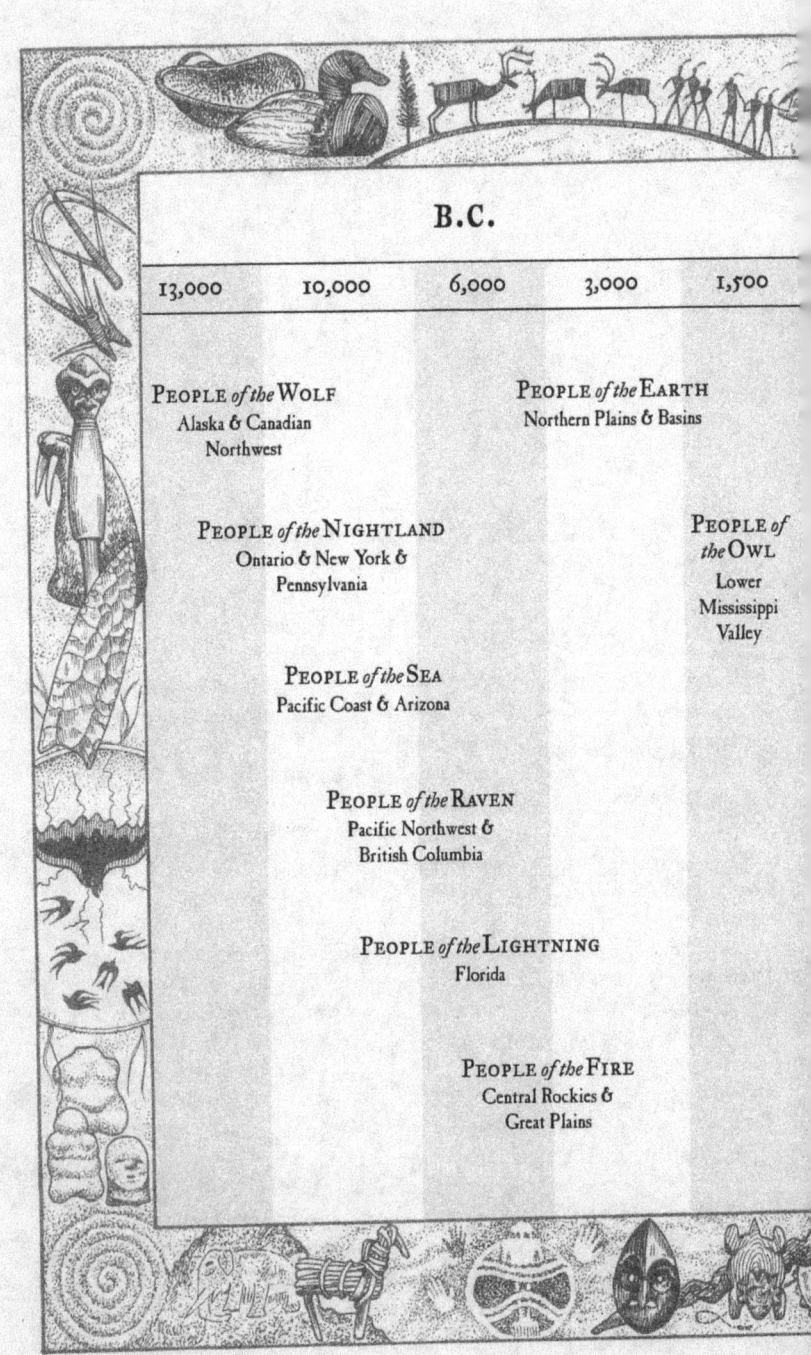

B.C.

| 13,000 | 10,000 | 6,000 | 3,000 | 1,500 |

PEOPLE *of the* WOLF
Alaska & Canadian Northwest

PEOPLE *of the* EARTH
Northern Plains & Basins

PEOPLE *of the* NIGHTLAND
Ontario & New York & Pennsylvania

PEOPLE *of the* OWL
Lower Mississippi Valley

PEOPLE *of the* SEA
Pacific Coast & Arizona

PEOPLE *of the* RAVEN
Pacific Northwest & British Columbia

PEOPLE *of the* LIGHTNING
Florida

PEOPLE *of the* FIRE
Central Rockies & Great Plains

A.D.

| 0 | 200 | 1,000 | 1,100 | 1,300 | 1,400 |

PEOPLE of the LAKES
East-Central Woodlands
& Great Lakes

PEOPLE of the WEEPING EYE
Mississippi Valley
& Tennessee

PEOPLE of the MASKS
Ontario & Upstate New York

PEOPLE of the THUNDER
Alabama & Mississippi

PEOPLE of the RIVER
Mississippi Valley

PEOPLE of the LONGHOUSE
New York
& New England

PEOPLE of the SILENCE
Southwest Anasazi

PEOPLE of the MOON
Northwest New Mexico
& Southwest Colorado

PEOPLE of the MIST
Chesapeake Bay

BLOOD LIGHTNING

1

Sleet pattered on the roof of the longhouse, creating a faint chatter that competed with the crackling fire and the whispers in the Council House at Bur Oak Village. Fires blazed down the length of the house, lighting the faces of the people who'd assembled to hear Gonda's story.

"Give me just a—a moment." Gonda, Speaker for the Warriors of White Dog Village, lifted his hands to massage his temples. He was a thin, wiry man with a moonish face and brown eyes. He'd seen thirty-eight summers pass, most of them in Yellowtail Village. Never, in all that time, had he felt this weary. Evil Spirits had been cavorting in his head since the attack two days ago, plunging stilettos behind his eyes as though trying to puncture a way to freedom.

When the pain had eased a little, he lowered

his hands and prepared to finish the telling. He stood beside the central fire, examining the faces of the Ruling Council of the People of the Standing Stone. Concentric rings of benches encircled the fire. Each person had his or her place. The six clan matrons and High Matron Kittle sat on the innermost ring of benches closest to the fire. Behind them, on the middle ring, sat the village chiefs and village matrons. The outermost ring was crowded with the Speakers. Each of the five villages had four Speakers, elected representatives who conveyed various group decisions and asked questions on the group's behalf. The Speakers for the Warriors sat on the outermost northern benches, including the War Chief of Bur Oak Village, Skenandoah, and War Chief Deru of Yellowtail Village. The Speakers for the Women sat on the eastern benches. The Speakers for the Men occupied the western benches, and the Speakers for the Shamans filled the southern benches.

Gonda responded, "The sickness began the same day the baskets of corn arrived. Our village was deeply grateful for the food sent by the Ruling Council. Portions were divided for each longhouse. By nightfall, most people were so ill they could barely stand. The attack came at dawn the next morning." As he spoke, the whispers quieted, and expressions went somber. "Those who could carry a weapon did so, but we couldn't defend all three palisades. Our war chief, whose name I cannot speak for he is traveling the Path of Souls, ordered all of our fighters to stand on the outermost palisade. As each palisade was overwhelmed, we moved to the next. We were simply too weak to defend the village. The battle was over in less than two hands of time."

Matron Kittle stood. Still, an extremely handsome woman, the firm contours of her oval face had just begun to sag. He could see it in the slight wrinkles at her throat and the lines at the corners of her deeply set dark eyes. She wore her black hair pulled back and twisted into a knot at the base of her skull and fastened with a tortoiseshell comb. Her beautiful white cape, reserved for council meetings, glimmered with circlets of seashells. "Forgive us for keeping you here, Speaker. We realize you are tired, but we must understand what happened so that we can immediately begin planning a response."

Gonda nodded. "I understand."

Kittle continued, "Are you suggesting that it was the baskets of corn that sickened White Dog Village and made them vulnerable to attack?"

"Yes, but we cannot say for certain that the corn was to blame. If we'd had more time, High Matron, we could have verified our suspicions. As it was, we barely had time enough to escape with our lives."

"High Matron," a deep voice called from the eastern benches, and a very tall woman rose to her feet.

Gonda's gaze fixed on her. She'd cut her gray-streaked black hair short in mourning, and it made her small narrow nose and full lips seem all the more beautiful to him. Despite all the unpleasantness that had gone between them over the twelve long summers since she'd divorced him, his heart gladdened. Just the sight of her was like the feel of a war club in his hand; it gave him confidence that he could face anything.

"Koracoo, Speaker for the Women of Yellowtail Village, proceed," Matron Kittle said.

Koracoo folded her arms, and firelight played through the reddish fur of her woven foxhide cape. "In recent days, we have all heard similar stories from the survivors of Sedge Marsh Village. It must be obvious to this council now that someone is poisoning the baskets of corn that we send to needy villages."

"High Matron?" War Chief Deru said from the northern benches. His massive bearlike body rose and loomed in the murky shadows. Oddly, firelight pooled in his caved-in cheek, turning it amber while the rest of his features remained dim.

"Proceed, War Chief," Kittle acknowledged him.

"If Speaker Koracoo is right, someone is trying

to make it look as though we are poisoning these villages. Which of our enemies is clever enough to accomplish this?"

"It must be a man or woman who can freely walk through both Hills and Standing Stone villages," Koracoo said. "A Trader? Or a messenger traveling under the white arrow?"

Kittle lifted her pointed chin and surveyed the council. "Since both Sedge Marsh Village and White Dog Village were attacked by Atotarho's warriors, the man behind it seems clear. The question is, who is Atotarho's poisoner?"

Daga, Matron of the Turtle Clan in White Dog Village, braced a hand on the bench and grunted as she rose to her feet on spindly legs. Her fifty-six summers showed in her snowy hair and the deep wrinkles around her toothless mouth. "As you all know, I was here attending the betrothal feast of the high matron's granddaughter when the attack came on my home. Because of that, there are many things I do not know about what went on in White Dog Village. Speaker Gonda, what is your opinion about the poisoner?"

He ran a hand through his black hair. "I cannot even offer a guess, Matron Daga. The day the corn arrived was a day of joy for us. Every longhouse feasted. Many people honored the gift by wearing their best clothing, jewelry, and painting their faces. Identifying a stranger would have been difficult."

Chief Yellowtail lifted a hand. He stood right behind Kittle. As he rose, his shoulder-length dark gray hair swayed around his wrinkled face. "If the Ruling Council of the People of the Hills is to blame, is it trying to provoke us into attacking Atotarho Village?"

"Blessed gods, I pray not," Gonda said. "They have four times as many warriors as we do. Such an assault would be doomed to failure and a foolish waste of our young warriors' lives."

Murmuring filled the council house. Gonda spread his feet and waited. He needed to get back to his sick wife, Pawen, who lay in the Bear Clan longhouse being tended by his daughter, Tutelo. Pawen had been very ill before the attack, but after the poisoned corn and the long journey here...

"High Matron, how can we be sure it was the corn, and not some other evil? Perhaps a spell was cast upon White Dog Village by Atotarho's army of witches?" War Chief Skenandoah asked. He had seen around thirty-four summers, and had a square chin and thin lips. He was of medium height, and his short black hair had started to gray at the temples.

Gonda replied, "We aren't sure, War Chief. I apologize if I gave that impression. We suspect the corn was poisoned, but the illness may have been witchery. Who can say?"

The phrase "army of witches" was whispered throughout the council as nods went round. Gonda stumbled and righted himself.

High Matron Kittle noticed. "If there are no objections, perhaps we should dismiss this council and reconvene tomorrow. Speaker Gonda needs to rest, and it will give us all time to consider his words. Do I hear any objections?"

There were none.

Kittle called, "We will reconvene this council tomorrow morning just after dawn. Go in peace."

People began to file out of the council house. Gonda didn't wish to be jostled by the crowd, so he continued standing by the fire, biding his time. When most of the councilors had gone, he saw Koracoo looking at him. She excused herself from the group of Yellowtail matrons that had her surrounded and made her way through the benches to get to him.

He gave her a tired smile. "You look well."

"And you look like you can barely stay on your feet. How is Pawen?"

He shook his head and looked away. "Tutelo is with her. I—I don't know."

Koracoo put a gentle hand on his shoulder. "She's young and strong. She'll get well."

He jerked a nod and changed the subject. "You

must tell me about Sky Messenger's Dream. I've already heard five different versions."

She looked around at the few people still standing nearby, then slipped her arm through his. "Let us speak in private. I have much to tell you."

"Are the Yellowtail matrons finished with you? They look like they're still waiting to talk more."

"They have my answer. They're just discussing the timing."

She tightened her hold on his arm. At her touch, he realized that, without being conscious of it, he'd needed her closeness. This was the first time they'd seen each other in two summers. Not so long ago, even a glance from her would have fired his veins. Now, her touch was as warm and comfortable as a worn pair of moccasins. She looked down at him, for she was taller than he, and smiled in the old way he loved—smiling as though they'd never said hateful things to each other.

"I swear I'm getting old and decrepit," she said.

"Well, the good thing about being a legendary former war chief is that few men will ever be brave enough to suggest it."

She smothered a chuckle. "Then I am more fortunate than I deserve."

He clutched her arm as they made their way out of the council house and across the plaza through the cold sleet. When they stood beneath the porch of the Bear Clan longhouse, Koracoo stopped.

"Let's speak of the important things out here."

He nodded. "Of course."

Her warm smile turned into a bleak, tight-lipped expression. "First, I want you to know that I believe battle with Atotarho Village is a certainty."

"Why?"

"War Chief Hiyawento was just here. He came to deliver a message from the Hills Ruling Council."

"A threat, no doubt."

"Yes. They told us not to attempt to make any other alliances with Hills villages or they would destroy us. Many members of our Ruling Council believe that it is foolish to live in fear that they will carry out their threat and wiser to attack them first."

Gonda bowed his head. "That would be a grave error. They will cut us up and lay us down like a summer hailstorm does the corn. Are you trying to talk sense into them?"

"Trying without much success."

"Is this just pride or—?"

"No, it's Sky Messenger's Dream."

For a long, quiet moment, they gazed at each other. Between them lay many summers of warring side by side, of mad, desperate passion, of two beloved children stolen and rescued and now grown to adulthood...so many intimate moments unthinkingly shared. And he could tell from the way she ground her teeth that she needed someone to talk to, someone she trusted.

Gonda said, "He Dreamed the end of the world, or so I've heard."

"He says that we must end this war, and if we do not, there is a great darkness coming."

With a touch of irony, he said, "You, naturally, believe that means making peace with our enemies. Matron Kittle, however, thinks it means annihilating them. Is that pretty much it?"

A small, hard-edged smile curved her lips. "Pretty much."

Gonda squinted out across the plaza, watching the sleet fall. It bounced from the frozen ground as though alive. "With your mother gone, you will soon be the Yellowtail Village matron, won't you?"

"I have agreed to the Requickening Ceremony, yes. That's what the matrons were discussing in the council house."

"When will the ritual take place?"

"Tomorrow, midmorning."

He sighed. "Then this is the last day of our lives when I will be able to call you Koracoo. Tomorrow, you will become Matron Jigonsaseh. The following day, you will have considerably more power to direct the future course of the nation."

Her expression tightened. "Village matrons have power in their own villages. In the Ruling Council, however, each voice is just one of many."

He remembered all the times he'd called her a "peacemaker" with loathing in his voice. Apparently, so did she. She had a guarded expression on her face, as though preparing to hear the same words she'd always heard from him.

Instead, he said, "Let me speak with what's left of the White Dog Village council. Perhaps I can convince them to back your peace efforts. The Spirits know we cannot win a war against the Hills People. There simply aren't enough of us to wage the fight."

When he looked back at her, he saw an unsettling mixture of relief and old love in her eyes. "I would like to have Bahna present Sky Messenger's vision to your council, if you think that would be acceptable."

"I'm sure they'd rather hear it from your lips, but I'll ask."

She walked forward and drew aside the entry curtain. Warm air rushed out, and when it struck his face, he shivered.

She said, "Let's tend to those who need us. Perhaps, if you are not too tired, we can speak more later."

"I'd like that."

Just before Gonda ducked through, Koracoo

said, "Gonda, immediately after the Requickening, I'm leaving."

"Leaving? This is hardly the time for the new matron of Yellowtail Village to be away."

She gazed at him without blinking, as though worried how he was going to respond to what she was about to say. "Sky Messenger asked me to carry his vision to Chief Cord."

A tiny thread of old jealousy went through him, which amused him. It had been twelve long summers since she'd removed Gonda as her deputy war chief and installed Cord in his place. What did it matter now?

"Well," he said, "we need more warriors. If you can convince Cord to join us, even just for this battle, it will help."

She gave him a grateful smile, and Gonda ducked beneath the curtain and headed for Tutelo's chamber, where his ill wife rested.

Cord. Why did it have to be Cord?

2

Four nights later, Taya and Sky Messenger made camp in the hollow of a toppled pine. The deep hole had been gouged when the old giant had blown over in a windstorm. It was filled with rocks and gravel and, in her opinion, created the worst place possible to try to sleep. They'd stowed their canoe, hidden it in a pile of brush along the river, and now were traveling on foot through the trackless wilderness of enemy territory.

As she arranged the kindling on the small island of dirt at the rear of the hole, she morosely glanced around. The hole, deeper than she was tall, didn't give her much to look at. High above, crooked pine roots zigzagged over her head, and beyond them, the campfires of the dead filled the sky and sparkled through the treetops. Her gaze drifted over the brush that fringed the rim of the hole—a mixture of ironwood saplings and dense holly. The forest canopy was luminous. Moonlight streamed between the sycamores, bleaching the bark where it struck or draping inky weblike shadows through the forest.

She couldn't see him, but she knew Sky Messenger was gathering wood. At night, he moved with the stealth of a cougar. Were it not for the occasional snapping of twigs, she wouldn't know he was out there. She couldn't hear Gitchi at all, but the wolf was at Sky Messenger's side. He always was.

Taya finished arranging the kindling, pulled her cape closely around her, and flopped back against the cold dirt wall. Rocks poked into her back. She shifted to avoid them.

When water started soaking through her cape, Taya jerked forward and dragged the doeskin around to look at the wet spot. Leaning forward, took a good look at the floor of the hole. Water glistened.

"Wonderful. Just wonderful," she groaned. This was the most abominable place he'd yet chosen to camp. Was he trying to punish her for wanting to go home? This just made her long for the warmth of her longhouse even more.

The brush rattled softly as Sky Messenger shouldered through the holly and carefully worked his way down into the hole. The old gray-faced wolf came through behind him. Taya watched them with an annoyed expression on her face. Sky Messenger carried a small pile of branches in the crook of his left arm.

"That's not nearly enough wood," she complained. "There's water in this hole." She pointed to the puddles. "We'll have to build a really big fire to dry it out."

"We can't, Taya. We're in the middle of Hills country. Our fire will have to be very small. Even that is a risk. You can have my blanket tonight. I'll be plenty warm wrapped in my cape." Sky Messenger knelt and placed the wood beside her kindling. As he pulled his pack off and drew out the little pot where he kept coals from their morning fire, she frowned at him. Grandmother Moon cast a queer silvery sheen over his cape and hair and threw the planes of his face into sharply contrasting arcs of gray and black. Sky Messenger carefully tucked the coals into her twig pile, added some dry leaves, and began blowing on the coals. It seemed to take forever before they reddened and flames licked through the tinder. She instantly extended her cold hands to the tiny blaze and sighed. "Thank the Spirits."

"Here, this will help." Sky Messenger reached into his pack and pulled out his carefully folded rabbit-fur blanket. Composed of worn, sewn-together rabbit pelts, it resembled a shabby patchwork. As he draped it over her shoulders, he said, "Why don't you also pull your blanket from your pack? Then you—"

"Please, do so."

He blinked as though annoyed, then he picked up her pack and tossed it at her. "I'm sure it's in there."

Indignant, she roughly rummaged through her pack and jerked out the wadded pine marten blanket. The thin strips of marten fur, woven tightly together, were beautiful and kept her very warm. She tugged it over her shoulders.

Sky Messenger added twigs to build up the blaze, but it was barely a palm's width across.

"Why can't we make a bigger fire?"

As though irritated because he'd already explained, he said again, "We're in Hills country. A big fire will reflect from the trees and can be seen from a good distance. It will also produce a lot of smoke. The scent carries. On a dark night, billowing smoke wouldn't matter so much, but tonight, there's a full moon. Streamers from a big fire would rise over the treetops and stretch out across the sky like a trail. Anyone could follow it to us."

"But a small fire will produce light and smoke, too."

"Yes, but not much, if it's built correctly. Down

here in this hole, a small fire will be almost invisible to passersby, and what little smoke rises will be diffused by the breeze and the thick branches over our heads. If anyone gets close enough, they'll still smell the smoke. Every fire is a risk."

She cocked her head and thought about it. "That makes sense. I guess I'd rather be alive than warm."

"I'd rather you be alive, as well."

They sat in silence, listening to the crackling of the fire, while he set up the dinner pot. The size of two fists put together, the pot held barely enough to feed them both, but since he always cooked, she never complained. It was a little like being at home in the longhouse where the newly adopted war captives cooked for her family. She wondered if he realized that and did it to make the nights easier for her or if it was just his way. Because it was small, the pot did boil faster, which allowed them to get more sleep. She liked that.

Sky Messenger drew his chert knife from his belt and sliced up the squirrel they'd snared at dusk, letting pieces drop into the pot, occasionally tossing a piece to Gitchi. After he'd poured water over the top and set the pot at the edge of the flames to boil, he sat down cross-legged beside her. His black cape spread around him in sculpted folds.

"Are you certain you'll be warm enough

without your blanket? I want you rested tomorrow."

He glanced up as though intrigued that she cared. "I'll be fine. I am accustomed to the cold."

He tossed another twig on the meager flames. Sparks sailed into the air. He frowned uneasily at them until they winked out amid the sycamore branches.

"Sky Messenger?" she said hesitantly. "This friend who saved you, the man we'll be stopping to see on the way home, who is he?"

Even pitched low, as it was tonight, his deep voice was startlingly beautiful. Gitchi eased down and propped his big muzzle in Sky Messenger's lap. Sky Messenger stroked his head. "He's a war chief. He taught me everything I know about honor and duty." More softly, he added, "And about self-sacrifice."

"Really?" She brightened. If he was a war chief, when they got there, they'd be feasted and showered with gifts. Her world was brightening. "I probably know him. Standing Stone war chiefs come to see Grandmother all the time. What's his name?"

"He's not Standing Stone, though he was born among our people."

It took a moment for her to digest this news. "You can't mean...are you trying to tell me that we're going to walk into an enemy village without a war party at our backs?"

"I think we'll be all right."

"You *think?*"

He leaned against the dirt wall and worked to find a comfortable position before he replied, "I can't be sure. I haven't seen him in a long while. And it won't be easy getting close to his village. But if we make it, I think he will protect us."

"What nation is he?" Her eyes slitted.

"He was adopted by the People of the Hills. The woman he loved was there. He went to her. They have three beautiful daughters." While he scratched Gitchi's ears, he gazed at the moon-glittered water that pooled between the rocks in the bottom of the hole. "I am happy for them, though I miss them very much."

Indignantly, she said, "And is your mother happy that you are friends with an enemy war chief? She was once a great Standing Stone war chief. Doesn't it worry her?"

"I'm sure it does." Love and respect softened his voice. "Especially now that she is the Speaker for the Women."

"And she will soon be the Yellowtail Village matron."

"I suspect she will, yes."

When his grandmother, Jigonsaseh, journeyed to the afterlife, the matrons of the Bear Clan would almost certainly cast their voices to requicken Jigonsaseh's soul in her daughter, Koracoo.

"We will all mourn the loss of your grandmother," Taya said sincerely. "She is a great leader. Matron Jigonsaseh must have been distressed when you told her you were giving up your weapons for good, and—"

"I haven't told her. The one time I got to speak with Grandmother...I had more pressing concerns. I needed her advice."

He seemed to be concentrating on the twinkling campfires of the dead.

Or perhaps he was assessing how much smoke from their fire was escaping through the treetops into the sky beyond.

"Her advice about what?"

"My...treason."

"So this was before your clan heard your vision?" It must have been, since afterward they'd absolved him of the crime, but his expression appeared uncertain.

He pulled a horn spoon from his pack and bent over the cooking pot, stirring it. The delicious smell of boiling squirrel wafted into the air. As the rising steam coated his tanned face, it seemed to flow into the lines at the corners of his eyes, making them appear deeper.

"It won't be long now," he said in a mild voice.

"You must be starving. We've been canoeing hard, and we walked a long way today."

He kept staring down into the pot, stirring it, and she tried to fathom what he could possibly be thinking. He looked like he wanted to tell her something but had decided against it. And she had the feeling it was more than just his discussion with Jigonsaseh about his treason. He was hiding something. His gaze had that haunted look that was becoming so familiar. He was no longer here with her but traveling some war trail in the past. Perhaps, with *her*.

"You're dreaming about her again, aren't you? Do you wish she was here instead of me?"

He looked up. The moonlight sheathed his eyes with such strength she could see her own reflection. "She *is* here. They all are." He touched his cape over his heart. "My friends never leave me."

"I don't understand what that means. I don't see them here."

His brows lifted as though not surprised, then he drew wooden cups and another spoon from his pack. "Let's eat so that we can get some rest."

As he ladled soup into the cups, Gitchi watched him, perhaps hoping for the last dregs. Taya took the cup Sky Messenger handed her, and her gaze wandered as she blew on the hot stew to cool it. Just when she started to sip, she saw something in the branches overhead. Her cup halted halfway to her lips. "Did you see that?"

"Hmm? What?" he asked around a half-chewed bite of squirrel.

An eerie chill prickled her spine. She went very still, as though her body sensed a predator nearby, even if her eyes didn't see one. The moonlit sycamore limbs seemed unusually bright against the night sky. Faint tendrils of smoke threaded the canopy, but nothing seemed amiss. Gitchi, however, silently rose to his feet and stared at the same place in the canopy.

Sky Messenger instantly set his cup down and followed Gitchi's gaze.

His brow furrowed as he examined the trees. Barely above a whisper, he repeated, "What did you see, Taya?"

"Probably just one of Grandmother Moon's tricks. A flicker of light, nothing more."

That didn't seem to soothe him. He stared at her fixedly, not blinking. "A flicker of light?"

"Well, yes." A breath of wind swirled around the hole, and the flames leaped, casting a gaudy gleam over his concerned face. "It was nothing, Sky Messenger. Just eat. I'm sorry I said anything." She took a drink of her squirrel soup, swallowing a chunk of squirrel whole, and forced a smile.

This time, he didn't smile back. "What color was the light?"

"I don't know, bluish, like a string of tarnished copper beads—"

In less than a heartbeat, he'd leaped to his feet and kicked dirt over the tiny blaze to smother it. Gitchi seemed to have turned to stone. Only his eyes moved as he watched Sky Messenger part the holly to stare out at the forest beyond.

Taya set her cup down, rose, and went to Sky Messenger's side, whispering, "Did you hear something?"

He patted his lips with his hand, instructing her to be silent.

She had to stand on her tiptoes to see through the dense brush. Out among the forest shadows, she thought she made out the dark, looming shapes of deer running the trail. It was a small herd, perhaps six or seven animals. She squinted as one animal veered closer to their hiding place. It must be a large buck for it...against the tracery of black shadows, the elusive wink of moonlight flashed on shell.

Her breathing died.

Sky Messenger used a hand to gesture for her to be perfectly still, but it was unnecessary. She'd already gone rigid.

The figure moved as though not tethered to the ground, drifting through the moonlight like one of the Flying Heads. Awful creatures, they were just heads with long trailing hair and huge paws that were continually grasping at things, for they were forever hungry. Or it might be one of the *oki,* Spirits who inhabited Powerful beings, including the seven Thunderers, rivers, certain rocks, valiant warriors, and sometimes lunatics. Even shamans, witches, or others who possessed supernatural Power had a companion oki that helped them.

Taya kept her eyes on the figure. The only sounds in the night were the soft hissing of her breathing and the panicked hammering of her heart.

Moonlight caught in the shell beads sewn to his cape, and there was a prolonged glimmer. Was he examining the brush where they hid?

The hair at the nape of her neck felt like it was on fire.

Warriors. Had they followed them from Bog Willow Village? Other shadows closed around the first. From the bristly ridge of hair down the center of their scalps, all but one were of the Flint People. The last man, the man with long black hair, hung at the rear. It was difficult to see him. The warriors hissed to each other and sniffed the breeze.

Taya turned to...

Sky Messenger hissed, *"Not one word."*

She had to lock her knees to keep standing. There was something horrifying about the sudden quiet. It was unnatural. The wind had stopped. The silvered branches resembled thousands of ancient knobby fingers reaching down to grab her, and Gitchi stood like a grass-stuffed dog skin, his unblinking yellow eyes on Sky Messenger.

The lead warrior said, "I don't see anything. I thought you said they'd be here. Isn't this the place your *hanehwa* told you about?"

Taya shuddered. Hanehwa were human skins that had been flayed whole by a witch and served as guards. These skin-beings never slept. They warned witches of danger by giving three shouts.

There was a pause and then the man with long black hair replied, "They're here. Somewhere close by."

Another warrior said, "You've been saying that for days. I was sure I smelled smoke, but I don't smell anything now."

"You imagined it," the lead man said, and swung his war club up to rest on his shoulder. "Come on. Let's keep searching. I want to get home before dawn."

Their words affected her bones like war clubs, striking and trembling them until she felt certain her skeleton would splinter to dust. A witch was hunting them, sending out his hanehwa to fly over the land and bring back information about their movements. That's the only thing it could mean. When she knew she was going to collapse from sheer terror, Sky Messenger slipped an arm around her shoulders and physically held her up. All she could do was squeeze her eyes closed and lean heavily against him.

Finally, she heard their steps moving away and held her breath, listening for voices. When they seemed to be gone, her fingernails dug into Sky Messenger's cape. He wrapped his arms around her and hugged her tightly.

"It's all right," he whispered. "They're gone. We're all right."

Terrified beyond rational thought, she stood dumbly, feeling the hard muscles of his thighs pressing against her and the large shell gorget he wore beneath his cape, crushing her breasts. A strange sensation, bewildering and frightening, came over her. Her thin body rigid with fury, she wildly slammed her fists into his chest, and just above a whisper, wept, "If you'd had weapons, I wouldn't have been so afraid! At least you could have kept a few of them busy while I made a run for it! Let me go, you *coward!*"

Rage and hate flowed into her. She wrenched her body from his arms, and her quaking knees instantly buckled. She collapsed to the ground in tears and sat there with her shoulders heaving, not making a sound. Dear gods, she wanted to be home!

Sky Messenger took one last look out at the forest. When he seemed certain they were truly gone, he knelt before her and lightly touched her hair, stroking it comfortingly. "We're going to be all right."

"How can you say that? We're being hunted by a witch! Didn't you understand that?"

"I've been hunted by witches before. We're going to be fine."

She wiped her eyes on her cape. "How could you escape a witch? They have armies of hanehwa and gahai, and—"

"Just do as I say, and we'll make it home. Can you stand up?"

"Of course I can." She rose on shaky legs.

He whispered, "The last man in line, the one with long black hair and big ears, looked over his shoulder again as they left. He wasn't satisfied with the decision to move on. He may return to search this spot."

She scrambled for her pack. Sky Messenger kept watch while she hastily packed their things. His face was grim, and for the first time, she saw the sweat pouring down his temples. It had glued his black hair to his cheeks.

"Why is a witch hunting us, Sky Messenger?"

With a warrior's deadly agility, he climbed out of the hole and extended a hand to her. Gitchi slid past her leg like warm smoke and eased through the holly. She reached for Sky Messenger's hand.

As he pulled her up, he whispered, "Evil needs no reason."

3
SKY MESSENGER

I quietly examine the dark shapes that fill the forest. The warriors are gone, but there is still something out there. I catch glimpses of it as it moves between the trees, pale and flickering. One of the gahai?

"What are we waiting for?" Taya asks.

"There's something I need to look at more closely."

"What do you mean?" She grips my sleeve in terror.

"Just wait here for me. If you see anything suspicious, dive back in that hole. I won't be long."

As I trot for the place where I saw the light, she calls, "Don't get out of my sight. Do you hear me? I want to be able to see you at all times!"

I lift a hand, showing that I've heard, and slow down to enter the thick trees. Gitchi moves at my side with ghostly stealth. When the wolf utters a barely audible growl, I subtly turn to look in the direction he's pointing.

As soon as my eyes adjust, I see them. Two small balls of light wander close to the ground. Prior to two moons ago, I'd never seen such things. Since then, I've seen more than I wish to, most floating aimlessly around destroyed villages.

"They aren't gahai," I whisper to Gitchi.

Gahai move purposely, in straight lines, because they always know where they are going. These lights float in one direction, then another, clearly confused.

I tiptoe forward and lean my shoulder against the trunk of a gigantic hickory to watch them. A herd of four deer emerge from the trees and keep watch on the lights, trailing them as they head into a narrow clearing, surrounded by plum trees. The bucks are young. Their forked antlers blaze whitely when they pass through the thin bars of moonlight.

Gitchi has probably always seen lost souls roaming the forests, but it is relatively new to me. I am fascinated and still learning about them.

I shift against the hickory trunk, and the scent of wet bark rises. These lights are tiny, barely larger than my thumb. Are they the lost souls of children?

The two lights bob into the meadow with the deer trotting behind them. When the bucks can see the sky clearly, they playfully kick up their hooves and charge headlong for the glowing balls. The souls seem to understand. I sense a happiness in the air, or perhaps it is relief that someone has found them. They hover perfectly still, allowing the bucks to scoop them into their antlers and toss them into the air, high over the treetops.

In awe, I watch them climb into the night sky until they disappear among the glittering campfires of the dead that crowd the Path of Souls.

"They're on their way now."

Yes, as you should be.

The words are so soft I'm not sure whether I actually heard them or if they exist only in my souls. When moccasins crunch the dry leaves to my right, I turn slowly.

He stands four paces away, with his gaze focused on the bucks in the meadow. There is an eerie quality to the man, a stillness so complete it is as though he has been standing beside me unnoticed all my life, just waiting for me to see him. His pale hands are folded in front of him. Against his black cape, they appear pure white. He wears sandals, apparently immune to the cold, or perhaps it is warm where he stands. He seems to be looking around the forest, and sadness pervades the air.

"Why are you here?" I ask.

"The cold."

"I don't understand."

His cape waffles as though touched by wind, though I do not feel a breeze.

"The cold has worked its way into the hearts of all living creatures and twined around the roots of the sycamores and oaks. It's killing us all. Especially him."

"Who?"

The Voice is unsettlingly soft: *"He has no afterlife soul. She locked it in her soul pot."*

Deep inside me, memories flash. The tormented faces of children.

Terror congeals like the impact of an arrow. "Are you talking about Hehaka?"

Twelve summers ago, the old woman who held us captive used an eagle-bone sucking tube to suck out the boy's afterlife soul. Hehaka. Zateri's brother. He'd seen eleven summers. She blew Hehaka's soul into a pot where she imprisoned the souls of anyone who crossed her. The old woman used the pot to threaten Hehaka, telling him to do as she ordered, or when he died, she'd take his soul far away and release it to wander among enemy ghosts for eternity.

Suddenly, I understand. "Are you saying that Hehaka is the witch who's hunting me? Was he the man with the Flint warriors?"

"You know where it is."

He says the words with a strange serenity far more frightening than a shout.

"The pot? Yes, I—"

"He needs it."

I shake my head. "Is that why he became a

witch? Is that what you're telling me? His afterlife soul is still locked in that pot?"

The Voice moves its pale hands and reclasps them. It is an inhuman gesture, as quiet as the frost. *"Help him."*

"Help Hehaka?" I say angrily. "Why? Don't you recall that he betrayed us to the old woman? I hope I never see him again. For many summers, I prayed he was dead."

He turns toward me. Inside his hood is only darkness. Both Tutelo and Wrass have seen his face. Why won't he show it to me? Just empty blackness fills the space where eyes, nose, and mouth should be.

"If you are to find brothers in all human beings, you must start with the most abandoned. There's something you've forgotten. He has not."

I become acutely conscious of the blood pounding in my ears. Memories struggle to rise. Images burst in my mind like bubbles on a pond—I'm back in the clearing with the other children...

Wrass asks, *"Do you know what they'll do to you if they catch you?"*

Zateri lowers her eyes, and her face flushes. "I'm not going to lie to you. I'm scared to death of what they'll do...mostly scared of what they'll do before they kill me. But I can stand it, Wrass. If I know you're all safe, I can stand anything."

A faint smile touches Wrass's lips. "What if one of us gets injured escaping? He will need you and your

Healing knowledge. I think you're the only one of us who is not expendable, Zateri."

Zateri's mouth quivers. "But I—"

"You're too valuable. Not you, Zateri."

He does not look my way, but I feel Wrass thinking about me. Waiting for me to speak.

Baji sits up straighter, girding herself, and smooths long black hair away from her face. She knows from firsthand experience what the warriors will do to her before they kill her. How can she volunteer?

Baji says, "Me. I'm the one, Wrass. I'll do it."

"You?" I say in panic. "Why—"

Wrass grasps my arm to stop me from continuing. He nods at Baji. "Baji may be the only one of us who can get close enough."

"Why do you think that?" I demand to know.

With tears in her eyes, Baji answers, "Because, silly boy, I'm beautiful. I can make the men want me enough that they'll carry me right into their camp and sit me down by the stew pot. No matter what happens, by the end of the night, I will have dumped the Spirit Plants in that pot." Her eyes are stony, resolved to do what must be done.

I...

The Voice intrudes: *"It wasn't your fault. You must stop blaming yourself because you did not volunteer. If you had, well...we wouldn't be standing here now."*

The emotion in the words never touches the glassy stillness of his tall body. He remains oddly motionless, as if eternity has taught him that, like the white hare hidden in the snow, survival rests in closing your eyes and freezing as solid as the drift.

When I do not respond, he turns and starts walking away through the trees.

I clench my fists. "If I can, I will help Hehaka."

He stops. His back is to me. His hood moves in a nod, which is, at best, a faint imitation of an earthly gesture.

As I watch him blend with the night, there is an instant of terrible certainty where I know my Spirit Helper is an evil monster in disguise, a deceiver biding its time, waiting to leap until its chosen prey grows careless. I don't believe I'm his prey...but I sense that I am important for his final kill.

Or perhaps I am just frightened. All men are bound in the swaddling clothes of their deepest fears, and the truth is that I am more afraid of the dead now than the living. Dancing soul lights, Spirit Helpers, ghosts—they are far more my world today than the land of the living.

Twigs crack, and I glance back over my shoulder at Taya. She has crouched down beside the toppled pine and is studying me. Waiting impatiently for me. She is certain I am mad. I can see it when she looks at me. Of course, she isn't alone. I heard many people at the betrothal feast whispering behind their hands that the last battle was too much for me. They said it had driven my afterlife soul from my body, leaving an empty husk of a man.

Taya stands up, obviously wondering what's taking me so long. My fingers lower to gently pet Gitchi's head. "Let's go back, old friend," I whisper, and the wolf trots for Taya.

I gaze longingly at the Path of Souls for a time, imagining what that brilliant, glittering silence must be like. Like all warriors, sometimes I yearn for it.

"Come on!" Taya says.

I walk back.

Taya clutches my sleeve as though her life depends upon it. "Let's go."

I say, "We must be very quiet."

"I will."

This time, I think she finally understands.

Ohsinoh stepped from the cold shadows of the boulder, and the night breeze blew his long black hair around his triangular face. He smoothed the locks behind his oversized ears. The Flint warriors he'd been traveling with were long gone, headed home. The only other human sounds in the forest were the soft voices of the two people on the trail ahead of him. He knew Sky Messenger. He'd been watching him, dogging his path, since they were children, though he doubted Sky Messenger had the slightest idea.

They were only thirty paces in front of Ohsinoh. He had to be cautious. His enemies said he had ears like a bat, but Sky Messenger's hearing was even better. It had been honed by many summers on the war trail when missing a strange sound could have cost him his life.

He glanced around, wondering what had happened to his gahai. Had the deer and the lost souls scared them away?

With the stealth of a big cat, he moved from tree trunk to tree trunk, hiding long enough to listen to the forest. Finally, lights flickered to his right, out in the trees. When he turned to look at them, they sped away, heading straight for Sky Messenger.

He smiled and followed.

4

As the two warriors dipped their paddles to steer around the bend in the river, the canoe rocked beneath Koracoo, and water slapped the hull, shooting spray over her white hood and cape. She wiped the drops from her face and returned her gaze to the shoreline, searching the maples and red cedars, expecting to see a war party emerge at any instant. Despite the fact that she'd sent a runner ahead with a white arrow, she kept CorpseEye resting across her lap, just in case. She didn't trust the Flint People to honor the request. In fact, it would not surprise her to find her runner's body on display, lying gutted on the bank, when she arrived.

Pale pink shards of broken dusk light scattered the river, twinkling and shifting as Wind Mother touched the branches that overhung the water.

Koracoo—*no, I am Jigonsaseh now*—Jigonsaseh took a few moments to appreciate them before her thoughts returned to the Flint People.

After they started bickering last summer, their alliance dissolved, and the relationship between the Standing Stone and Flint peoples had gone from bad to worse. It had started with war parties clashing on the trails, then a few raids where warriors had attacked people harvesting crops and stolen their food, and finally, they'd fallen upon each other like wolves. When the Ruling Council had ordered War Chief Deru and Deputy Sky Messenger to attack a Flint Village, there had been no going back.

The low, harsh *kak-kak-kak* of a gyrfalcon sounded overhead. She looked up. Against the pastel sky, the bird's sleek body resembled an arrow in flight as it plummeted toward the ground. Every other bird in the forest launched itself heavenward, flocking together for protection. The air was suddenly filled with warning chirps and batting wings. When the gyrfalcon disappeared into a copse of oaks, the flocks of smaller birds seemed to calm down. In barely ten heartbeats, the sky was empty again, except for three ducks circling over the glassy river ahead.

Deputy Wampa, kneeling in the bow, lifted her nose and scented the air. She wore a slate gray cape painted with brown spirals that blended with the leafless trees and brush. Fear had glued her shoulder-length black hair to her cheeks, making her nose seem wider and her lips more narrow. "Matron Jigonsaseh? Do you—?"

"Yes, Deputy. I smell the smoke." She could also hear the far-off sounds of the village: people chopping wood, dogs barking. Her fist went tight around the smooth wooden shaft of CorpseEye. He was cool in her hand, which made her nervous. CorpseEye always grew warm when there was danger, or he was trying to show her something. How could there not be danger ahead?

A short while later, warriors appeared on the right bank and ran along the river trail, paralleling her canoe. They carried nocked bows, but the bows were not aimed at her. Instead, the warriors' gazes scanned the trees, as though searching for anyone who might wish to harm Koracoo and her party.

"What do you make of that?" Wampa said.

From the rear of the canoe, Jonsoc replied, "It looks like they're here to protect us. I'm intrigued. Maybe my relatives won't have to requicken my soul in another body after all."

"Don't get overconfident," Koracoo warned. "It could be a ruse to make us feel safe."

"Yes," Wampa agreed. "It's a lot easier to hack people to pieces when they're inside your palisade than outside where they can run."

As they came around the curve in the river,

Koracoo saw the crowd at the canoe landing. There had to be thirty people.

"What's this?" Wampa hissed, and her eyes narrowed.

"I don't know, but I don't like it," Jonsoc said.

"Wait," Koracoo breathed and clutched CorpseEye tighter.

Standing near the front of the assembly was a tall man with a black roach of hair down the middle of his shaved head. As the canoe slid closer, she could see the snake tattoos on his cheeks. He'd seen forty-one summers now and had moved up through the ranks from war chief to the Chief of Wild River Village. He wore a black cape decorated with turtle shell carvings, symbols of his clan.

When Jonsoc dragged his paddle, steering them toward the landing, Chief Cord walked out of the crowd and down to the water's edge. As the canoe came slapping in over the waves, Cord reached out, grasped the bow, and dragged it ashore.

Wampa leaped out first and stood beside Cord with her hand on her belted war club while she gave him threatening looks. "You are Chief Cord?" she asked.

"Yes, warrior."

Wampa extended a hand. "May I present the esteemed matron of Yellowtail Village, Matron Jigonsaseh."

Cord's gaze warmed when he looked at her. She gave him a small smile, for old times' sake, and he walked forward and extended a hand to help her from the canoe. Jigonsaseh took it and stepped onto the sand. He must have been standing outside waiting for her for a long time. His grip was iron and ice. The knife scar that cut across his jaw had puckered from the cold, and his long, pointed nose was flushed.

In a deep voice, he greeted, "You are welcome in Wild River Village, Kor...forgive me, Matron Jigonsaseh."

"It's all right, Chief. It is new to me as well."

He nodded. "My warriors have orders to protect you and your guards with their lives. We have prepared chambers for you, if you wish to spend the night here."

"That is gracious. We will consider it."

"Good. If you'll follow me, I'll escort you to the council house."

Jigonsaseh turned and handed CorpseEye to Wampa. "Please take care of him while I am gone."

Wampa took the legendary war club. Her eyes widened, as though she felt his Spirit tingling her fingertips and then her gaze shot back to Jigonsaseh. "Gone? What do you mean, gone?"

"I want you and Jonsoc to remain with the canoe until I return."

Wampa's mouth fell open. "But, Matron, you need a guard! What if they—?"

"I trust the chief," she said with soft, implacable precision and started bravely walking through the enemy crowd toward the palisade gates.

The villagers pushed and shoved each other, trying to get closer, to see her. No Standing Stone matron, least of all a member of the Ruling Council, had ever set foot in Wild River Village. Their expressions were mixtures of awe and suspicion, but there was an undercurrent she didn't quite grasp. They were too calm. Not a single stone had been hurled yet. If a Flint matron had suddenly appeared in Yellowtail Village asking to meet with the chief, Jigonsaseh would have had to order half her warriors to encircle the matron for protection and had the other half put down the violent protests.

Cord walked easily at her side. His voice was measured and peaceful, a little reproving. "If you'd come earlier, I doubt our alliance would have collapsed."

"I couldn't have done much, old friend. Four moons ago, I was not in a position to influence war policy. As Speaker for the Women, I only relayed decisions."

His gaze scanned the black bear paw on her white cape. "That has changed, I see. I was saddened to hear of your mother's death. She was a strong, courageous leader."

She turned. Very few men were as tall as she. It was strange to look at someone eye-to-eye. "You didn't have to say that. It was kind, especially given what happened at Flatwoods Village."

His bushy black brows drew together. "That is something we will speak of, I hope."

"Yes."

As they neared the upright log palisade, he lifted a hand and warriors scurried to pull back the heavy gates. The men and women on the catwalk watched her with tight eyes, but not a single weapon shifted in her direction. Koracoo nodded in admiration.

"Your warriors are well trained."

"I take that as a compliment to my war chief. She will be pleased to hear you said that."

Cord guided her across the plaza, where children stood staring at her with frightened eyes, but the women calmly continued pounding corn in hollow logs. A few old men reclined against the longhouse walls, enjoying the last warmth of the day, smiling as they talked. Jigonsaseh studied the four longhouses. They were around three hundred hands long, arranged in a square around the plaza. Covered with white birch bark, the longhouses had a pearlescent sheen in the evening glow. Several smaller houses dotted the edges of the plaza. Cord was leading her toward the circular house that stood straight across from the central fire. Two warriors waited outside, standing guard.

"Warn me," she said. "Who will attend the meeting?"

"Myself, Village Matron Buckshen, who is also the matron of the Turtle Clan, Wolf Clan matron Gahela, and Bear Clan Matron Kiska. Others may be called in as necessary."

"Has Matron Buckshen given you any indication of whether she views my mission favorably or unfavorably?"

"I think our entire village council wishes to hear Sky Messenger's vision."

Jigonsaseh breathed a quiet sigh of relief. Often, such councils turned into shouting matches where both sides hurled accusations. She prayed that would not be so tonight.

Cord halted. "Before we enter the council, may I ask you something?"

"Of course."

"Why did you choose Wild River Village? You could have gone to more prestigious and powerful Flint villages. Why here?"

"I didn't make the choice, Cord. Sky Messenger asked me to come here. But I believe he selected your village because of you. Despite the horrors between our peoples, he has trusted you since he was a child. He respects you a great deal."

"And I, him." He drew back the leather door curtain and gestured for her to enter.

She ducked inside. For a time, all she could see was the shaft of light pouring through the smoke hole over the fire pit, and then, as her eyes adjusted, she saw the three women sitting on benches around the fire. They all wore red capes, but each was uniquely painted with the clan images of turtles, wolves, and bears.

"Let me introduce you," Cord said.

As she followed him across the hard-packed floor, she looked at the sacred False Face masks on the walls. Their crooked noses and misshapen mouths were expertly carved and painted. She could sense their Spirits watching her, judging her. When she gazed into their empty eye sockets, she wondered what conclusions they'd come to.

Cord walked sunwise around the fire and halted between Matron Buckshen and Matron Kiska. "Allow me to present Matron Jigonsaseh of the Bear Clan in Yellowtail Village, and member of the Ruling Council of the Standing Stone nation."

She bowed deeply to the matrons. They dipped their heads in return. "Thank you for agreeing to meet with me."

Matron Buckshen stared at her. White turtles painted her red cape. Perhaps sixty summers old, a white haze covered her eyes. She must be half-blind, but she had a kind face, round and deeply wrinkled, framed by thin gray hair. Buckshen extended a hand to the empty bench to her right. "Please sit down, Matron Jigonsaseh. You have been on the water many days and must be very tired."

"Thank you. I am." She seated herself, and her white cape fell into soft folds around her feet. She took a few moments to study Gahela and Kiska.

Around forty summers, both had black hair, but silver threads shone in Gahela's. The matron of the Wolf Clan, Gahela, had slitted brown eyes and a hard mouth. She looked at Koracoo with her jaw set. Kiska of the Bear clan, however, appeared relaxed, even happy to see Koracoo—which she doubted. It was probably just that Kiska's thin, childlike face and soft brown eyes gave her a friendly appearance.

Cord seated himself across the fire from her, on the bench beside Kiska, and said, "Please tell us why you've come, Matron Jigonsaseh."

She took a deep breath, preparing herself. The fragrance of burning hickory encircled her. "My son, Sky Messenger, asked that I come to you. He—"

"You are his mother," Matron Buckshen softly said, "but we are his People."

Jigonsaseh's eyes narrowed, confused. "Forgive me. I assumed that after he returned to Yellowtail Village and became a deputy war chief for our nation that you would have considered him to be a traitor and unadopted him."

"No," Kiska said. "In fact, many of our people consider him to be a hero."

Jigonsaseh sat back on the bench and looked to Cord for some sort of explanation.

He turned to Matron Buckshen. "If you will allow me, Matron?" When she nodded, he continued, "After the Flatwoods Village battle, your son released the captives, shoved a log into the river, told our women and children to grab hold, and then he led the enemy warriors away. He risked his own life to save them. Many of the survivors came here to Wild River Village. Those women and children speak his name with great reverence."

Matron Kiska added, "Without Dekanawida, the man you call Sky Messenger, they would be dead or serving as slaves in enemy nations."

Matron Buckshen shifted on the bench, and all eyes turned to her. "You see, after hearing their stories, we realized that he had never turned his back on his adopted nation. Instead, he'd been serving our people the entire time."

Koracoo felt a little bewildered. She wasn't sure she liked the idea that they believed her son had been acting as a spy in the Standing Stone nation. But if it helped her today…

"It was at that battle," she said respectfully, "that the Spirits of your relatives came to him."

The matrons went silent, listening intently, and the crackling of the fire seemed louder. "Just before he released the women and children, the Spirits of the dead rose up from the battlefield and encircled him. Hundreds of bobbing soul lights followed him to where the captives were being held, and guarded him while he made sure they got away. After they were safe, Sky Messenger's Spirit Helper called him into the forest, where he was tormented with Spirit Dreams for many days. Visions of our future."

Almost breathlessly, Matron Buckshen said, "We have heard the stories the Traders tell, but did not know how much to believe. As you know, Traders are not always reliable. They like to embellish to make the stories more entertaining."

Koracoo smiled. "Yes. I know."

Her voice light and disinterested, Matron Gahela asked, "So, is the world really going to end?"

A log in the fire split, and green flames erupted from the crack. Jigonsaseh watched them until they faded to amber again. "When Sky Messenger's Dream begins, he can't feel his body, just the air cooling as the color drains from the world, leaving it gray and shimmering. A great cloud-sea moves beneath his feet, a restless dark ocean punctured by a great tree with flowers of pure light—"

"The World Tree," Kiska whispered. Her eyes are bright and alert.

"Hush, Kiska," Matron Buckshen said. "Let her finish."

"Oh, forgive me."

Jigonsaseh waited a few instants before continuing, "...punctured by a great tree whose roots sink through Great-Grandmother Earth and plant themselves upon the back of the Great Tortoise floating in the primeval ocean below. Suddenly, the birds in the trees tuck their beaks beneath their wings, roosting in broad daylight, and butterflies secret themselves in the clouds at his feet. A strange silence descends."

The matrons shifted. Kiska leaned forward, bracing her elbows on her knees, while Buckshen inhaled a deep breath. Gahela just stared at Koracoo with a sour expression.

"Dimly, Sky Messenger, Dekanawida, becomes aware that he is not alone. Gray shades drift through the air around him, and he knows they are the last congregation, the dead who still walk and breathe. A voice calls his name, and he turns. Beyond the cloud-sea, a darkness rises and slithers along the horizon. Strange black curls, like gigantic antlers, spin from the darkness and rake—"

"Horned Serpent?" Kiska hissed, then clapped a hand to her mouth and looked apologetically at Buckshen. "Sorry."

"Please go on, Matron Jigonsaseh," Buckshen instructed.

Jigonsaseh focused on the fire. The red coals winked as the flames danced. "The antlers rake the bellies of the Cloud People, and Elder Brother Sun trembles in the sky. There is a brilliant flash, and white feathers sprout from his edges. As he flies away into a black hole in the sky, a crack sounds, and when Sky Messenger looks down, he sees a great pine tree pushing up through Great-Grandmother Earth. As it grows, its white roots stretch out to the four directions, and a snowy blanket of thistledown rains upon the world." She hesitated, not sure she wished to tell them the whole Dream. "Then the Dream bursts, and for a time, there is only blinding light. Finally, Sky Messenger sees the flowers of the World Tree fluttering down, down, and he falls through a hole in the cloud-sea, and keeps falling, tumbling through nothingness surrounded by petals of pure light. Wisps of cloud trail behind him."

When she stopped, she looked up and found Matron Buckshen's white-filmed eyes on something insubstantial, perhaps living the Dream. The other two matrons contemplatively stared at the fire. Then Matron Kiska closed her eyes with desperate effort, as though to blot out the images. Only Cord was looking at her, and he had a slight frown on his handsome face.

"That is his Dream."

"And what does Dekanawida make of this Dream?" Buckshen asked.

Jigonsaseh wasn't accustomed to his Flint name yet. It took her a moment to answer. "He thinks our war is killing Great-Grandmother Earth and will cause Elder Brother Sun to turn his back on us. He wants the war to stop."

Matron Gahela's eyes went strange, almost accusatory. "Are you trying to talk us into another alliance? The last one didn't work out too well. Many of our people are dead. Ask the survivors of Flatwoods Village. They—"

"Gahela," Buckshen softly chastised. "We all grieve with you over the loss of your relatives, but—"

"*She* does not grieve with me." Gahela's eyes blazed at Jigonsaseh.

Jigonsaseh calmly returned her gaze. "I was not a member of the Ruling Council at the time, Matron Gahela. If I had been, I assure you I would have voted no. We had no cause to attack Flatwoods Village. It was a bad decision, and I grieve both for your losses and ours."

That seemed to somewhat mollify Gahela. She lowered her eyes but continued to grind her teeth.

Buckshen said, "What does Dekanawida wish us to do to end the war?"

"He said to tell you that there will come a time

in the very near future when we must tie our people together again to fight for peace. He asks that you consider joining us, and if you agree, then you should prepare yourselves. He will send a messenger when he needs you to join the fight."

"When will that be?"

"I cannot say." She sat back on the bench and heaved a breath. "When I left Yellowtail Village, we were preparing to attack Atotarho Village. I pray that is not the battle my son needs you for. I suspect it will be long and bloody."

Kiska blinked owlishly. "But what if it is? Atotarho is an evil sorcerer. His witchery has killed many of our children, and his warriors have killed the rest! If we band together to destroy him, will that stop Elder Brother Sun from turning his back on us?"

Matron Gahela snorted disdainfully. "You're not thinking, Kiska. Dekanawida's request makes no sense. He says he wants us to join the Standing Stone nation to fight for peace. Does that mean he wishes to fight, or not to fight?"

Buckshen said, "That is a good question. Matron Jigonsaseh?"

Koracoo gestured uncertainly. "I'm no Dreamer, Matrons. Just a Dreamer's messenger. I leave all interpretations up to you. But I suspect, sooner than any of us wish, we will all know the answer to that question."

Buckshen tilted her head, and the firelight reflected from her white-filmed eyes, turning them into amber mirrors. "The council will need to deliberate on this matter, then we must seek the opinions of our clans."

"I understand. I will return to my own village and await your decision. I thank you with all my heart for agreeing to hear my son's Dream." She stood and bowed deeply to the council members.

Cord stood up. "Matron Jigonsaseh, if it would not delay your journey, I would offer you something to eat and drink. Our village makes an excellent walnut bread."

She dipped her head in gratitude. "I would very much enjoy that."

She and Cord walked across the council house to the door curtain.

When they stepped outside, the light had changed. A lavender veil had fallen over the land, and with it, a hush. The village was calm, the warriors on the catwalk unconcerned.

"Well," Jigonsaseh asked. "What do you think?"

"I think they're worried this is a trick. But I also suspect they believe you."

She jerked a nod. "I wish Sky...Dekanawida... could have been here to present his vision himself. They would have had no doubts."

"Maybe."

There was an awkward moment where neither of them said anything.

Then Cord gestured to the closest longhouse. "I had hoped you could spend an extra hand of time here. My niece has already prepared supper for us and carried food to your warriors. Will you join me?"

She smiled. "Yes, thank you."

The warmth in his eyes caught her off guard. How was it possible that the old attraction between them had not died in the past twelve summers of war?

The two of them, enemies, made a strange pair as they walked across the plaza—he dressed in black, she in white, talking like the old friends they were.

5
SKY MESSENGER

Wind Mother rampages through the twilight forest, whipping my black cape so wildly that I can scarcely walk. Taya is having an even tougher time. She has her thin, willowy body leaning into the gale, but is still stumbling. I walk back and take her hand, helping steady her steps as we plod toward White Dog Village. I need to see my father, Gonda, to hear the gossip. I especially need to know if War Chief Hiyawento is out on the war trail. If so, I needn't risk traveling to Coldspring Village.

Taya asks, "Do you smell that?" Despite the wind, she's been trying very hard to keep her voice low.

"Yes." The faintest hint of smoke rides the air.

I lead her off the main path and onto a narrow deer trail that slithers between trees and massive head-high boulders. All around us, the forest shrieks, and branches crash together. A constant shower of leaves and twigs pelts our faces and capes. Taya has one arm up to protect her eyes.

"Sky Messenger?" Her voice is almost lost in the gale. "How much farther to White Dog Village?"

"By now, we should see the firelight reflecting—" I stop suddenly and sniff the wind again. "Blessed gods," I say when the distinct scent of burning longhouses reaches me. "Stay here! Gitchi, don't let her follow me!"

I release her hand and break into a dead run.

As I round the curve in the trail, the dark bulk of the still-burning village, with its high log palisade and skeletons of charred longhouses, looms like a black wall. I feel as though I've just been kicked in the belly. Firelight halos the village, but the surrounding forest is uncommonly dark and blustery.

"No!" I run, duck through a charred hole in the palisade, and dash across the plaza toward the Snipe Clan longhouse, the clan my father married into. Discarded arrows cover the ground. Baskets, broken pots, and dropped capes are scattered everywhere. Hungry dogs lope through the devastation with their tongues hanging out, looking frantic, or in despair. Their masters are gone, probably dead, but they do not know that, and won't leave the chaos of charred ruins until they search every crevice and nook.

I can tell now that the village was attacked days ago. The longhouses are little more than piles of ash, the remaining poles and log benches fanned to flames by today's gale. If Father is alive, he is not here. He fled with the other survivors. I pray they made it to Bur Oak Village.

From outside the burned palisade, Gitchi barks, and I hear Taya shout, "Let me go!"

I trot back to the hole in the palisade and duck outside. Gitchi, still obeying me, has his teeth embedded in Taya's sleeve and is tugging her backward. She must have tried to follow me.

"Let me go!" Taya screams in rage and shakes her arm, trying to dislodge the wolf's massive jaws.

"Gitchi, it's all right," I call. "Let her go."

Gitchi releases her and leaps back to avoid Taya's fists. "I *hate* this animal!" she shrieks.

Panicked by her loud cries, I dash back. "Are you trying to attract the attention of the attacking warriors?"

"No, I—"

I grab her hand and drag Taya into the shadows of nearby trees, pausing only long enough to examine the forest for hidden warriors, or desperate survivors who will kill anyone not from their village. Beneath the cacophony of wind and storm, the faint whining of village dogs rides the gusts.

With Gitchi at my side, I drag Taya to a small meadow ringed by black oaks. The shiny ridges of bark on the trunks glisten in the fading light. Swirling leaves and the pungent scent of the ferns crushed by our feet trail us to the fallen log.

"Sit down," I order. "I need time to think."

"I don't understand," Taya says. "Why are we stopping? We should keep moving. This is dangerous! Can't you think while we run?"

"No. I need to be here, Taya. Since the villagers are gone, my only choice is to wait until tomorrow morning to get the information I need. There's someone I have to meet." My thoughts race, thinking about the Trader's rounds, trying to figure out...

"But there must be enemy warriors and hundreds of angry ghosts roaming the forest!"

I close my eyes for a long moment, calming myself, then lift my gaze to the clearing. "I'll keep watch tonight, just in case either warriors or survivors return."

"What good will that do? You have no weapons to protect us." Taya jerks her cape more closely about her, pouting. "When did this happen?"

I clench my fists to keep from saying something that will hurt her. "Four or five days ago. There are no bodies along the main trail, and I don't see any scattered around the palisade, which means the survivors already collected the remains of their dead relatives."

"But if it happened five days ago, why are the flames still so high?"

"The wind kicked up this afternoon. It must have fanned the embers smoldering beneath the charred piles of bark and timber."

She grabs her flying hair when a particularly brutal

gust sweeps the forest, cracking limbs together and hurling a barrage of acorns and twigs at us. When it passes, she asks, "Do you think your father is alive?"

I rub my hands over my stunned face. I can still feel Father's breath moving inside me, as I can my sister's and mother's, and a handful of friends. But hope often masquerades as truth. "I pray he is."

She studies me, notes my expression, and says, "Who do you think attacked the village?"

"In the morning, I'll be able to tell by the decorations on the arrows, but tonight? My guess is Mountain People."

"But we're far from the lands of the Mountain People."

"Doesn't matter. A large enough war party makes territorial boundaries meaningless."

We ate supper earlier—at her insistence—and I am suddenly grateful. It would be impossible to get a fire going in this wind, and I have no appetite at all. As I look around, the scene takes on the wavering and misted edges of a Spirit Dream. Thoughts hang like raindrops caught in a spiderweb—shiny, fragile. I can make no sense of this. But I must. And I must face the possibility that Father and dozens of cousins are dead.

Taya's head moves, turning to examine the dark forest, as though afraid. "I don't like it here. Please, let's move on."

"We can't leave until after dawn tomorrow."

"Why not?"

"I need to meet someone."

"But I don't wish to stay here!"

"If my father were here, we wouldn't have to stay. Since he's not, we must. I need more information before we head for Coldspring Village. There's a Trader who is always here on the last day of the moon. It's part of his regular rounds. He will know all the gossip."

As the stunned sensation begins to drain away, a cold new light illuminates the political ramifications. Whoever attacked White Dog Village has earned a swift and devastating response from Matron Kittle, and I—

"Sky Messenger?"

Curtly, I say, "Taya, there's a soft bed of leaves right over there. Why don't you try to sleep? I'm going to go stand guard beneath that oak." I point.

Panic trembles her voice. "But you'll stay in my sight, won't you? If I awake and look for you, I'll see you?"

"I told you. I'll be right there." Exasperated by this constant refrain, I turn my back and walk to the oak to take up my position.

Occasionally, when the wind shifts, ash and billows of black smoke completely obscure my view of the trail as it snakes down the hill and into the narrow dusk-cloaked valley beyond. A large pond fills part of the valley. Battered by the wind, it appears to be boiling, sloshing back and forth.

When the White Dog survivors arrive at Bur Oak or Yellowtail Village and ask for help, the matrons will be obliged to give it, and there is simply not enough food. At this very instant, Grandmother must be calling in elders from all the surrounding villages, preparing them for the worst.

I glare at the tormented forest and think about the quagmire that is clan politics, of my own stake in it, and of matrons like Taya's grandmother, who scheme and lie and plot so her own kin will remain in power. For many summers, High Matron Kittle has been amassing warriors, keeping them close. In the past, villages were widely separated, many days apart. They couldn't protect each other. So Kittle convinced the other Standing Stone villages to move closer to Bur Oak Village. That way, in time of need, they could pool their warriors and defend each other against attacks. It made sense. It also meant that she had five thousand warriors at her command—providing the individual village councils approved her schemes. And provided they had warning that an attack was imminent. White Dog Village must have been taken completely by surprise. Kittle's rage must be tearing the nation apart.

"Sky Messenger?"

Startled, I spin around. "What *is* it? I thought you were going to sleep?"

She stands three paces away with her blankets pulled tightly around her slender body. "No." It is almost a sob.

When I frown at her, she looks at the ground and nervously moves one moccasin back and forth through the fallen leaves. She looks very young, and though she probably doesn't know it, very beautiful. Her long hair blows about her pretty face.

"What's wrong, Taya?"

"Sky Messenger, I want you to come to the meadow. Please. Come and lie down with me? I'm cold and I'm afraid to be alone tonight."

"I'm only eight paces away. I need to keep watch on the main trail."

"You never try to understand how I feel!"

I suck in a breath and hold it to keep my temper in check. "Explain it to me, please."

"I'm lonely! At Bur Oak Village, my longhouse had almost three hundred people in it. There was always someone to talk to, or conversations to listen to as I fell asleep at night. Dogs to pet as they trotted by. Here…" She looked up at the violently nailing branches that filled the sky. "There's no one. No one but you and Gitchi. Please, I don't want to be alone."

When she lifts her gaze to look at me, I see desperation, and it occurs to me that my own qualms about this journey have made me impatient and callous. Seeing her first burned village has probably stirred up her fears.

"Yes. All right, Taya. I'll come—"

"Thank you." She runs forward and throws her arms around my waist. The setting...the smell of war...her arms...memories of the war trail overwhelm me, memories interlaced with pain.

I am with her...exhilarating, striking more deeply than anything else in my life. At the end, I'd known exactly what I wanted...and did not. Exactly who I was, and was not.

"Sky Messenger, if you need to watch the main trail, I can sleep right here beside you. That way, you won't have to sleep with me. But I'll be close to you. I'll be able to hear you when you move."

The empty wasteland inside me yawns wider. I ask, "Are you cold?"

"Freezing."

Against her hair, I say, "Perhaps I can find a way to warm us both up."

6

Cord held the door curtain aside for Jigonsaseh to enter the Turtle Clan longhouse. When she ducked past him, he caught the scent of pine needles, and found it strangely powerful. On the war trail, he had spent many summers sleeping on soft beds of pine, spruce, or juniper needles. The fragrance brought back those days, and with them, the odd co-mingled thrill of victory and the despair of friends lost on long-ago battlefields.

"My chamber is on the right," he said as he let the curtain fall closed behind him.

She politely waited for him to remove his black cape and hang it on a peg on the wall, then followed him into his chamber. The space was small, fifteen hands across. He hosted so many visitors that benches lined all three walls. His belongings were neatly stowed in baskets and pots beneath the benches. His niece had arranged the wooden trays of food and cups of tea in the center of the floor mats, then spread soft hides around them.

He extended a hand. "Please, sit."

Jigonsaseh gracefully removed her white cape and knelt on the deer hides. He couldn't help but stare at her. She wore no jewelry, just a simple tan doe hide dress that conformed to her slender, muscular body, and red knee-high moccasins. She had seen thirty-nine summers pass, and though a few silver threads glistened in her short black hair, she was as beautiful as he remembered. Her small, narrow nose and full lips were perfectly balanced in her oval face, and her jet-black eyes...a man could get lost in those eyes. A long time ago, he had considered it, but it hadn't been the right time for either of them. And now? Their peoples were at war.

Cord sat down across from her, removed the lid on the teapot, and dipped a cup into the warm liquid. When he handed it to her, their fingers touched for a lot longer than he suspected either of them intended. She gave him a tight smile and drew the cup away.

As he divided the walnut bread between the two bowls, he said, "How were your harvests this year?"

"Poor. And with all of the attacks on our people, our remaining villages are flooded with refugees. I doubt our supplies will last the winter. Which, as you well know, means we will be forced to take what we need from our enemies."

He blinked. Revealing such vulnerabilities was not a wise military strategy. She knew better, so he wondered why she'd said it. "I had forgotten how frank you are."

She sipped her tea, and a shiver went through her. After many nights of camping in the open, the cold must have settled in her bones. He knew from experience that it would take a long time for her to get truly warm. Slowly, she replied, "I'm sorry, I did not intend—"

"Don't be. I'm sick to death of all the deception and political maneuvering. It's good to hear honest words."

She shifted positions, turning slightly away so that she could bring up her knees and prop her cup atop them. From this side view, she looked even more slender, almost frail. It touched something inside him, some illogical masculine need to protect—as if legendary War Chief Koracoo needed anyone to protect her. He suspected many men before him had felt this same protective urge and were now dead because they had hesitated when they'd had the chance to kill her.

"I appreciate your willingness to hear honest

words. May I ask you some questions?" The glimmering light from the longhouse fires reflected in her dark eyes.

"Certainly." He handed her the tray of walnut bread and dipped himself a cup of tea.

"How were your harvests? Will you need to attack us this spring?"

His brow furrowed. Thoughtfully, he set his teacup down. "Matron, the fever took a great toll on our villages. We do not have the number of mouths to feed that you do. We have enough food, I think." In a low earnest voice, he added, "But understand that if we are attacked and our food stores taken, we will have no choice."

"Yes, that's how it works, isn't it? You strike us. We strike you. The Mountain People strike us both, and it goes on and on. Sky Messenger is right. This has to end before there's no one left to fight."

He studied her. She looked tired. He picked up his teacup and let it warm his cold fingers before he said, "The question is, how? Every time my people move their villages to a new location and get settled, someone attacks us. We end up running for our lives. Our war strategy is based upon that fact. We don't want to run any longer. In fact, we won't. This is good bottom country. Our crops grow well here. We plan to keep it. That means we have to kill anyone who tries to take it away." The subtle question in his comment did not escape her notice.

"Chief, I assure you I will vote no if anyone in the Standing Stone nation suggests attacking a Flint Village. I give you my oath."

That intrigued him. He pulled his head back in mock amazement. "It eases my souls to hear you say that, but we both know that food is the greatest of all tools for manipulation." He paused. "And High Matron Kittle is not a friend to the Flint People."

Jigonsaseh took a bite of her walnut bread and ate it slowly, apparently relishing the flavor. "This is excellent, Cord. Please give your niece my thanks."

"She will be delighted that she pleased you."

Cord bit into his chunk of walnut bread and took a moment to enjoy the sweet flavor. Made from a mixture of acorn meal, walnuts, and bear fat, with a pinch of wood ash for leavening, it tasted wonderful.

They ate in silence for a time. When she'd finished her second piece of bread, she dusted the crumbs from her hands and softly said, "These are not easy times. I pray people hear Sky Messenger's vision and heed it, for I fear we are on the verge of destroying our own world."

He lightly stroked the fine wood grain of his bread bowl. "The Flint People will lay down weapons two instants after the Standing Stone People do—which will be three instants after the

Hills People do, five instants after the Landing People do, and one full day after the Mountain People do, since they are the least trustworthy."

She smiled at that and lifted her hand to cover a yawn.

"Shall we cut this short? You look very tired. We've prepared a chamber..." When he started to rise, she reached across to touch his sleeve. He could feel the chill of her tanned fingers through his shirt.

"I'd much rather talk with you, if you don't mind."

A tingle went through him. He lowered himself back to the hides. "I don't...but I'd appreciate it if we could abandon the war talk. I haven't seen you in so long and there are many things I'd prefer to discuss."

"I am agreeable to that."

"May I ask about your family?"

"What do you wish to know?"

He paused for only an instant, but it was uncomfortable. "Have you remarried?"

She smiled. "No. After Gonda and I parted, I had two children to raise, and my duties as war chief, which entailed many nights on the trail. When I returned home I wanted to spend what few moments I had with Odion and Tutelo. And truly, there was no man who interested me. Which perhaps says more about me than it does them. And you? Did you remarry?"

She sounded like she was genuinely interested. "I remarried ten summers ago. She gave me a strong son. But we divorced two summers ago. I have not had the strength to consider another marriage, though my clan keeps insisting. As I'm sure yours does."

"With regularity."

He laughed softly and saw the lines around her eyes crinkle in return. "And Gonda? A Trader once told me he remarried and moved to White Dog Village. Is that correct?"

Her smile faded. She looked away. "It was. White Dog Village was destroyed by the Hills People—"

Cord sat forward. "Blessed gods, when?"

"Five days ago."

Cord stared down the length of the longhouse, absently noting the movements of the people as they cooked supper or washed their children's faces. Two dogs wrestled three compartments down. "Is Yellowtail Village overrun with refugees?"

"Yes, and Bur Oak Village, too."

He turned his cup in his hands. Somehow, they had circled around each other and returned to talking about the war. They fell silent, gazing at each other, both of their faces lined with concern.

A small connection of warmth grew between them, like hands reaching across time and clasping tentatively, then strengthening. When he started to feel it in all the wrong places, he dropped his gaze and frowned into his teacup. In the pale green liquid, his black roach of hair appeared faintly purple.

"How is Baji?" Jigonsaseh asked, changing the subject. "I think of her often."

"She's still strong-willed and too confident for her own good, but my adopted daughter is well. Her warriors elected her war chief three moons ago."

"Well, that does not surprise me. Even as a child, she had a powerful presence. She was a born leader." A tender smile came to her lips.

Cord tried to hide his pride, but his voice showed it: "Yes, she is. It will sadden her that she missed seeing you."

"She is away?"

"Yes, and won't be back for days."

She politely did not ask why, and it relieved him that he didn't have to hide the fact that Baji was out on the war trail.

Jigonsaseh sipped more tea. "I pray that Sodowego does not see her face. Has she married?"

Cord shook his head. "No. You know why, I suppose."

Her delicate black brows pulled down. "No, why?"

"I'm surprised Dekanawida didn't tell you. It's a lengthy story." Cord stretched out on his side on the mats, propping himself up on one elbow. As his sleeve slipped down, the tattoos covering his arms were revealed. She seemed to be studying them, perhaps remembering. "My grandmother has tried to marry Baji several times to good men. She has refused."

"Does she give you any reason?"

"Of course not. But the reason is clear. No man equals your son."

Something about the softness in her expression touched him, building a warmth below his heart. He longed to speak of more personal things, things between the two of them, but he couldn't let himself. He feared where it might lead.

"Why did they part, Cord? He's never told me." She drained her tea, set the cup on the floor, and laced her fingers over her knees. Her beautiful face had a pale yellow gleam.

"Oh," he said through a taut exhale. "I only know part of it. Baji is not one to openly speak of such matters. I heard they had a violent battlefield squabble over captives. There was an infant, a little boy, that Baji wished to bring home and adopt. Dekanawida objected. Apparently, they had a pact that neither would ever take a child captive."

"Had she changed her mind?"

He lifted his shoulders in a shrug. "I think,

perhaps, she wished to make an exception in the baby's case. I wonder if her lack of a child is not beginning to bother her. Every other woman in the village who has seen twenty-four summers has five or six children. Baji has none."

Jigonsaseh blinked thoughtfully at the floor. "I felt that way once after a raid. There was a baby boy crying in the midst of a collapsed house. I couldn't leave him there. Gonda and I brought him home and raised him as our own."

"Odion?"

"Yes."

"Does he know that?"

"Oh, yes, we told him the story as soon as he could understand, at four or five summers."

Cord watched the silver glints in her hair reflect the firelight that filled the longhouse. "Then I am especially surprised he didn't help Baji raise the child. They would have made good parents, I think."

"What happened to the infant boy?"

"I have no idea. I only know that no one brought him home."

Few warriors dared to adopt infants. Almost no one could afford the luxury of carrying and feeding a baby for days on the war trail. His lips pressed tightly together. "I regret that they parted. I looked forward to having Dekanawida here. Not only because I liked and respected him, but because he was a very fine warrior. We could have used him."

Through a long exhalation, she said, "Well, he's decided that he will never touch a weapon again. So..." She tilted her head as though to say *who knows what the future will bring*. Then she exhaled, and her face suddenly appeared haggard.

"Will you spend the night, Matron?"

"No, but I thank you for the offer. We must get home. Our village councils are deliberating the issue of attacking Atotarho Village at this instant. When the vote comes—if it hasn't already—our war chiefs will begin planning the assault. I must be there."

"How many days until the battle?"

"Hard to say. At least six or seven. I pray we have more time."

As she started to rise, he said, "Perhaps..." She looked up, saw his expression, and sat back down. "Perhaps I should send a war party with you. If my people decide to join yours in the fight, there will be no time for us to ready ourselves and get there before the arrows start flying. At least you would have a few more warriors—"

"That is a kind offer, and I appreciate it. But that would be dangerous for you. If your people vote no, they will ask why Flint warriors were engaged in a fight they did not authorize. No, Cord.

Wait. I will send a fast runner when the time comes."

"Very well."

She started to rise again, and he got to his feet and instinctively offered her a hand. She put her fingers into his, and he helped her to her feet. When she looked up at him, time seemed to stop. Conflicting emotions danced across her beautiful face: a magnetic attraction to him, fear, desperation. They stood less than two hands apart, holding hands for so long that blood began to rush in his ears.

"I wish you would stay the night."

"I can't." She gently pulled her hand away. "I wish I could. Truly. But I must get home."

"At least allow me to walk you back to your canoe," he said. "That will give us a few more moments."

"I would welcome that."

She shrugged her white cape over her shoulders and ducked beneath the door curtain into the darkness. Cord, two steps behind her, thought: *Blessed gods, we haven't seen each other in twelve summers, and I'm still in love with her.*

7

Taya woke to the rich smell of cooking grouse. When she opened her eyes, she saw Sky Messenger crouched before a fire, adjusting the roasting stick so the bird would cook on the other side. The faint gray rays of early morning outlined his muscular body. Last night, his tenderness had left her breathless. Her gaze moved from his shoulders to his narrow waist and legs, and it occurred to her that he wasn't wearing his cape, just his knee-length buckskin shirt and leggings. She looked down and saw that he'd draped his cape over the top of the blankets to keep her warmer through the night.

"Are you awake?" he called.

Taya dragged herself to a sitting position and rubbed her eyes. "Barely."

Gitchi's head turned from where he lay beside

the fire, tearing a rabbit apart. Blood covered his gray muzzle. He gave Taya an unnerving appraisal, then went back to his rabbit.

The wind had died down. Only a few leaves cartwheeled across the trail. She reached for her pack and drew out her carved antler comb. Yesterday's gale had turned her hair into a snarled mess. While he cooked, she took her time, combed the waist-length strands smooth, and then plaited them into a long braid. She knew the style accented her perfect oval face and made her dark eyes seem larger, and she wanted to please him this morning.

He dipped a cup into the pot at the edge of the flames, then rose and brought it to her. "It's spruce needle tea. The grouse is almost ready."

"Thank you." She took a sip of the hot tea and let the tangy flavor filter through her waking body.

"You're beautiful this morning." He stroked her hair and went back to turn the bird again. As fat dripped onto the flames, they sputtered.

It was comforting sitting with the warm blankets coiled around her waist. She was hesitant to leave them. She drank more tea and studied the burned village. Smoke still scented the air, but there were no flames this morning, at least none she could see. The charred palisade—burned through in many places—resembled a gigantic mouth of rotted black teeth. Through the holes, collapsed houses were visible, standing in smoldering piles, but she saw no dead bodies, just a few roaming dogs.

Taya shoved her blankets aside and rose with her cup in her hand. "Did you see anyone in the night?"

Sky Messenger's brown eyes lifted and narrowed. He seemed to be watching someone right now, someone moving through the destroyed village. But he said, "No. Come and sit down. I'll fill our bowls."

As she walked toward him, he slid the grouse off the stick and into one bowl, then used his fingers to quickly rip it in half and deposited the larger portion in her bowl. Afterward, he sucked on his fingers as though he'd burned them.

She sat down beside him, placed her teacup to the side, and picked up her bowl. As she blew on the grouse to cool it, she said, "You could have used my knife"—she touched the hafted chert knife on her belt—"to cut up the grouse."

"Yes, thank you. That would probably have been acceptable."

"Acceptable?" She pulled off a succulent strip of dark meat and put it in her mouth. The delicious flavor coated her tongue. "This is good. When did you have time to hunt? I didn't hear a thing."

"It wasn't much of a hunt," he said, and swallowed a bite of meat. "The bird fluttered up on that fallen log five paces away. I killed it with a rock, a lucky throw, then I skinned it and slid a hickory stick through the middle."

"Yes, the hickory flavor is wonderful."

As they ate, she smiled at him, and he seemed confused by it. She felt so happy this morning. When she'd eaten everything but the leg, she picked it up and placed it in his bowl. "You need more food than I do, Sky Messenger, though I appreciate you for taking care of me."

He glanced at the leg and suspiciously said, "Are you sure? I don't want you to get hungry on the trail."

"I'll be fine." She rubbed her greasy fingers in the dry leaves to clean them and reached for her teacup again. As she sipped, she watched Gitchi. He was taking his time eating the rabbit. His tail wagged often. "You should have taken that rabbit away from him and cooked it for us. Then neither of us would have to worry about being hungry on the trail."

Sky Messenger replied, "It's his rabbit. He hunted it."

"You could give him a leg, or maybe even two, but he's a wolf. He doesn't need as much food as we do."

"The rabbit belongs to Gitchi."

Annoyed, she chastised, "You protect that old gray-faced wolf like he's a human being, Sky Messenger. He's not."

Sky Messenger reached out to pet the wolf's head, and the love in Gitchi's eyes touched even her. "He's my friend."

Taya frowned into her teacup. She hated to admit it, but she was jealous of the affection he lavished on the decrepit wolf. She turned the cup in her hands and decided to change the subject. Anything to keep the morning filled with warmth and conversation.

"What did you mean when you said it would have been *acceptable* to cut up the grouse with my knife?"

The wrinkles across his forehead deepened. He finished chewing the bite in his mouth before he replied, "I'm still finding my way, discovering what I can and cannot live with."

"I don't understand. What's wrong with cutting up a grouse with a fine chert blade?"

"I just need to think about it for a time longer."

This confused Taya, who tried to decipher what he meant. *A knife is unacceptable to him.* Why? She could understand, no matter how ridiculous, that he didn't want to carry a bow, spear, stiletto, or war club—he'd stopped fighting—but a knife?

"So," she said, "you consider a knife to be a weapon?"

His head waffled, as though uncertain. "I'm just at the foolish stage, Taya. Don't waste too much time trying to figure it out. I don't understand it myself yet."

"But, you mean you're at the stage of figuring out what is a weapon and what is not?"

"Yes." He picked up the leg she'd given him and concentrated on eating it. When he finished, he lowered the bone to his bowl and wiped his greasy hands on his leggings. Many people did that because the oil helped to keep water from soaking into the leather. Sky Messenger rose to his feet and extended a hand. "May I take your bones away?"

She gave him her bowl. It was considered disrespectful to the animal to throw its bones on the ground. He walked away to the sycamore and carefully placed the bones in the crook of the tree. Then he said a soft prayer, thanking the grouse for its life, and walked back to kneel in front of her. When he bowed his head, his heavy brow cast shadows over his brown eyes, and his black hair fell forward.

"A knife is a tool, Sky Messenger, not a weapon. A leather punch is a tool. An awl is a tool."

"Yes, in most hands. But in my hands"—he opened his palms and stared at them distastefully—"they have often been weapons. I can see the faces of each person I killed with a bone awl, a punch, or a fine chert blade."

"You were a warrior fighting for your people. Of course, you used whatever you could find to defeat the enemy. You should be proud of it. Not ashamed."

The few brief moments of happiness between them vanished. The curtain closed over his eyes again. He rose and walked away to stare down the trail toward the distant pond, which shone a deep blue.

Taya drank her tea and frowned at his back. Was he going to start refusing to use tools? If he wouldn't touch an axe, how could he chop wood to keep them warm? If he wouldn't touch a knife, how could he skin animals for their food? What good was he if he wasn't willing to be a warrior, a hunter, or perform any other manly duty?

Blessed gods, does Grandmother know this?

Sky Messenger folded his arms and walked out into the trail, apparently waiting for the Trader.

Beyond the rolling tree-whiskered hills, dawn had begun to blush color into the day. A swath of deep purple limned the eastern horizon. High above it, the brightest campfires of the dead continued to gleam.

When she'd finished her tea, she silently gathered up their things and packed them—a menial duty she usually left to him. Then she set both packs beside the trail and went to grab his cape. It smelled of wood smoke and crushed grass. She held it to her nose for a time, just breathing in his scent, before she walked to him and draped it over his shoulders.

It must have startled him, for he jumped slightly and looked at her. "Thank you," he said softly. He pulled it forward and tied it beneath his chin.

Taya touched his arm. "I'm sorry. I know you'd like to thrash me for the things I just said."

"You exaggerate."

"I'm just trying to figure you out, probably as hard as you're trying to—"

He threw up a hand to silence her and squinted down the trail. "There he is."

An ugly little man with five pack dogs trotted toward them. He was humming a tune, watching his feet. When he lifted his head and saw Sky Messenger standing in the middle of the trail, he stopped suddenly. Greasy black hair framed his scarred face. "What are *you* doing here?"

Sky Messenger called, "I came to find you, Raloga."

"Me?" The man's hand flew to his chest. "Why? What did I do? Where's your war party?" His gaze darted across the forest.

As he walked forward, Sky Messenger pulled something from his belt pouch and handed it to the Trader. "White Dog Village was burned several days ago. There's no need for you to stop. I will pay you to deliver a message for me, but it must be done quickly."

The man took the exquisite pearl bracelet, turned it over in his hands, and eyed Sky Messenger suspiciously. "This is valuable. You must want me to do something dangerous. Where would you have me go?"

"To Coldspring Village."

Raloga glanced at Taya, then looked back at Sky Messenger. "And who am I to see?"

"I want my message delivered exactly, do you understand?"

The Trader nodded.

"Tell War Chief Hiyawento that Odion wants to meet him in the aspen meadow at midnight."

Taya's blood went cold. *Hiyawento?* He was one of the most feared war chiefs among the Hills People. *He* was Sky Messenger's old friend? The man who'd saved him? He was a monster!

"Umm," Raloga said. "Who is Odion?"

"Just tell him. He'll understand."

Raloga shrugged and grinned, revealing four yellow teeth in an otherwise toothless mouth. "You are paying me well for such a simple message. Is it risky?"

Sky Messenger's voice took on a timbre Taya had never heard before—threatening. "I'm not paying you to ask questions."

Raloga's smile drooped. "Fine. That's fine. I

didn't mean to anger you. I'll deliver it exactly as you said."

"Then you will live a long and happy life, my friend." Sky Messenger slapped him on the back hard enough to make the Trader stumble.

"Er, yes, well...then, if you don't mind, I'll be on my way." He lifted a hand and quickly trotted away with his dogs surrounding him. He cast two backward glances, apparently to make certain he wasn't being followed, and vanished up the trail.

Taya walked to stand beside Sky Messenger. Her cape flapped around her legs. "What are you trying to do? Hiyawento is married to Chief Atotarho's daughter! We can't go see him. Atotarho is an evil cannibal sorcerer. If he captures us, he'll cut our hearts out and eat them for breakfast. Do you want to die?"

Sky Messenger's gaze remained on the point where the Trader had disappeared. "We should be there by midnight. I'll be able to answer your question then."

8

Raloga scratched his itching armpit. He'd had to run hard to get here in time, and sweat-drenched his shirt. It was almost midnight, yet people crowded the plaza of Atotarho Village. Everywhere he looked, cook pots boiled near huge bonfires, and the scent of sweet corn cakes baking in ashes rose. Drum beats pounded the air. Arranged in a rough oval around the plaza were four longhouses, four smaller clan houses, and a prisoner's house. The magnificent longhouses—the biggest ever built—were constructed of pole frames and covered with elm bark. The Wolf Clan longhouse was truly stunning; it stretched over eight hundred hand-lengths long and forty wide. The others were shorter, two or three hundred hands long, but still impressive. The arched roofs soared fifty hands high. Was

Hiyawento in council with the matrons? Or the elders? He might have just been meeting with War Chief Sindak, or various war deputies.

"There must be three thousand people here. What's happening?" His five dogs pricked their ears and looked at him. "Come on, we don't have much time."

As he shouldered through the crowd looking for War Chief Hiyawento, he passed people in brilliant capes, wearing elaborate shell, copper and carved wooden jewelry. Sounds of laughter and singing echoed from somewhere ahead.

He tapped a youth of perhaps sixteen summers on the shoulder. "What's happening?"

The young warrior's face was alight. He wore his hair pulled back and fastened in a tight bun. "We captured two hundred prisoners in our last raid. The matrons are deciding who will be adopted into the clans and who will be tortured to death." He clapped Raloga on the shoulder. "There's plenty of food. Fill a bowl and join the celebration."

"Actually, I'm trying to find War Chief Hiyawento. The guards at Coldspring Village told me he was here. Have you seen him?"

The youth craned his neck, spied what he was looking for, and pointed. "His personal guards are standing over in front of the Wolf Clan house. He's probably in council."

Raloga smiled. "Thank you. Have an enjoyable night."

He strode away with his dogs trailing behind him. Each time one growled at a village dog, he shouted stern words, and his dogs put their tails between their legs and fell into line again.

The guards standing at the southern end of the longhouse scowled at him as he approached. "A pleasant evening to you, brave warriors," he greeted. "I am Raloga, and I carry an urgent message for War Chief Hiyawento."

The tall woman sneered. Perhaps twenty-nine or thirty summers, she had short black hair and an oval face. "Who is the message from?"

Raloga wouldn't dare say Sky Messenger's name in this company. That would get him cut into tiny pieces and fed to the village dogs. "A man called Odion."

The guards looked at each other and exchanged annoyed glances. The shorter man with a broken nose and scars the width of a man's finger running across his right cheek, said, "I've never heard of him. Have you, Kallen?"

"No," the woman replied in a bored voice.

"Nonetheless, the message I carry is extremely important."

"Yes, yes," Kallen said as though she'd been hearing similar claims all day. "Sit down over there, and when the war chief is available, I'll let him know you're here."

"No, friend, you don't understand," Raloga pressed. "I must see him immediately."

Kallen said, "*Sit down* before I crack your skull with my club." She swung it to emphasize her point.

Raloga swallowed hard. "I have another solution. I will be perfectly content to give the message to you, his trusted guards, and have you relay it to him. That way, the responsibility for delivering it in a timely fashion rests with you."

"Very well," Kallen said, "what is the message?"

"Come closer. I don't wish anyone to overhear it."

Kallen bent down and let the ugly little Trader whisper the message in her ear. She straightened. "That doesn't sound urgent to me."

"Trust me, friend, the war chief will think it is." Raloga bowed slightly, gave them an ingratiating smile, and trotted away with his dogs at his heels.

As Raloga hurried across the village, Kallen shook her head. "He's an onerous character. I've never liked him."

Gosha stared after the Trader. "What did he say?"

"Just that Odion, whoever that is, wishes to meet the war chief in the aspen meadow at midnight, and he's traveling with a woman."

Gosha adjusted his weapons belt, shifting it on his hips. "Should you interrupt the war chief? Midnight is fast approaching, and if the aspen grove at issue is the one just outside of Coldspring Village, it's a hard run to get there in time."

Kallen jerked an irritated nod. "Hiyawento said he did not wish to be disturbed. Matron Tila has never called a council meeting in her chamber before. Everyone important is there."

"I know. If this is some sort of joke, I'd rather not be the one to pull the war chief out of the council."

"Stop looking at me. I don't want to do it," Kallen exclaimed.

Gosha distastefully examined the celebration. Atotarho had attacked White Dog Village six days ago, and his people considered him a hero. The fact that his actions might split the Hills nation in two did not seem to worry him. The attack had stunned Hiyawento and the Coldspring Village council, and at least two other villages had been forced to put down riots over the outrage. Whispers of civil war were running rampant across Hills country.

Given the stakes, who knew what "a message from Odion," might mean?

Kallen looked at the longhouse door curtain. Firelight glimmered around the edges, creating an enormous luminous square. Inside, she could hear Hiyawento's deep, measured voice making some point.

"All right." Kallen straightened. "I'm going in. If he kills me, make sure my family finds my body."

"He won't dismember you. No one would allow it. You're an honored deputy war chief."

Gosha gave Kallen a confident nod, which slightly unnerved her. She took a deep breath, pulled back the curtain, and stepped into the firelit warmth of the longhouse. Forty fires burned down the length, lighting each family's compartment and reflecting from the faces of the council members. Matron Tila sat on the bench in the back wrapped in so many hides she resembled a fat furry animal, except for her pain-stricken face. Matron Kelek of the Bear Clan sat to Tila's left, apparently holding her up. The other council members—Hiyawento, Zateri, War Chief Sindak, Matron Ganon of Turtleback Village, and Matron Kwahseti of Riverbank Village—were seated on mats around the fire. Kwahseti's war chief, Thona, stood just behind her with his war axe shining on his belt. Next to him stood Negano, the chief's personal guard. The sight of Atotarho made Kallen's bowels go watery. A beautiful black ritual cape, covered with circlets of bone cut from human skulls, covered his twisted, deformed body. Gray hair, braided with rattlesnake skins, haloed his bony face. When he gestured at Hiyawento's wife, Zateri, his bracelets, made of human finger bones, rattled.

Atotarho said, "You seem to have forgotten you are my daughter. Have you lost all respect for the elders of this nation?"

Matron Zateri calmly stared him straight in the eyes. She was stately but unattractive. Her face was too round, and her front teeth stuck out slightly, but she had a powerful presence. "I respect those who obey the will of the people, Father. You consulted no one before you and your village council decided to raid White Dog Village. It seems to me it is you who has shown disrespect. Did you think the other village councils would not care?"

Atotarho's eyes narrowed in anger, but his voice came out with deadly softness. "I expected them to be grateful. The destruction of White Dog Village has demonstrated to the Ruling Council of the Standing Stone nation that we will not be toyed with. Perhaps in the future, they will not take our threats so lightly."

Hiyawento said, "They did not take our threat

lightly, Chief. In fact, I'm sure from High Matron Kittle's response that they are already preparing for our attack. If we were wise, I think we would try to arrange a meeting to discuss the situation before it gets out of hand."

War Chief Sindak said, "I agree with Hiyawento. We are standing on a precipice. Any wrong move now and we will all fall into chaos. Many lives will be lost."

Matron Kwahseti tucked gray hair behind her ear and let out a sigh. "I am also forced to agree with Hiyawento. We should all take a step back. My village council is outraged by the attack on White Dog Village, and we will not stand by and be drawn into this conflict. We—"

Matron Kelek's raspy voice called, "You would take sides against your own people, Kwahseti? You would fight against your relatives? How many times have we sent our warriors to protect your village from Mountain war parties? Hmm? How many times?"

Matron Kwahseti lowered her eyes in shame. "Many times, Matron, but—"

"There are no *buts*. Either you are part of this alliance, or you are not. Choose."

Zateri softly said, "None of us should be forced to choose, Matron Kelek. But you are right. That is where we stand, as War Chief Sindak says, *on a precipice*. Before we all push each other over the edge, let us calm our voices, and..."

While Zateri continued talking, Kallen eased up behind Hiyawento and knelt. The war chief was a tall man with sharp eyes and a hooked nose. Black hair brushed the collar of his buckskin shirt.

Without looking at her, Hiyawento asked, "This had better be critical, Kallen."

"A Trader came through. He said he had a message for you."

"Yes?" He still didn't look at her. His gaze moved back and forth between Zateri and the matrons, judging their expressions. "What is it?"

"Odion wishes to meet with you in the aspen meadow at midnight."

Hiyawento seemed to stop breathing. His eyes widened. He leaned closer to Kallen. "What do you mean? He's here?"

"Apparently."

"Dear gods, is he alone?"

"No, the Trader said there's a woman with him."

"A woman! Why wasn't I informed immediately! They need protection. Organize six guards and meet me at the aspen meadow. Hurry."

Hiyawento scrambled to his feet and strode for the door curtain. Everyone in the meeting stopped to stare. Leaving without the consent of the elders was considered a grievous insult to the council.

Atotarho leaned back and glowered at Hiyawento's back. Matron Zateri just watched him, concerned.

Kallen apologized, "Forgive him. A minor emergency. He meant no disrespect." She bowed to the council and swiftly backed outside into the cold night.

9

Taya could not say what made the first sight of War Chief Hiyawento so impressive. He had no guards, no attendants, no extraordinary jewelry, none of the trappings of prestige and power—the man was not even armed. When he first glimpsed Taya and Sky Messenger in the forest, he stood alone, frozen, silent. A formidable man, tall, with a narrow beaked face and burning eyes, black hair blew around his shoulders. Dressed in a worn, knee-length buckskin shirt, he was dwarfed by the soaring height of the Coldspring Village palisade behind him. But if there had been hundreds of people assembled in this clearing, none of them would have had eyes for anything but this man. He was clearly a war chief to be reckoned with.

Sky Messenger's words were like pebbles

striking at the silence. "Wrass, it does my heart good to see you."

The war chief strode forward and embraced Sky Messenger so hard his muscular arms shook. "Blessed gods, Odion, I have dreamed of this day a thousand times."

They should have long ago given up their childhood names, and perhaps they had with every other person in the world, but it struck Taya as strangely intimate.

They continued to hold each other, their muscles bulging through their shirts, until the war chief pushed back. "I can't believe you made it this far. Why are you alive?"

Taya noticed that Sky Messenger had tears in his eyes. "I know I'm placing you in danger, forgive me, but I had to see you."

"What's wrong?"

Sky Messenger extended a hand. "First, let me present Taya, granddaughter of High Matron Kittle. The woman to whom I am betrothed."

Hiyawento's mouth opened slightly, as though he didn't know what to say.

Taya stepped forward, uncertain how to act but then her grandmother's training took over, and she extended her hand to the man who was the sworn enemy of her people. "I am honored to meet you, War Chief Hiyawento."

He took her hand, and when he felt the slight

tremor in her grip, he said, "You are here under my protection. Don't be afraid."

Warriors emerged from the trees, six of them, carrying nocked bows and quivers bristling with arrows on their backs. Hiyawento instructed, "Fan out. I don't want anyone to get close enough to see my guests."

The warriors ghosted away into the shadows, and though she knew they had to be close, she could not see them.

Sky Messenger and Hiyawento walked into the small clearing in the middle of the aspen grove and sat down on the fallen log. Taya trailed behind them. It was very late, and she was exhausted from running all day. Despite Hiyawento's guarantee of safety, they were Hills People. They couldn't be trusted. She kept glancing around, trying to see if anyone was sneaking up on them.

Hiyawento and Sky Messenger just stared at each other for a time, smiling, as though memorizing the other's face.

Hiyawento finally said, "I returned from Bur Oak Village just last night. Were you aware of that?"

"No. Why were you there?"

"I delivered a message from our Ruling Council. Basically, it was a threat to destroy the entire Standing Stone nation if it ever attempted to establish an alliance with a Hills village again. You can guess how High Matron Kittle responded."

Sky Messenger nodded, but before he spoke, Taya said, "She must have shouted and threatened back. Believe me, she meant every word."

"I did believe it," Hiyawento said.

Sky Messenger propped a fist in his lap. "Mother will try to ease the situation."

"Yes, Speaker Koracoo is a peacemaker at heart, but I'm not sure she can. We have a tidal wave of rage building here. I fear this next battle is going to be long and bloody. You heard the news?"

Sky Messenger's forehead wrinkled. "No. We've been on the trail. What news?"

"Blessed Spirits, I thought that's why you'd come."

Hiyawento leaned forward and braced his elbows on his knees. "Six days ago, Chief Atotarho, without consulting any of the other village councils, decided to attack White Dog Village. He—"

"Yes." The rush of air behind the word made it sound like a gasp. "I know. We passed by it on the way here. How is the Hills nation reacting?"

Hiyawento hesitated. "Aren't you concerned about your father? I heard Gonda and his wife escaped, along with most of the elders."

"I'm greatly relieved to hear that, but right this instant, I am more concerned about how your people are taking the news."

"Badly. It could mean civil war. The attack was not sanctioned by the Ruling Council. Coldspring Village is not the only Hills village upset by the outrage. Riverbank Village and Canassatego Village are both up in arms."

Sky Messenger let out a breath that fogged in the cold air and then he stared up at the firelight reflecting from the aspen leaves. As the golden leaves trembled in the breeze, the light fractured and flashed in hundreds of places at once. "After everything he did to us, I don't know how you can live here and not kill him."

"He's Zateri's father. If I didn't love her so desperately, I assure you"—he glanced around to make certain his warriors could not overhear their words—"I'd have killed him when I first came here. His words are like an eel in your hand, slippery. You can never quite get hold of them."

In a warm voice, Sky Messenger asked, "How is Zateri?"

"She is well. But she's going to be devastated that she didn't get to see you."

"I was hoping to see her," Sky Messenger said, disappointed.

"You won't. She'll be in council for most of the night. And you, my friend, are going to have to leave here before either of us wishes it."

"How soon?"

"Very soon. Before anyone finds out you're here. We have, perhaps, one-half hand of time."

"Then I should get to the point." But he hesitated and wiped his palms on his cape.

Hiyawento noticed the action, and with great care, said, "I was glad to hear that Matron Kittle reversed your death sentence." He cast a meaningful glance at Taya. "Your vision was on everyone's lips."

"Yes, it's a long story, and that's why I'm here." Sky Messenger massaged his forehead. "I've been having Spirit Dreams. I don't know what to make of some of them."

Hiyawento straightened. "Is there more than one, or is this the same Dream that started when you'd seen eleven summers?"

Taya's head jerked around to stare. He'd been having the *same* Spirit Dream for twelve summers? Did Grandmother know that? Or any of the Ruling Council? Blessed gods, if it were true...

"It's basically the same Dream." Blood flushed Sky Messenger's cheeks. Even in the pale light, Taya could see it. "It's changed slightly over the summers. Images get added, some are deleted, as though not even the Spirits know the final shape of the story."

"Does the Dream come every night?"

"Recently, it's afflicted me two or three times in a night. I just abruptly find myself walking in a strange glittering world where Elder Brother Sun—"

"*Covers his face with the soot of the dying world?*"

Taya's spine tingled. She glanced at Sky Messenger.

He shuddered as if he'd been doused with ice water. Just above a whisper, he said, "Blessed gods, Wrass, those words are as powerful today as the day you first said them. They still strike at my heart."

Hiyawento leaned closer to Sky Messenger. "Mine, too. I remember the day I heard them as though it were this morning."

Sky Messenger hesitated. "Could you tell Taya the story of what happened to you that day, Wrass?"

Hiyawento was quiet for a time, as though preparing himself for the memories. "It was twelve summers ago, just before War Chief Koracoo and her search party found us. I was lying in the old witch's canoe. The beatings I'd taken the day before had left me badly fevered. I was lying with my cheek on the cold gunwale when a man walked through the water toward me. He had a bent nose, like one of the Faces of the Forest."

Sky Messenger whispered, "Shagoniyoh. The Voice."

Taya sat down hard in front of them. Her knees

had gone weak. Sky Messenger's Spirit Helper had also come to Hiyawento? That meant Sky Messenger might not be a mad fool. "Then what happened?"

Hiyawento's dark eyes took on a troubled expression. "I was afraid. I asked him if he was one of the hanehwa."

Instinctively, Taya's gaze went to the forest, searching for flits of gray slipping between the trees. "What did he say?"

"He said, *'We are all husks, Wrass, flayed from the soil of fire and blood. This won't be over for any of us until the Great Face shakes the World Tree. Then, when Elder Brother Sun blackens his face with the soot of the dying world, the judgment will take place.'* I swear the words are burned into my afterlife soul. I hear them in my sleep, on the war trail, when I'm playing with my daughters. I wish I knew what they mean."

The lines at the corners of Sky Messenger's eyes pinched. He shoved his cape aside and reached into the red Power pouch tied to his belt, where he drew out the splinter of charred skull. Attached to it was a tightly wound strand of black hair that had been tied with a cord—as though it were precious to him—and she wondered if it belonged to Baji.

Sky Messenger tenderly tucked the hair back into the Power pouch and held out the piece of skull. "This has something to do with the *judgment*."

Hiyawento frowned at it.

Sky Messenger flipped it in his hand. "This skull ties you and me to the Dream. I just...I'm not certain how yet. But I must find out."

Hiyawento extended his hand, and Sky Messenger placed the piece of skull in it. The war chief's black brows drew together over his hooked nose. He examined it carefully. "Where did you find this?"

"Just north of Bog Willow Village. It belongs to the...do you...do you remember the Mountain war chief...the one who took me out into the forest?"

A swallow went down Hiyawento's throat. His voice came out filled with hatred. "Yes."

"What did he do to me, Wrass? What happened out in the trees?"

Hiyawento bowed his head and shook it, as though to ease the memories. "I didn't see it, Odion. I know he hurt you. You told me he did. But I don't know for sure. Something...something terrible. Why do you ask?" He handed the piece of skull back and rubbed his hands hard on his shirt as though to rid them of the taint.

Sky Messenger tucked it into the red pouch again and pulled the laces tight. "At the end of my Dream, I hear his voice."

Hiyawento paused. "What does he say?"

"It's as though he has his lips pressed to my ear. He orders, 'Lie down, boy. Stop crying, or I'll cut your heart out.' Then a great hole opens in the cloud-sea beneath my feet, and I fall and fall. Wisps of cloud trail behind me as I tumble through nothingness surrounded by glittering petals shaken from the World Tree."

Taya sat stunned. Blood pounded in her ears. *Blessed gods, what did the war chief do to him?* A sensation of pained awe filled her. It was real. The Dream was true, and it was tied to whatever had happened to both Sky Messenger and Hiyawento twelve summers ago. She had thought his soul was loose. But if Sky Messenger and Hiyawento had the same Spirit Helper and both were having the same Dream...great ancestors!

"Taya and I just came from the Dawnland country. I spent a day walking the old campsite and the forest, trying to remember that part. The last thing I recall is being taken by the hand and dragged into the forest. The rest...the rest is just gone."

Softly, Hiyawento asked, "Why is it so important to remember, Odion? There's nothing but pain there."

"Old Bahna says that before I can stop Elder Brother Sun from turning his back on the world, I have to remember." Sky Messenger clenched his fists. "Wrass, there's something I must ask of you."

Hiyawento said, "Long ago, I promised you on my life that I would be there with you. At the end. I mean to keep that promise. So be careful what you ask, for I will do it without question."

For a time, Sky Messenger just stared into his friend's eyes. Finally, he said, "Great-Grandmother Earth is dying. Our war is killing her. We have to stop it."

"I agree, but how? It's been going on for generations."

"Will you ask Zateri to speak to the matrons of the other Hills villages about establishing a truce so that I may tell them my Dream? I know Atotarho won't listen, but perhaps they will."

"I will ask her. And what do you wish me to do?"

Sky Messenger took a deep breath. "I hesitate to ask, because I know what it will cost you. Will you, War Chief Hiyawento, speak against war in your next council?"

Hiyawento straightened. The ramifications must be sinking in. A war chief who argued for peace was likely to find a stiletto between his ribs.

Finally, Hiyawento nodded. "Yes, I will. And you know Zateri will do everything necessary to support you. She..." Hiyawento's expression slackened, as though something dire had just occurred to him.

"What is it?"

"Nothing, it's just...nothing." He shook his head as though denying some inner warning. "I will speak with her. That's all."

He was holding something back. Sky Messenger said, "If there was any other way—"

"Don't get sentimental," Hiyawento replied. "We both know the price of your Dream. We've known it for more than a decade."

They smiled at each other, the smiles of men who've known each other since boyhood, fought side by side through the worst of times, and are ready to fight again. Men who share an unbreakable bond of trust.

The price of the Dream. For the first time, Taya considered the possibility that Sky Messenger might truly be the prophesied human False Face. Along with that shocking moment came the realization that his vision—the same vision of War Chief Hiyawento—might also save both of their peoples from the abyss that yawned before them. *It might save all of the peoples south of Skanodario Lake.*

She sat back and looked at the two men. She couldn't believe it. The man she was betrothed to might actually be a prophet. Taya had to concentrate to keep her stomach from rising into her throat.

10

Taya swallowed hard. "May I speak?"

Sky Messenger swiveled on the log to look at her and blinked as though he had forgotten she was there. "Yes, of course, Taya."

She wet her lips. War Chief Hiyawento seemed to be staring right through her. Fear and excitement had conjured the unthinkable in her heart, and she didn't know how to deal with it. But...but she was beginning, dimly, to understand why Bahna had said she had to go with Sky Messenger on this journey.

Shakily, she said, "I was wondering if perhaps more alliances like the one Grandmother established between the allied Standing Stone villages and Sedge Marsh Village might be possible?"

Hiyawento shifted. Set against the background of firelit palisade, he looked vaguely unreal, his hair dancing around his dark face. "Why do you ask?"

Taya gestured helplessly. "I have spent my life listening to Grandmother's political lectures, so I know something of what our people need, and perhaps, a little of what the Hills People need. If our two peoples could just agree to protect each other from Chief Atotarho"—she wet her lips again—"I mean, he's the problem, isn't he?"

"So far as I'm concerned, he is," the war chief responded.

Sky Messenger stared at her as if confused. And why wouldn't he be? Just a few days ago she'd argued that they had to kill all of their enemies to survive. "I was thinking that if we could agree on that one thing—that Chief Atotarho should be destroyed—and we could create an alliance to do that...well, it would be a start."

Hiyawento's eyes narrowed enough to let Taya know he was suspicious of her motives. "Before the destruction of White Dog Village there might have been a chance, but why would High Matron Kittle agree to such an alliance now? I suspect that at this very instant she's engaged in whipping up a fervor to kill every Hills person alive."

"But your village was not involved in that attack."

"No. Most of our nation didn't even know about it until it was long over. Nonetheless, rage and pain tend to simplify the world, Taya. Your grandmother and the Ruling Council will see only that the Hills People just attacked a Standing Stone village. Such an act demands a response. Your people must be preparing for it as we speak. Our people certainly are."

"Even Sindak?" Affection laced Sky Messenger's voice.

"Of course, my friend. He is an excellent war chief. Protecting our people is his sole responsibility. He'll do whatever it takes to stop a Standing Stone attack. As you would, if the reverse were—"

Sky Messenger shook his head. "No. I've given up my weapons. For good. I'll never touch a bow, or club, again, never raise my hand in violence, not even to save my own life, or the lives of people I love."

Hiyawento appeared stunned. He hesitated, before quietly saying, "Odion, I'm not sure that this is the time for—"

Taya cried, "Yes, please, tell him how foolish it is! He should take up his weapons and return to being deputy war chief before it's too—"

Sky Messenger interrupted, "The *only* position I would accept now is that of *peace* chief." He gave Taya a disgruntled look.

"Peace chief?" Hiyawento leaned back and chuckled softly. "I like the sound of that. It implies something not of this earth."

Taya flapped her arms against her sides. "Let's get back to the subject. I'm telling you, if Grandmother knew the truth about what really happened to White Dog Village, the matrons would vote not to attack the Hills villages that weren't responsible. Grandmother hates Chief Atotarho—she says he's an evil cannibal sorcerer who deserves to die—but she can be reasonable. Perhaps, if Sky Messenger and I can get home quickly enough, we can redirect Grandmother's rage."

"What do you mean? Redirect it?" Hiyawento asked.

"Perhaps we can use it like pine pitch, to glue our peoples together for one purpose: to destroy Atotarho. Please listen to me. I'm sure Grandmother would like that idea, as would the other matrons. Even if it required an onerous alliance with you to achieve it, killing the enemy chief responsible for the deaths of so many Standing Stone women and children would be worth it."

In an ominous voice, Sky Messenger said, "We are all talking treason. Let us not forget that. If we do this, it will have to be done with the stealth of Cougar stalking Hare. Are we all prepared for that? Taya? Are you?"

Am I?

She took a deep breath and exhaled the words: "By the time we reach Bur Oak Village, I think I will be."

Sky Messenger and Hiyawento both nodded to her, as though understanding perfectly well that it took time to brace the body and souls for the possibility of being executed. But then, both men had already committed treason, at least in the eyes of some—Hiyawento for allowing himself to be adopted into the Hills nation, and Sky Messenger for releasing the Flint captives. They understood, as few men ever can, the price of loosing the whirlwind. Once released, its path was almost impossible to control.

"Then we will speak with our matrons about this," Sky Messenger said.

"And I will speak with Zateri about gathering the Women's Council to consider a truce to hear your vision. But don't get your hopes—"

A tall woman warrior, silent as a wolf on a blood trail, trotted out of the darkness, her short black hair flapping around her taut face. "War Chief? You must hurry. Several of Atotarho's warriors are coming. They mean to bring you back to the council meeting."

Hiyawento leaped to his feet. "Kallen, pick two warriors and take my guests to the Bur Oak Village trail. Be back by morning. I don't wish anyone to know you were gone."

"Yes, War Chief."

Hiyawento and Sky Messenger embraced one

last time. Hiyawento whispered, "Before you go, tell me of Baji? Is she well?"

"I don't know. I've had no news from Wild River Village for moons. I pray she's safe."

Baji is from Wild River Village...

"Be off, my friend. I'll send word as soon as I know if the matrons will hear your vision."

Sky Messenger gripped Taya's elbow and turned to Kallen. "We're ready."

"We must move quickly." Kallen took the lead, pointing to warriors as they emerged from the forest. Two men fell into line behind Taya.

As they trotted away, Taya said, "Why didn't you tell me that Shagoniyoh had come to both you and Hiyawento?"

Sky Messenger shoved her ahead of him and took up the rear. "We are not the only two people who have been visited by him."

"Others have seen the Spirit, as well? Blessed gods! If I'd known, it would have made a difference." She shook her head. "I'm still terrified, but—"

"You can still change your mind, Taya."

"No, not after tonight. Not after what I heard. I am with you, my future husband. To be against you is even more scary."

11

Ohsinoh followed the mob at a distance, lagging behind the others as they crossed the plaza of Atotarho Village and proceeded on to the sacred platform. Ten hands tall, three upright logs stood in the center of the platform. Some of the most impressive longhouses in the country formed a square around it. People crowded near the platform, their gazes fixed on the man who staggered in the midst of the warriors. He'd been captured seven days ago, and had managed to survive the torture until this moment. His two friends had not. Their bodies hung limply from the two poles on the sides. The crows and magpies had been at them for days. Their eyes were blood-blackened sockets, and the flesh had almost been completely stripped from their faces, leaving gape-mouthed skulls to stare down upon the people of Atotarho Village.

Ohsinoh stopped, allowing the party to continue without him, and knelt to dip a handful of water from a puddle. It tasted earthy and dank. He sang a little to himself as he drank, *"The crow comes, the crow comes, pity the little children, beat the drum..."*

The words had been stuck in his head since childhood. He heard the tune all day and all night, repeating over and over as though seeping up from a black door inside him. There were times when it drove him so mad he beat his head with rocks, trying to make it go away.

People glanced at him, wondering why he didn't simply help himself to the large pots of rainwater that stood near the houses. But he would never do that. He'd never share water with these people. The Wolf Clan had abandoned him to horror when he'd seen just four summers. Everything here was unclean, full of contagion. If a man stayed too long, he felt certain a part of his soul would remain behind, condemned to wander the village until the last timbers rotted to dust.

Two old women passed, pointed at him, and whispered behind their hands. He gave them a grim smile, and they made the sign against evil and hurried away.

When he dipped his hand again, he saw his

reflection. He'd painted his face to hide his identity. His white face paint was decorated with black stripes. Though the paint did not hide his oversized ears, upturned nostrils, and small dark eyes, it obscured them, as the striped shadows of the forest did the deer. Few people ever recognized him when he wore face paint. Those who did didn't live long.

As he rose to his feet, his heavy moose hide cape waffled around his tall body. Powerfully built, he'd seen twenty-three summers pass. His thick eyebrows were obsidian black and formed a single line over his slitted eyes.

A flock of children veered wide around him, laughing, running to see the latest spectacle. Their dirty feet were bare and caked with mud.

Warriors marched the doomed man up the platform steps and tied him to the middle pole. Ohsinoh couldn't tear his gaze away. He had never even met the victim, but—like everyone else here—he yearned to watch him die. The prisoner was a warrior from White Dog Village, a village of the Standing Stone People. That was enough reason to hate him.

The man's head hung down, and he breathed heavily. His muscular body had endured much over the past few days. Slashes and punctures adorned his flesh. All had been cauterized with fiery brands. Even from this distance, Ohsinoh could smell the taint of burned skin and muscle.

The esteemed and powerful Atotarho emerged from the Wolf longhouse and with great ceremony marched toward the platform. Two holy men followed him. As he climbed the steps to stand before the doomed man, the circlets of human skull on Atotarho's black cape flashed. The prisoner had no strength left. His chest heaved, and he panted as he licked parched lips. With little ceremony, Atotarho drew out his flint knife and slit open the man's belly. When his entrails fell onto the platform, the man let out one final wail and slumped. As was his right, Atotarho cut the still-beating heart from the warrior's chest and presented it to the glorious war chief, Sindak, who'd won the battle. Sindak bowed and strode away to eat his prize in private.

Ohsinoh chuckled. The rest of the human carcass was soon cut up and distributed among the villagers. Three little girls ran by him carrying bloody pieces of meat, their faces alight.

When the crowd dispersed, Ohsinoh stood for a while gazing up at the three dead men. They'd gotten better than they deserved. The Standing Stone People were savage beasts, cowards not worthy of life. Even Wrass and Odion had chosen to be adopted by other nations.

He moved a little closer, standing in the rear,

waiting to catch the great Atotarho's gaze. The chief stood atop the platform speaking with the holy men.

Finally, Atotarho turned, glimpsed Ohsinoh, and paled. His crooked body careened down the platform steps, his walking stick clacking. "I told you *never* to come here. You were supposed to send a messenger telling me where to meet you."

"But, Father, I wished to see my home. Surely I have that right. I've been away too many summers. I'm certain my relatives have missed me."

He smiled at the old man, and the chief's eyes narrowed. Atotarho looked around to see who was watching and whispered, "Give me your message and leave."

"I've accomplished both tasks."

Atotarho blinked. "Really? Because it isn't apparent. If anything, my daughter's husband is even more a problem now than before. Last night in council he urged peace. *Peace!* And after everything we've gone through, his words had power. Two clan matrons sided with him and the Coldspring Village council. It was a disgusting display of arrogance."

Ohsinoh leaned down to whisper in an amused voice, "Sky Messenger has pitied the little children, and soon, very soon, the Crow will come to sit upon Hiyawento's head."

"That's gibberish. Are you saying you've seen Sky Messenger?"

"Oh, yes." Ohsinoh chuckled. "Sky Messenger met with Hiyawento last night outside of Coldspring Village, just before Hiyawento rejoined your council meeting."

It took a few instants for the words to sink in, then rage twisted the old man's wrinkles into frightening lines. "Are you certain of this?"

"I personally followed him from Atotarho Village to Coldspring Village. I saw them sitting together in the aspen meadow."

Atotarho stamped his walking stick on the ground as though to punish Great-Grandmother Earth for allowing such an abomination. "My own daughter's husband is conspiring with the Standing Stone People behind my back? What did they talk about?"

"I couldn't get close to hear, but given what he said in council, it isn't hard to figure out."

Enraged, Atotarho said, "Very well. You've brought your message. Now get out of my village before someone recognizes you. When it is clear to me, and it isn't yet, that you have accomplished both of the tasks I gave you, I'll send your payment to the usual place."

Ohsinoh laughed and gave him an exaggerated mocking bow. As he strode across Atotarho Village, he drew magical symbols in the air, cursing his relatives. When people noticed, they hastened to flee from him. Even the dogs trotted away growling.

12

That night Zateri knelt before the fire in the longhouse, stirring a pot of cornmeal mush filled with strips of venison jerky and pine nuts. The rich scent of the jerky mixed with the sweetness of the corn and scented the air. Hiyawento sat on the mat beside her, staring at the fire as though praying hard the flames would speak to him and tell him what to do next. The council meeting had not gone well. Hiyawento had been openly accused of cowardice and collaborating with the enemy. At the end, it had almost come to blows.

Across the fire, their three daughters played with a cornhusk doll, handing it back and forth, tousling its long corn-silk hair, rattling the beaded fringe on the doll's leather dress. It was a pretty thing. She wondered where Hiyawento had gotten it.

Barely above a whisper, Hiyawento asked, "What about the other matrons?"

She shook her head. "I don't know. Grandmother wishes to hear Sky Messenger's vision. She agreed to send messengers to the others. She'll inform us if there is a consensus that he should be heard. But this is the worst possible time to be asking such a thing. The turmoil in the nation is growing worse."

Early that morning she'd run to Grandmother's chamber in the Wolf longhouse and told her about Sky Messenger's visit. She'd also begged Grandmother not to tell Father for fear that he'd immediately dispatch a party to hunt down and kill Sky Messenger and Taya. Grandmother, who'd barely been able to lift her head from her bedding hides, had reluctantly agreed.

"What are you thinking about, my husband?"

He stretched out on his side on the mat and propped his head on his hand, watching the girls play. "About the Dream. He said it changes, as though not even the Spirits know the final shape of the story, but he's certain it has to do with what happened to him that last night in the old woman's camp. He asked me if I'd seen what happened."

Her heart twinged. "He doesn't remember?"

"No." Hiyawento grimaced at his teacup.

"Which I think is a blessing, but he says he must know."

"He's always been touched by Spirits. I wish I'd seen him. I would have so loved that." They had endured so much together as children. He was almost as much a part of her souls as Hiyawento was. "What did you think of his betrothed?"

"Hmm?" Hiyawento blinked as though just hearing her. "Oh, his wife-to-be? She's very young, fourteen summers. Pretty. Actually, she looks very much like her grandmother, High Matron Kittle."

"In that case, she's not pretty, she's stunningly beautiful."

He shrugged and fiddled with his empty teacup, turning it where it rested upon the mat. She watched him closely. His thoughts seemed far away.

"What else did Sky Messenger say? The thing you haven't told me. Was it Sky Messenger who asked you to argue against war in the council?"

Hiyawento looked at each person who was close enough to hear them, then he lowered his voice. Barely audible, he said, "Yes, but he's right."

"But in a war council?" She felt slightly ill. "Urging peace in a village council meeting is one thing, but in a war council?"

"Zateri, someone has to stand up for peace. You know it as well as I do. I don't mind being the first."

She placed the horn spoon upon one of the

hearth rocks and sat down beside him to stare into his worried eyes. "Peace, no matter the cost? Even if we are attacked by Mountain warriors?"

"Yes." He squinted at the flickering flames.

"He can't be suggesting you refuse to defend our village?"

"If we are attacked, I'm sure he knows I will fight to my last breath to protect our people. Just...I think he wants one war chief out there who always, in every case, counsels against war."

"He must know, however, that if the Ruling Council approves an attack, you will have no choice but to lead our warriors into the fight. He does understand that, doesn't he?"

"All he asked was that I vote no in council. He said nothing about what happened when everyone else voted yes."

She drew up her knees and propped her elbows atop them, trying to imagine how the council had gone. The other members of the war council must have been furious, especially if they'd just lost loved ones in the White Dog Village battle. Hiyawento had told her he'd been accused of both cowardice and treason, but she suspected a few people had also probably threatened his life. If anyone attempted to carry out that threat, it would be catastrophic. Murder was the worst crime. It placed an absolute obligation upon the relatives of the deceased. They had to seek revenge, or retribution. Often grieving family members claimed the life of a member of the murderer's clan—his mother, grandmother, even the clan matron—as was their right. Blood feuds could and did escalate into civil wars. And the nation was already on the verge of splitting down the middle.

She asked, "Does Sky Messenger realize that always voting no will make you appear to be a simpering weakling? Not to mention a fool?"

"He's thought it through, Zateri. He needs a symbol."

"A symbol?"

"A war chief who preaches peace. He needs me to become *a peace chief*. He says he will never pick up a weapon again, never raise his hand in violence, not even to save his own life, or the lives of people he loves."

Zateri frowned at the sooty shadows clinging in the corners. The firelight turned them into spectral dancers, their dark feet pounding out the sacred rhythms that had created the world. A strange, almost bizarre notion was forming in her heart. "He's trying to launch an unarmed revolt."

He lifted his head. "What do you mean?"

"I mean, if village matrons followed his example and simply refused to cooperate—to attend council meetings—the Ruling Council could never vote to dispatch warriors."

"Any matron who refuses to attend a meeting

of the Ruling Council will be labeled a traitor." As he thought about it, Hiyawento's brows drew together over his hooked nose. "For the renegade matrons to remain steadfast will require a great deal more bravery than swinging a war club at an enemy warrior."

Zateri considered the ramifications of refusing to attend the next council. Blunting the arrows of war through noncooperation would be very much like swinging an invisible war club at her own relatives. Could she, with her minimal influence, gather enough matrons together to accomplish anything meaningful? "Do you believe his vision?"

Hiyawento didn't even hesitate, "You know I do."

"Then you also believe you will be there when the World Tree shakes, and Elder Brother Sun covers his face with the soot of the dying world?"

He answered in a sober voice. "Yes, and he'll need me more at that moment than at any other time in our lives."

When he looked up at her, his eyes were like night stars. Too bright. She had to look away. She prayed to all the ancestors who had ever lived to give her, and Hiyawento, the strength for the trials ahead. "When is the next war council?"

"Tomorrow. The war chiefs are afraid that Kittle's retribution will be swift. Every village is preparing to be attacked."

"What will you say to them when they suggest striking first?"

Firelight fluttered over his tense features. "I will counsel against war, as I did today."

"Then you had best take ten warriors with you to guard your back. I don't want you waylaid on the way home."

He smiled. "That would make me appear afraid. I can't afford such—"

Across the fire, a shrill, *"You're ruining it!"* erupted, and Zateri looked up in time to see Kahn-Tineta rip the cornhusk doll from her youngest sister's mouth. As she wiped the drool on her cape, she cried, "Look what you did, Jimer! Now it's going to fall apart!"

Three-summers-old Jimer let out a yowl and tried to grab it back.

"Here, give it to me." Zateri held out her hand.

Kahn-Tineta's lower lip quivered. She clutched the doll to her chest. "Mother, it's my turn to play with it. Jimer and Catta have been chewing on it for the past hand of time!"

"Give it to me *now*, Kahn-Tineta," Zateri ordered, and extended her hand farther.

Kahn-Tineta grudgingly handed it over, and Zateri placed it on the mat beside the hearth ring. When she turned back to Hiyawento, he was struggling to suppress a smile.

"The doll is a pretty thing," he said. "Where did you get it?"

"Me?" she asked in surprise. "I thought you brought it to them. I've never seen it before tonight."

They both turned to stare at their daughters. Jimer's gaze was still fixed on the doll, while Kahn-Tineta glared at Zateri, and Catta seemed to have found something fascinating on the bottom of her moccasin.

"Kahn-Tineta," Zateri asked, "where did you get the doll? You didn't take it from another child in the longhouse, did you?"

"No, Mother! I wouldn't take something from one of my relatives. Catta brought the doll to me this afternoon. She said a man gave it to her."

"A man? Catta, who gave you the doll?"

Catta's five-summers-old face took on a guilty expression. She licked her lips nervously. "I don't know his name. He was scary. He said the doll came from Sedge Marsh Village and he wanted me to have it—though he said it was really more of a gift for you, Father, than for me."

Hiyawento lifted his head slowly, his eyes unblinking. "What did the man look like, Catta?"

She drew lines across her young face. "He had his face painted white with black stripes. He said he was a friend of yours."

"A friend...to me?"

Someone from the war council.

Catta nodded vigorously. "And to Mother. He said he'd known you both since you were children."

When Zateri turned to meet Hiyawento's eyes, she found him staring not at her, but at the cornhusk doll. "Did the man say anything else?"

Catta swallowed hard. Her enormous eyes were shiny with tears. "No."

Zateri's gaze burned into Hiyawento's. "There's something I have to tell you. I—I've been meaning to. Sindak came to me. He said...he—he wasn't going to tell me anything until he was sure."

"What about?"

"Hehaka. And Ohsinoh."

With the swiftness of lightning striking, Hiyawento grabbed the doll and threw it in the fire. The dry corn husks instantly caught and burst into flame.

"Father!" Catta groaned. "No!"

Zateri glanced at her chastened daughters, then at the charred doll in the fire pit. It was little more than a human-shaped clump of ash now. The polished stone beads that had decorated the dress fringe had split apart and rolled across the logs. The holes in their centers, where the beads had been strung, resembled tiny glowing eyes.

Hiyawento dropped his face into his hands and

massaged his temples. "Blessed gods, I pray Sindak is wrong. I..."

Kahn-Tineta screamed, *"Mother!"* just as Jimer toppled backward and went into convulsions. Her body flopped and jerked across the mats. Before Zateri could even get to her feet, Catta collapsed with her mouth foaming and her limbs twitching like a clubbed dog's.

Hiyawento lunged to his feet and grabbed Catta. "Zateri! What's happening?"

"I don't know!" She scrambled around the fire and stared down at Jimer's face. The little girl's eyes rolled in her head as her jaws clapped together. She lifted her head and shouted, "Pedeza, go find Ahweyoh!"

Her cousin ran.

Zateri dropped to the floor and pulled Jimer into her lap, holding her daughter, praying that the seizure would end soon, and she...Jimer's body suddenly went limp. Zateri lifted her up and pressed her ear to her daughter's chest. She couldn't hear a heartbeat. She shook Jimer until the girl's head flopped. "Jimer? Jimer, no!"

Hiyawento cried, "Blessed Spirits, this can't be...what's happening?" Hiyawento clutched Catta tightly against his chest. He was rocking back and forth with tears streaming down his face. Catta's head flopped with his motions. Half the longhouse had crowded around them. A buzz of hushed conversations rose.

"Hiyawento?" A sob caught Zateri's throat. "Is Catta...is she..."

"She—she's not breathing."

Kahn-Tineta burst into tears. "Mother! Father!" The last word became a wail.

13

Zateri gazed down at Ahweyoh while the old Healer examined Catta and Jimer. Ahweyoh had seen almost sixty summers and had thin, chin-length white hair and a face like a shriveled scrap of leather. He wore a tattered buckskin cape over his sleep shirt. Everyone in the longhouse had crowded close, whispering, and shaking their heads as they watched.

The little girls rested on Zateri and Hiyawento's bedding hides. Their faces looked so peaceful. Their mouths were ajar, their eyes closed. Catta's head tilted to the left, spilling black hair across her right cheek. Jimer lay on her back with her arms over her head. Ahweyoh pressed Jimer's ribs, then his hands moved lower to prod her belly. A strange moldy scent issued from her mouth. Ahweyoh leaned forward to sniff her breath. Finally, the old

Healer's somber expression slackened, and he stood. Ahweyoh glanced at the far corner of the chamber where Hiyawento sat holding Kahn-Tineta. Kahn-Tineta had her face buried against his shoulder, weeping softly. Hiyawento patted her back and spoke into her ear, but his face had gone deathly gray, wiped clean of all except the hideous realization that his two youngest daughters were dead.

Ahweyoh said, "It was musquash root, probably in the doll."

"In the doll?" Zateri asked.

"Yes, I suspect the powdered root had been folded between the corn husks."

At the expression on Hiyawento's face, Zateri's heart went cold. Three women nearby sobbed. Zateri kept her eyes on her husband, for he looked as though he longed to be dead himself. His expression had contorted. He couldn't take his gaze from his little girls.

"Are you certain? I need to know," Zateri asked. She felt numb, not really there. None of this seemed real. But she knew, all too soon, her world would come crashing down. As her gaze flicked to the people standing close by, her breathing went shallow. She was the village matron. No matter what personal loss she sustained, she could not appear weak or ineffective. She had enemies. Every matron did. Give them one small opening, and they would slit her throat politically.

Ahweyoh searched Hiyawento's face, clearly cataloging the extent of Hiyawento's strain, perhaps wondering what he might do next. "Yes, I'm sure."

Hiyawento lifted Kahn-Tineta's chin to look into her brimming eyes. "Your mother and I must speak. Could you stay with Pedeza for a time?"

"No, Father, don't leave me!" she wailed. "I'm afraid!"

"You'll be all right. Go on now. We won't be long."

Kahn-Tineta shrieked as she ran across the house and grabbed Pedeza around the legs. Pedeza petted her hair. "Come, let's make a cup of tea and talk."

Hiyawento wiped his nose on his sleeve and got to his feet. He was shaking badly. "Come with me, Zateri. Outside."

"Let me grab my cape."

She swung it around her shoulders and followed him out of the house into the icy night wind.

Hiyawento led her to the central village fire, where a bed of coals glowed. He kept his back to her, trying to hide his face. Her heart ached for him. He was on the verge of drastic actions, but she did not know whether they were based upon grief, or rage.

A strange, eerie clarity had come over Zateri. Unlike the people in the longhouse, Zateri did not make futile, anxious gestures or sob. Her souls were busy, piecing things together. The instant she'd understood without a doubt that her daughters were dead, she'd started asking why, how, and who. As the truth took shape, it loomed over her like the shadow of a dark, clawed beast.

Hiyawento sank down on one of the log benches that surrounded the fire and dropped his face into his hands. She saw his wide shoulders shake and heard the desperate choking sounds he made. When he raised his head, and she glimpsed his face, she swiftly went to him and sat down on the log.

"Hiyawento," she began. His arms went suddenly around her waist, and he crushed her against his broad chest.

"Dear gods, what have I done?"

"You?" she said in confusion. She stroked his shoulder-length hair. "You're not to blame."

"It's the war council. I should never have..." His grip tightened around her waist, and he began speaking rapidly, babbling incoherent words while he pressed his cheek against hers. "I knew it would be dangerous...when I agreed...but I thought... Zateri, you know I'm right!"

He continued, speaking against her hair, words blurred, indistinct, saying things she could not decipher. "Stop this," she said. "There is something important I must speak with you about."

"Dear gods," he wept, "they...can't be...can't be dead."

She shoved away and forced him to look at her. His face had contorted. "Listen to me. Try to concentrate."

"What is it?"

"I don't think this has anything to do with your peace initiatives in the war council."

"How can you say that? You know what they accused—"

"Listen to me. Just after Ahweyoh arrived, I heard a rumor that Ohsinoh was in Atotarho Village today."

He didn't seem to comprehend her implication. "The Bluebird Witch wouldn't dare walk into a village. He'd be killed on sight."

"Apparently, he wore elaborate face paint."

"Face paint..." Hiyawento's voice faded. "Like the man who...who gave our daughter the doll?"

"Pedeza heard that his face was painted white with black stripes. Think about this: He said he was a friend of ours, and that he'd known us since we were children. I think, maybe, Hehaka is Ohsinoh."

A frightening mixture of rage and fear creased

his face. "Even if he is, why would Hehaka want to destroy our family? We never did anything to him—except free him from slavery."

"He may see things differently."

"What do you mean?"

Two people emerged from the Snipe Clan longhouse and proceeded across the plaza. They spoke in low, ominous tones as they cast glances at Zateri and Hiyawento. Already, the news must have spread through every longhouse in Coldspring Village.

"He loved that old woman, Hiyawento. Our clan abandoned him when he'd seen four summers. For all practical purposes, she was the only mother he'd ever known. He probably also saw her Outcast warriors as his family—"

Hiyawento's bloodshot eyes fixed upon her face. "But they enslaved and tortured him!"

"Yes, but the old woman and her men were all he had."

"...And we killed them."

A haunted sensation filtered through her. His words repeated in her head, spinning around, mixing with memories of Hehaka's facial expressions from twelve summers ago. After Koracoo's party had rescued him, Hehaka had fought like a caged bear to get back to the evil witch.

"You didn't kill the old woman, my husband. Baji, Odion, and I did."

Hiyawento seemed to wilt. He sagged against her, burying his face in her long hair. "I killed several of her men. He must blame all of us."

"So...this is the Law of Retribution? We killed the old witch and her guards, and he believes that gives him the right to—"

"Your father could just as easily be to blame. He consorts with witches! Do you think he's responsible?"

"I can't believe he would murder his own granddaughters. Even my father—"

"He's a monster, and you know it!" he replied. "He's capable of anything. Even this." Hiyawento suddenly swung around to look at the longhouse with blazing eyes. "They can't be dead!"

He leaped to his feet and marched away so swiftly, Zateri had to grab the log to keep from falling. She called, "Hiyawento, come back."

"No, I—I have to check them again. Maybe they're breathing now." He broke into a run.

Zateri rubbed her cold arms. The red coals in the fire pit flared when Wind Woman breathed upon them, shimmering and casting reddish light across the longhouses. Where had Ohsinoh gone after he'd left? He was her brother. Or at least, it seemed likely. Was he still here, perhaps watching her? They had no proof that it was Ohsinoh who'd poisoned the cornhusk doll. Many people painted their faces white with black stripes. It was common enough, but...

Did my father pay a witch to kill my daughters?

Somewhere in the quiet depths of her soul, details churned, some matching, some not. All relevant if she could just keep the overwhelming grief at bay long enough to figure them out.

Her gaze moved over the plaza. Blue smoke curled from the smoke holes in the roofs and hung over the village like ghostly serpents. They twined together and slithered upward, flying for the Sky World.

Memories seeped up from the deep recesses of her heart. In the background, Zateri could hear Baji screaming...then Hehaka's voice: *"Sometimes, the men want boys. You should be ready. They're going to hurt you."*

"Tonight?" Wrass asks.

Hehaka shrugs. "I don't know. Maybe."

Wrass looks around and says to Odion, "Hehaka is just guessing. How could he know that?"

Hehaka crawls closer, his batlike face alight. He has seen eleven summers. "I know. Believe me. There are a few men who keep coming back just for me."

The horror of that memory snapped Zateri back to the plaza, but not before a thin wail started deep in her lungs. She had to shake herself to force it down. If she lived to see ten thousand summers pass, the pride in Hehaka's voice—his words spoken against a background of Baji's screams—would still ring in her ears.

Shouts rose in the Wolf longhouse. Hiyawento yelled, "They're my daughters! Give them to me!"

Zateri dragged herself to her feet.

For a few terrible moments, she continued staring out at the firelit darkness, trying to imagine what life would be like without the running patter of their small feet, without the feel of their arms around her neck or the sound of their laughter in her ears. The shining eyes that had looked up at her with such love...gone.

Pedeza shouted, "Leave Kahn-Tineta alone! She doesn't know anything else!"

Zateri squared her narrow shoulders and started back.

14

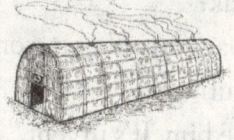

As Pedeza marched across the plaza of Atotarho Village, people raced around her, flying in and out of longhouses, carrying water and firewood, already preparing for the Standing Stone attack that everyone knew was coming. All, that is, except for the young men. Most of them huddled around the council house. Some had their ears pressed to the walls, listening. She wondered why they needed to, for she could hear the raised voices from here.

Two guards stood outside the council house door, their faces set into hard lines, war clubs braced upon their broad shoulders. She hated this village, hated Chief Atotarho: He had brought so much pain to the Wolf Clan. If her lineage achieved prominence, the first thing it would do would be to remove Atotarho.

She was dressed in a long buckskin cape without decorations. Her black braid bounced upon her back as she hurried through the cold wind.

When she halted before the guards, her voice sounded small, even to her. "Please. I need to see War Chief Sindak?"

"There's a war council going on, woman. Can't you hear the shouting?

"I need to see him. It's urgent."

"Urgent?" The guard hooked a thumb over his shoulder. "They're talking about annihilating the entire Standing Stone nation before it can attack us, and you want me to disturb the discussion? Go away. Come back later."

Pedeza wrung her hands. "Please. If I don't see Sindak, someone he cares about is going to die."

The guard's expression changed. He looked at her from the corner of his eye, apparently thinking about the ramifications if Sindak's friend died because he'd refused to deliver a simple message. Finally, the guard pulled his war club off his shoulder, set it beside the door, and stabbed a finger at her. "All right. I'll tell him, but if you're wrong and Sindak slits my throat for this—"

"He won't. I swear. He'll reward you. Maybe even make you deputy war chief. It's *that* important."

The man scowled at her, ducked beneath the curtain, and vanished.

While Pedeza waited under the second guard's alert gaze, she paced. Last night had been the worst of her life. She'd loved those little girls. Watching them die, seeing them lying cold and still in the firelight, had been like dying herself. Then the parade of relatives and Healers had begun and hadn't ended until this morning. Pedeza was exhausted and heartbroken. Zateri had met each person, consoled their grief, and thanked them for coming. All the while, she'd watched Hiyawento disintegrating like a sand sculpture in a rainstorm.

Sindak ducked beneath the curtain. When he saw her, his narrow face creased with worry. He wore a pure black cape—the color of war and death—and had his hair tied back with a cord. The style made his lean face appear even more narrow. "What is it, Pedeza?"

"Hiyawento…"

Misunderstanding, he said, "He's not here. The war council is livid."

She hesitated, uncertain where to begin. "Then you haven't heard about Matron Zateri's daughters? They're dead."

His deeply sunken eyes were bloodshot and red-rimmed, as though he hadn't slept in days. "Blessed gods, forgive me. No one told me. When did it happen?"

"Last night. Please, I know this meeting is critical, but if I could just have a few moments to speak with you in private—"

"I don't have much time," he said as he took her by the arm and led her into the middle of the plaza, out of hearing range of the guards. "How did they die?"

"I don't know everything—just that an unknown man gave the girls a doll, and it was poisoned. Our Healers say it was filled with ground musquash root. You know how children are. They put the doll in their mouths."

Sindak bowed his head. "That's terrible, but how can I help?"

She braced herself. "It's Hiyawento."

"Is he all right? I can't even imagine how he must be feeling. Those little girls were beautiful."

Suddenly Pedeza's tears began to flow. She lifted her cape and dried her eyes. "You have to come, War Chief. Matron Zateri has done the best she can, but Hiyawento has become a madman. I swear he's lost his soul."

"What do you mean?"

"He's gone crazy! Last night after he knew they were dead, he charged around the longhouse smashing pots, tearing down the bark partition walls, screaming at the top of his lungs. You know how much he loved those little girls. This morning at dawn, he carried them out into the forest and won't come home. He says he's never coming back to Coldspring Village."

Earnestly, Sindak replied, "Tell me quickly what Zateri needs. I'll help if I can."

"She wants you to speak with him. She says he needs a friend, a man he trusts, and you're the only man in our entire nation that he'll listen to."

Shouts rang out from the council house. Sindak turned to look, and his jaw went hard. He took Pedeza's arm in a friendly grasp. "Where is Hiyawento?"

"Between the aspen grove and Mallard Marsh."

"Very well. Tell Matron Zateri I will come as soon as I can."

"Yes. I will. Thank you, War Chief."

Pedeza watched Sindak stride back to the council house, his long legs eating the distance; and then she smothered her sobs and started back for Coldspring Village.

15

The scents of water and soggy leaves rode the evening breeze near the marsh.

Sindak halted at the edge of the aspen grove and stared out across the reeds and dead cattails. Golden leaves pirouetted through the frigid air around him, alighting on his shoulders and black hair. He paid them no notice. In the distance, a thin streamer of smoke spiraled into the dove-gray twilight. The thought of trying to talk sense into a man as grief-stricken as Hiyawento made him long to return to the insanity of the war council. What could he say? Nothing, nothing in the world, could lessen the pain of losing a loved one, especially an innocent child. Or worse, two. For a moment he hesitated, trying to imagine how the conversation might go, then he shook his head and tramped around the edge of the marsh toward the campfire. Somewhere out on the water, ducks quacked.

When he got close, Hiyawento shouted, "Go away or I'll kill you!"

Sindak suppressed the urge to pull his war club from his belt and called, "I'm a friend. At least I think I am. Correct me if I'm wrong about that?"

Hiyawento thrashed through the brush. When he stood no more than ten paces away, he looked at Sindak with bright glazed eyes. He held his nocked bow up, aimed at Sindak's heart. His jaw muscles trembled despite his efforts to clench his teeth—the action that of a man teetering on madness.

Sindak spread his arms. "I heard the doll was poisoned. Yesterday someone in Atotarho Village claimed he'd seen Ohsinoh talking with the chief. Have you heard this rumor?"

The bow lowered slightly, and Hiyawento's broad shoulders shook. In a choking voice, he said, "Yes."

"I need more information about your daughters' deaths. May I speak with you?"

Hiyawento relaxed and lowered the bow. "Come." He turned and walked back toward the campfire.

When Sindak made it through the brush, he found Hiyawento standing over the dead children.

They'd been laid out on their backs, their clothing smoothed, their hair combed. Each stared up at the sky with shrunken death-gray eyes. Their white faces shone in the firelight. No matter how long he lived, that wrenching image would never leave Sindak.

He knelt on the opposite side of the fire and watched Hiyawento stroking Jimer's face.

Sindak said, "Ohsinoh would never have had the audacity to enter Atotarho Village unless he knew he'd be protected."

Hiyawento's eyes went shiny. In a lethal voice, he said, "The man who gave my daughter the doll he—he had painted his face white with black stripes."

Sindak nodded. "That matches the description of the man who spoke with Atotarho."

Hiyawento's grip tightened on the elk hide over Catta's heart, and words tumbled from his mouth, hoarse and broken. "He told her that...it...the doll. Was more a gift for me than for her."

Sindak quietly released the breath he'd been holding. If he could keep Hiyawento talking, everything might be all right. "Listen to me. For the past nine moons, I've had a man tracking Negano. The chief has met with the Bluebird Witch several times, and Negano has delivered many bags of payment to a clearing two days' run from here. I think Atotarho has been working with Ohsinoh for a long time, perhaps for many summers."

"Blessed gods, Sindak, if he's been working with Atotarho, then the chief paid him to do this! He—the old man—he wanted me to watch my daughters die. He's punishing me for speaking out against war in the council. I swear before my ancestors that I will *kill* him! I will cut his heart out—"

"And I will help you do it," Sindak said, and waited for Hiyawento to turn so he could stare directly into the man's wild eyes. "But I must have proof."

"Proof?" Hiyawento cried and sprang to his feet. "I'm not waiting for proof! I'll kill anyone who tries to stop me!"

Sindak remained kneeling before the fire, but his thoughts were on the war club tucked into his belt. Could he get to it faster than Hiyawento could shoot an arrow through his lungs? Just as Sindak's hand started to edge for his club, Hiyawento seemed to deflate. He hung his head, and tears filled his eyes. "This is my fault, Sindak. All...my fault."

"None of this is your fault."

Tears ran down his face as Hiyawento hugged himself and looked back at his daughters. "Yes, it is. I should never have come to Hills country. I should have left Zateri alone. I—I loved her so. I'd loved her since we were children. We'd endured so much together. I thought...maybe, if I just...I tried to obey my clan and marry another, but...oh, gods. I'm leaving, I tell you. I'm killing the chief, then I'm leaving and never coming back." He put his head in his hands and squeezed as though to crush the thoughts. "Blessed ancestors, what have I done?"

"You made a life for yourself, a good life, that's what. And a good life for Zateri, too."

"If it weren't for me, none of this—"

"That's foolish." Sindak rose to his feet to loom over Hiyawento.

Hiyawento blinked and gazed up at him with a stunned expression. "You haven't heard a word I've said. I've been trying to tell you—"

"You're moaning like a twelve-summers-old boy. You still have a loving wife and daughter who need you more than they ever have. I saw Zateri on my way here. Kahn-Tineta was lying curled in a ball with Zateri stroking her hair. If you think you're dying inside, how do you think they feel? Zateri and Pedeza have laid out clean clothes and all the ritual necessities to clean your daughters and send them on their journey. If you cared at all about them"—he waved his hand to the dead girls—"you would take them back so that their mother could prepare them. Instead, the great war chief, Hiyawento, is out hiding in the forest weeping like an infant."

Anger twisted Hiyawento's face. Sindak didn't budge as Hiyawento leaned close and growled, "You're asking for a stiletto in your heart."

Sindak stared into those blazing eyes for several moments, assessing, before he replied, "Do you want to twist my head off and kick it around for the village dogs?"

Through gritted teeth Hiyawento said, "Yes!"

"Then you're sounding more like your old self. You must be feeling better. So I'm leaving now." He turned his back on Hiyawento and walked away.

When he'd gone twenty paces without an arrow in his back, he dared to exhale.

In another ten paces, he heard Hiyawento call, "Sindak?"

"Yes?" He turned.

Hiyawento wiped his eyes with his hands. His voice was stronger, if hollow. "How did the war council vote today?"

Sindak waited as Hiyawento tipped his head back and stared at the first campfires of the dead that gleamed along the Path of Souls. He seemed to be gathering his strength to speak.

"The vote was unanimous to attack the allied Standing Stone villages before they can get organized to attack us. The matrons promised to return with their final decision as soon as possible. I expect a decision tomorrow."

"Did anyone speak for peace?"

Sindak frowned. "No."

Guilt ravaged his face. He looked back at his dead daughters. As evening deepened, their small white faces picked up the wavering gleam of the fire. "This is just what Atotarho wanted. I played right into his hands."

Sindak didn't respond. If the chief had been responsible for the deaths of the man's daughters, he was right. It was a calculated move designed to eliminate Hiyawento's influence. And it had worked. If Hiyawento had been there, Sindak suspected the vote would have been split and never referred to the Ruling Council.

To silence Hiyawento, Atotarho was willing to murder his own granddaughters.

Hiyawento called, "War Chief?"

"Yes?"

Hiyawento wiped his face on his sleeve. "If you wouldn't mind, I'd appreciate it if you could help me carry my little girls home."

Sindak walked back. As Hiyawento scooped up Jimer and clutched her to his chest, Sindak gently lifted Catta into his arms. Her small body had grown stiff.

They silently walked around the marsh trail. Just before they reached the Coldspring palisade, Hiyawento halted and turned to gaze at Sindak with bloodshot eyes.

"I want you to answer a question. Do you believe Ohsinoh is Hehaka?"

Sindak tightened his hold on Catta's cold body. "I think so, yes."

Hiyawento didn't say a word. He just walked for the palisade gates.

16

High Matron Tila sat wrapped in hides on her bench, her back propped against the wall of her compartment. Without that support, she would have dissolved like a fistful of earth in a thunderstorm. The excruciating pain in her chest had left her trembling. She did the best she could to hide it as she looked at the old man pacing before her. Atotarho's crooked body made his movements more of a careening than a simple placing of one foot in front of the other. His gray hair, braided with rattlesnake skins, shimmered.

She listened to his walking stick thump on the hard-packed dirt floor. She had known him his entire life, but she had never hated him more than at this moment. The emotion was so powerful it felt like a dark miasma enveloping the world, turning it into something monstrous. The expression on his gaunt skeletal face told her something had surprised him, and he didn't like it at all.

Tila whispered, "Don't bother to deny it. I don't have the strength for lies. Did you know he'd kill your granddaughters?"

Atotarho's wrinkled lips pursed. He didn't answer for a time. Finally, he shook his head, and the circlets of skull on his black cape flashed. "No."

His voice was genuinely troubled, but he'd perfected that tone over the long summers, so she had no idea if he truly regretted his actions or not. "You've turned your daughter against you for good. There's nothing you can do now, or ever, to redeem yourself in her eyes. Do you realize that? You've lost her completely."

"She doesn't know I was responsible. She must think it was witchery, or perhaps—"

"You're a fool." Tila watched him try to indignantly straighten his hunched back without success. "She is *my* granddaughter. I guarantee you she will concentrate all her efforts on destroying you. You don't have long to rule, Chief."

Atotarho leaned heavily on his walking stick. In the firelight, the snake eyes tattooed on his fingertips seemed to wink. "I'll find a way to make it up to her. Perhaps start placing suggestions that her husband should be promoted to a higher position on the Ruling Council—"

Tila let out a low disdainful laugh. "You can't

make up for killing a woman's daughters, even if it was accidental. Besides, you won't have the chance. If I were Hiyawento I'd be plotting your murder this instant. He just has to bide his time until the moment is right." She sucked in an agonized breath. When she let it out, she said, "If I had the strength, I'd save him the trouble."

Atotarho's wrinkled face twisted with anger. He'd always hated hearing blunt words. "I tell you I didn't know the witch would do this. It wasn't my fault."

"Well, that doesn't matter now, does it?"

Stubbornly, he said, "It matters to me. I would never have harmed my own granddaughters! They are my legacy. The future rulership of the Wolf Clan depends upon—"

"You should have thought of that before you gave a witch free rein to take care of *your problem* however he saw fit."

Atotarho glared at the herb pots lining the wall to Tila's left. Softly, he answered, "I realize that now."

Tila sighed and let her chin fall to rest upon the bulky hides that wrapped her like a soft, multi-layered cocoon. It was so hard to breathe. Her souls were itching to be released from the sick cage of her body. When all this was over, and she found herself walking the Path of Souls with her laughing daughters surrounding her, perhaps then she would be able to think clearly. But tonight it was almost impossible. Any subtlety she had ever learned in her life was gone.

Brutally, she said, "You are unfit to rule this nation, but the council cannot afford to remove you on the eve of battle."

He jerked around. "Are you saying the Ruling Council has reached a consensus?"

"Not yet, but it will. Even though the attack on White Dog Village has split this nation down the middle, the council members do not have the heart to wait until we are attacked. The alliance will hold long enough to take the fight to the enemy. After that, I cannot say." She shook her head. "Old Yana just walked the Path of Souls. Gwinodje is now the village matron in Canassatego Village, and she does not wish this war with the Standing Stone People. Nor, I've heard, does Matron Kwahseti."

"Will they fight?"

"I believe they will. But they will do it under protest."

His lockjawed expression gnawed at Tila.

In a voice that could make muscles flinch, he said, "Then I will prepare our war chief."

"Sindak already knows. I told him myself. After all, he spent half the day trying to control his warriors during the council. He had a right to know. But there is something you could do."

He gave her an askance look. "What is it?"

"When each village has made its decision, they will send warriors to join us. Within days, I expect Atotarho Village to be overrun with hungry men and women eager to do battle. We must ration our food even more conscientiously. I want you to oversee the feeding of the war parties."

"Of course, High Matron."

Atotarho repositioned himself, and his polished finger bone bracelets glimmered like frost. He seemed to be trying to decide how to ask her a question.

"Ask," she ordered.

"I'm just curious about something."

"Yes?"

"I know you sent runners to each of the village matrons asking them to call a truce to hear Sky Messenger's vision. Have the runners returned?"

Tila's eyes narrowed. At this point, it did not matter what he knew, but it irked her. It meant that someone among her trusted few was his spy, and she'd missed it. As she struggled to lift her chin, her head tottered on the slender stem of her neck. "They couldn't agree. Kwahseti and Gwinodje wished to hear it. The others did not. Without a consensus, there will be no truce. And I..." She forced a breath into her burning lungs. "I must find a way to tell Zateri. It will be another blow to her heart, and it crushes my souls to have to do it."

Atotarho drew himself up and got that arrogant

look on his face that she knew so well—he hated Sky Messenger and was preparing to scold her for sending the runners. Tila said, "What makes you think I care at all what you have to say? Two of my great-granddaughters are dead, and you killed them. Leave me so that I may hurt in private."

He careened toward the leather curtain, flung it aside, and stepped out to where his guards waited for him.

Tila stared at the swaying door curtain. Atotarho's reputation for vengeance was legendary. In the old days she wouldn't have pushed him, but she no longer cared what he might do to her.

Outside, Atotarho's petulant voice erupted, ordering men around, as he took out his frustration on his personal guards. As they moved away, she leaned her head back against the bark wall. She didn't have the strength to lie down. If she tried, she would only manage to collapse and perhaps topple off her sleeping bench—which would create a flurry of activity that she couldn't stand just now.

She closed her eyes and sought sleep. She had endured the deaths of so many loved ones, but somehow the loss of her precious great-granddaughters was unbearable. Perhaps it was just that she was dying and that made life all the more dear, but she also had the eerie sensation that their deaths presaged disaster. Perhaps the darkness foreseen by Sky Messenger truly was coming. She could sense it right over the next hill, rolling down upon them like a massive boulder loosed by an earthquake, and she had the feeling there was nothing anyone could do to stop it, least of all her. Which felt...peculiar.

For most of her life she had been the power behind the Ruling Council of the People of the Hills. No matter the threat, she'd always been able to do something to protect her people. But in her current condition, she was powerless. She could barely prop herself up and stay there without crumpling. Dying was such a disgrace.

And that, perhaps, hurt most of all.

One hand of time later, Atotarho stood beneath the porch of the Bear Clan longhouse, waiting for Matron Kelek to dress. In the ochre firelight streaming around the door curtain, frost glinted, outlining the undulations in the bark walls and glimmering down the shaft of his walking stick. He was frustrated and freezing, and his patience was wearing thin. He'd ordered his guards to stand twenty paces away, so that no one could overhear the conversation he was about to have.

He knew now that his lifelong alliance with the Wolf Clan was over. He had to make other...

Kelek stepped through the leather curtain with

her chin elevated, regarding him as if he were a beggar. Her white hair and deeply wrinkled face appeared pale and drawn. She'd pulled a tattered bear hide over her shoulders to stave off the cold. "It's the middle of the night. What is it?"

He leaned on his walking stick. "I have a proposition I think you will appreciate."

17

"Will the Flint People join us?" Kittle asked.

As the Cloud People sailed southward, alternating splashes of darkness and brilliant sunlight covered Bur Oak Village, accentuating the worried expressions of the hundreds of people who had gathered to hear the news brought back by Matron Jigonsaseh. Jigonsaseh stood calmly beside Kittle, her hands held out to the warmth of the flames. She was so tall and slender, she looked statuesque. The long reddish hairs on her woven fox hide cape glistened. She remained still for so long that the silver threads in her short black hair caught the light and her head seemed to be covered with sunlit cobwebs.

In a strong voice, Jigonsaseh answered, "They did not say no. The matrons are consulting with their clans and will send a runner when they've made a decision."

A hum went through the crowd as people relayed her words to those farther in back who couldn't hear.

Kittle paced before the central plaza fire with her blue-painted cape flaring around her legs. Her shell rings and bracelets clicked with her impatient movements. Two of her spies had returned at dawn and told her they'd seen thousands of warriors at Atotarho Village. Worse, their capes and weapons indicated they'd come from all the surrounding Hills villages.

The news had left Kittle anxious and filled with dread. Of course Tila expected a response after the destruction of White Dog Village, but this could only mean one thing: The Hills People were preparing for a monumental attack. There was no going back. She had the uneasy sensation that the entire Standing Stone nation was little more than an autumn leaf balanced on Wind Mother's breath above a bloodbath. The instant she turned her head, they would be submerged, and she wasn't sure they could fight their way out—not without help.

"And what did your instincts tell you?" Kittle pressed. "Are the Flint People likely to agree to an alliance?"

Jigonsaseh quietly exhaled, and it trailed away

in a thin white streamer. "I don't know. The Wolf Clan matron, Gahela, did not seem inclined to agree. Which means the other matrons will be hard-put to gain a consensus."

"Then you are saying your instincts tell you they will not join us?"

Jigonsaseh tilted her head uncertainly. "My guess, High Matron—and a guess is all it is—is no, they won't. I think we're on our own."

Another low hum, this one like a swarm of angry bees, rose. Facial expressions changed, going from worry to despair. Many people started to wander away, heading back to the warmth of their longhouses, perhaps to hug their children and stuff a few more belongings into hide bags. Already villagers had begun burying precious belongings in the forest, praying they survived and could return to dig them up after the Standing Stone nation had been wiped from the face of Great-Grandmother Earth. As she looked around at the remaining people, the hopelessness seemed to congeal into a deadly creature of enormous proportions—a creature just as likely to kill them as the Hills nation.

Kittle announced, "Go home now. Nothing more is going to happen today. Prepare yourselves. We have the finest warriors in the world. We will triumph!"

Kittle took Jigonsaseh by the arm and dragged

her away toward the Deer Clan longhouse. As they walked, she said, "We must attack soon."

"Agreed. We're going to need every man, woman, and child who can wield a bow. Atotarho can mount an eight-thousand-person army if he wishes to. How many warriors can we gather?"

Kittle subtly shook her head. "The sickness and all the recent battles have gutted us. If we're lucky, we'll muster three thousand. The odds are overwhelmingly against us. We *need* the Flint People."

"I know, Kittle, but what else can we do?"

"Did they look hungry? We could send them food."

Jigonsaseh stared down at her. Her jet-black eyes had an odd tightness to them. "As it is, we don't have enough food to make it through the winter. But even if we didn't need the food, it wouldn't help. The fever has also taken a heavy toll in Flint lands. Chief Cord told me flatly that they have more than enough food for the people who survived. I fear our only hope is Sky Messenger's vision. If they believe it, they will join us. If they do not..."

She didn't finish the sentence. She didn't have to.

Kittle released her arm and drew her cold hands beneath her cape. Her fingers had turned to ice. Several onlookers trailed after them, whispering, trying to overhear their conversation. She kept her voice low. "Where is Sky Messenger? We need him here."

Jigonsaseh lifted her head, and her gaze scanned the towering chestnuts beyond the palisades. Their leafless branches swayed in the frigid breeze. As though she could sense his presence out on the trail, she said, "He's coming. He'll be here."

"I pray you're right, because we are on the verge of a battle that will devastate this entire country and cost thousands of lives. The least he could do is to march around spouting his vision to rally our warriors."

Jigonsaseh nodded. "He will be here, Kittle. He's coming."

18

The sound of pebbles striking rocks woke Taya. The *click-clack* rang with such clarity that for a moment she thought it was someone chopping wood in the distance. She roused herself, sitting up in her blankets to listen. Sky Messenger and Gitchi were gone. When panic seized her heart, her gaze instantly searched the starlit forest for them. A storm must be moving in. The bitter night air nipped at her face with particular intensity. Taya threw aside her blanket and followed the sound of rocks being hurled.

She and Sky Messenger had both endured a terrible night. One Dream after another had awakened him. It was as if the Spirits were tormenting him. Often he'd cried out in his sleep. She didn't know him well enough, and doubted she ever would, to guess whether it was Dreams of the future that woke him, or memories of the past.

I'll bet Baji can tell the difference.

Jealousy stung her, but only for a moment. And that was a major achievement. For the first time in her life, she was learning to see the world through the eyes of others, and it had broadened her view considerably. What did it matter if he loved another woman? He was going to marry her. And they both knew the marriage was a political alliance, nothing more. Though, she had to admit, she couldn't help wishing he loved her. On the other hand, she did not love him. She had only just come to the conclusion that his soul was still in his body and not out roaming the forest. She needed time for all of this to sink into her souls. However, she knew one thing for certain: She had to give up her girlish dream of marrying a man she loved. For the sake of her clan and her nation, she could do it.

When it occurred to her that Grandmother would be proud of her, she felt a little better.

In the past few days, she'd come to other conclusions, as well. She might, truly, become the wife of the greatest Dreamer in the history of their nation. That was worth a lot more than love...at least if the Keepers of the Stories spoke well of Taya of the Deer Clan, granddaughter of High Matron Kittle and one of the leaders of the

Standing Stone nation—for surely she would become a leader if her husband became a legend.

A small pond spread to her left, surreally bright in the gleam cast by the campfires of the dead. The trail wound around the water's edge. As she walked, she studied the owls sailing over the treetops, silent, deadly, hunting the darkness for mice or rabbits.

The clacking of rocks grew so loud she could almost feel them pounding against her skin. She followed the curving trail through a copse of maples and into a boulder-filled clearing. The rounded rocks appeared to have melted together, as though they'd spent thousands of summers conforming to each other's shape. Upon the top of the tallest boulder, Sky Messenger sat, his tall body limned in starlight. He had his handsome face tipped up, as though conversing with the ancestors who peered down upon him from the Path of Souls.

At the sight of him, a sensation of wonder came over her. He was right there. The prophet. As the truth filtered through her body, her muscles relaxed and her breathing slowed down.

For a timeless moment, she felt as though she'd crawled through a badger hole and emerged in a strange sanctuary nestled in the calm heart of the world. The fear that the Hills People would attack and kill everyone she loved had receded into nothingness. *I must be dreaming. Soon, I'll awake and the terror will return.*

The savory odor of wet leaves met her nostrils. She inhaled deeply and hugged herself. Taya silently walked down the deer trail to the place where Sky Messenger must have climbed up, for the rounded stones resembled steps. The rocks were cold and damp as she ascended. She couldn't see him for a while. Then when she glimpsed him at the top, she felt almost euphoric.

He *was* the human False Face.

When she emerged three paces away from him, he turned to her. Bathed in starlight, with black hair dancing around his broad shoulders, his gaze made Taya's heart stand still. A gust flattened his cape across his muscular chest. She carefully stepped across the slick boulders to reach him. He smelled faintly of crushed grass and forest-scented winds.

Sky Messenger said, "You should be sleeping."

When she tried to sit down next to him, her moccasins slipped on the wet rocks and she grabbed for his arm to steady herself. The hard muscles beneath the soft buckskin felt comforting. "As you should. What are you doing up here?" She eased down beside him.

"Throwing rocks."

"That's what woke me. Why?"

He shrugged. "It seems to ease the Dreams."

She gazed out across the sparkling pond to where a flock of geese paddled. The white feathers on their throats flashed as they bobbed up and down on the waves. "I missed you. The blankets grew stone-cold after you left."

He hesitated for a while. "I was too anxious. I couldn't lie there any longer."

She squeezed his hand. "How strange. You're anxious, and I feel so happy. Too happy. I'm sure I'm dreaming."

"Well, if you're happy, I suggest you don't wake. What I see coming will certainly ruin it for you."

Taya gazed up into his starlit eyes. "Tell me what you see. Please?"

Sky Messenger's eyes tightened. He kept staring at her, his gaze intense, searching. Probably measuring her sincerity.

Taya heaved a sigh and explained, "I believe you now. I didn't. I didn't believe any of it—until four days ago when you met with War Chief Hiyawento. I'm sorry. It's taken me a few days to come to grips with the truth that you're actually a great Dreamer and not a crazy man, but I think I have. I would like to know what you see coming. If you wish to tell me."

He looked out across the pond. As the trees swayed in the night breeze, the black limb shadows moved across the silver water.

Finally, Sky Messenger replied, "The beginning is almost upon us. In the depths of my souls, the air is cooling off, and the colors are leaching from the forest. My heart already sees that gray and shimmering world. And that world is the start of everything." He heaved a breath. "I feel like...like my heart is crumbling, sifting through the cracks in my soul a grain at a time, vanishing into eternal stillness."

His tone of voice, the lilt of the words, seemed to cast a spell upon her. Softly, she asked, "How long do we have before Elder Brother Sun covers his face with the soot of the dying world?"

The muscles in his arm went hard, as though straining against what was to come. "I don't know. The way the Dream plays out, I can't tell if the events occur over a single day, or several years. The images jump around, rearranging themselves in a different order. I—"

"'As though not even the Spirits know the final shape of the story,'" she repeated the words he'd said to Hiyawento.

The Power in his haunted eyes stunned her. "Yes, that's right."

The breeze that blew over the pond batted at Sky Messenger's hood where it rested upon his back. Taya nodded and said, "How may I help you?"

He inclined his head uncertainly, or perhaps it

was suspiciously. "I don't wish to place you in danger."

"I'm already in danger. I'm with you, aren't I? You may as well let me help."

He hurled another rock, which splashed in the darkness. "As I get closer, I suspect I'll have a better idea of what each of us can do. But right now, I honestly don't."

"All right. I'll be ready."

He frowned at her from the corner of his eye. "I think, perhaps, you've grown up some."

Taya wet her lips. Wind Mother whispered through the trees. A wall of dark clouds had formed in the north, blotting out the campfires of the dead. "Sky Messenger, since our meeting with War Chief Hiyawento, I've been thinking a lot about the Beginning Time story. It was Sapling, the Good-Minded Twin, who brought order after the creation. He made lakes and rivers, brought good weather, ensured the corn grew, and released the animals from the great cave where they were being held. It was his brother Tawiscaro, the Evil-Minded Twin, who tried to undo everything good that Sapling had accomplished. He sent bad weather and brought chaos and death to the world." She took his one hand in both of hers and held it to her heart. "I think, one day, there will be stories told about you. Great stories of life and death, and good and evil. I truly believe that you are the human False Face."

He flinched and drew his hand away from her. "I am not."

"How do you know? You wear that gorget that matches the stories, and you—"

"My gorget is a copy, it's not the original. Chief Atotarho wears the original—or half of it."

Annoyed, Taya said, "The stories speak of two gorgets crafted just after the creation. One must have been made first. So the other is obviously a copy. No one knows whether the human False Face wears the original or the copy. Yours could be the sacred gorget, and the other is just a distraction."

He hurled another rock. He appeared uncomfortable with the entire discussion of legends. "I am *not* the human False Face."

Taya shrugged. "All right. But maybe you are the person who clears the path for the arrival of the human False Face. That's still critically important."

His head dipped once. "Yes, it is."

In the distance, the geese started flapping their wings and honking, as though preparing to take flight. Their beautiful calls serenaded the night. "My Spirit Helper told me something tonight that worries me."

Almost breathlessly, she said, "Shagoniyoh was here? What did he say?"

He watched her closely, as if trying to anticipate how she would respond to what he was about to say. "He told me that I must dive headfirst into the darkness and blood. If I do, others will follow."

Taya's breathing went shallow. "But...that sounds like...it sounds like you're talking about dying. I'm mistaken, aren't I? That's not what you meant?"

Sky Messenger didn't answer.

Taya slid away from him. "If you're planning on dying, tell me now."

"Why? So you can start looking for another husband?"

"No, so I can beat you senseless for being an idiot!"

"Taya, I'm not planning to die, but if it's the only way—"

"It's not the only way!" She leaped to her feet. "We're going home to convince Grandmother that it's possible to create an alliance with several Hills villages to destroy Atotarho. That's the way to end the war."

"Yes, I hope so. But Taya, I have this feeling that things have gone too far, and we can't—"

"We're going to form this alliance and then everything will be all right," she insisted.

"I hope so." Sky Messenger rose to his feet and stood uneasily before her. After several heartbeats, she felt his hand stroke the long hair that draped down her back. "Earlier, you asked if there was something you could do to help me. I've changed my mind. There is."

"I will *not* help you die!"

They stood for a long time, looking at each other. He lowered his hand. "I would never ask that of anyone. But there may come a moment in the storm when I need someone politically astute to act as a negotiator on my behalf. I know you are young, but—"

"I can do it," she said with utter confidence. "I have watched and listened to my grandmother all my life." She drew herself up and faced him squarely. *"But..."* She pointed a stern finger at him. "Not if I know that you're planning on sacrificing yourself for the greater good, or some other stupid notion. Do you understand?"

His gaze went over her angry face as though memorizing it. "Yes. I understand."

They stood for a time, just gazing out at the glimmers of starlight on the pond, until Sky Messenger said, "I'm going back to camp and try to sleep. Are you coming?"

"Not yet."

He looked around at the darkness and seemed to be wondering why she wasn't terrified to be more than a few paces from him. She was wondering that herself.

"Very well. I'll be waiting for you."

She listened to his steps as he climbed down the slippery boulders. A short while later, she saw him slowly walking the trail back to the camp. He was alone. Where was Gitchi?

Taya climbed down the boulders and found the wolf standing with his ears pricked. He did not wag his tail. He merely gazed at her with shining yellow eyes, as though waiting for a command.

"Leave," she ordered, and flung her arm to point back to camp.

Gitchi stood his ground. The old wolf's graying head had a curious sheen in the silver light.

"I don't want you here. Go home. Go find Sky Messenger."

Gitchi licked his muzzle and sat on his haunches.

"Did Sky Messenger tell you to stay and protect me?"

He stared up at her, and she threw up her hands. "Gods, that means I'll never get rid of you. All right, come on."

Taya marched along the shore with Gitchi at her heels. When she reached the far side of the pond, she stared across the shimmering surface to where their camp nestled in the maples. She couldn't see him, but she knew Sky Messenger was there—it tore her souls apart. "Do you really think he's planning on dying?"

She slumped down on the sand and put her

head in her hands, trying to force sense into her worry-laced brain.

Gitchi eased forward, lay down, and rested his muzzle on top of her feet. When she looked at him, his tail thumped the ground as though he knew she was hurting, and he was trying to comfort her.

He was a curious animal, totally devoted to Sky Messenger. In all the world, the only person who really seemed to exist for Gitchi was Sky Messenger. Yet...here he was. Taya reached out and stroked his warm fur. "I don't really like you, and you know it, don't you?"

Gitchi wagged his tail.

Elder Sister Gaha pushed the air with a soft invisible hand, and Taya tugged her cape up beneath her chin. Gitchi watched her. When she shivered, the wolf got to his feet, walked around behind her, and curled his body warmly around hers.

Tears filled Taya's eyes. She slid a hand from beneath her cape to stroke his head. "We can't let him die, Gitchi. Even if he's foolish enough to think it's the only way. You'll protect him, won't you?"

The wolf's gaze suddenly shifted to the opposite side of the pond. A low growl rumbled his throat.

"What is it?"

Gitchi eased to his feet, his eyes still focused on the forest shadows across the pond. His muscles bunched as though ready to spring forward. She tried to see what he was looking at. By now Sky Messenger was wrapped in his cape and almost asleep—yet something moved near their camp. A black silhouette. It ghosted through the darkness.

Silent as the moonlight, Gitchi broke into a dead run.

The wolf shot around the pond like a silver arrow, its lean body gleaming in the night. Ohsinoh chuckled and took one last look at Odion. He would always be Odion to Ohsinoh, never Sky Messenger. Odion, the boy who was always afraid.

He'll be even more afraid. Very soon.

Long before Gitchi rounded the pond and hit the trail to camp, Ohsinoh turned and trotted into the deep forest shadows.

19

High Matron Tila lay on her sleeping bench with her great-granddaughter Kahn-Tineta snuggled beneath the hides beside her. Morning sunlight streamed around the leather curtain that led outside, casting lances of pure gold across the longhouse floor. As they flashed across the little girl's face, Tila's heart ached.

Many people scurried to and from the house today, securing the village, hauling in pot after pot of water and armloads of wood. Each time a person walked through the blue clouds that rose from the fires, smoke swirled and snaked upward toward the smoke hole in the roof high above.

She weakly stroked Kahn-Tineta's long black hair. "I know these are hard days, child, but things will get better."

In a pitiful voice, the eight-summers-old girl said, "No, they won't. Mother and Father are going to die, Great-Grandmother. Just like my sisters."

Tila frowned. From this view, she could just see Kahn-Tineta's profile. Tears sparkled on the girl's long eyelashes. "What makes you say that? Your father is a great war chief, one of the most respected men—"

"When Father left, he barely had the strength to lift his war club! Didn't you see him?" Kahn-Tineta rolled to her back to look at Tila. Her small face was white and strained. There was a luminous look of stunned disbelief in her eyes. The innocence of her expression struck Tila like a blow.

"I did see him." Tila shoved away the hair that had glued itself to the girl's wet cheeks. Zateri and Hiyawento had both come to bid her goodbye three days before. Though she was almost beyond feeling anything except her own agony, Tila had hurt for them, but especially for Hiyawento. The man who'd stood before her had been a pale haunted shadow of what he had once been. "I think your father's souls split apart for a time after your sisters traveled the Path of Souls. It will take time for them to weave back together again, but they will."

"But mother never cried. Not at all. Father—"

"Child, what your mother has to stand, the ancestors have given her the strength to stand.

Women were born to carry heavier loads than men."

Kahn-Tineta let out a tired breath and stared up at the sunflowers hanging from the roof poles. "Do we get that from Dancing Fox and the Wolf Clan matrons who lived long ago in the ancient darkness?"

"Yes. We do. The loss of your sisters has broken your mother's heart, but she'll bear that burden with a straight back and clear eyes. If for no other reason than your father needs her to."

A moment of pride warmed Tila's heart. Yes, no matter what came, Zateri could and would bear it. Wolf Clan women bent with the winds of change, but when the storm passed they stiffened their spines and got back to work building a better world for their clan and people.

"Great-Grandmother? Why did Mother have to go with Father? She almost never goes on war walks."

"Well, this is different. If we are successful, the full Ruling Council will need to be present when the Standing Stone nation falls. Your mother will stand in for me. Decisions may have to be made on the spot."

Kahn-Tineta anxiously ran her tongue through the gap left by her missing front teeth. "I wish Mother was home." Tears filled her young eyes.

Tila hugged her more tightly. "Can I tell you a secret?"

The girl's eyes widened. "What is it?"

"I'm going to name your mother as matron of the Wolf Clan when she returns, but you mustn't tell anyone. Can you keep my words locked in your heart until it is announced?"

"Oh, yes, Great-Grandmother," Kahn-Tineta said earnestly. "I'm good at keeping secrets."

"I'm glad to hear of it. Many people are not."

Kahn-Tineta's eyes narrowed slightly, as though something had occurred to her, but she wasn't certain she should say it.

"What's wrong?"

Kahn-Tineta glanced around the house to make sure no one could hear her and then she cupped a hand to Tila's ear and hissed, "Great-Grandmother, I'm not sure Mother wishes to be high matron."

"That's not a surprise. No one does." Tila poked a skeletal finger into Kahn-Tineta's young chest. "You remember I said that. Someday you will have to make the choice of whether or not to lead your people. It is an overwhelming responsibility. But I suspect in the end you will choose to place the welfare of the Hills nation above your own. You will shoulder the burden for the nation's sake. Just as your mother will."

"She will?"

Tila nodded. "I'm sure of it."

Kahn-Tineta crossed her legs and shook one moccasin while she frowned at the swirls of blue smoke gliding above her. "But Great-Grandmother, Father doesn't wish to move to this village. I've heard Mother and Father talking late at night when they think I'm asleep. Father hates Grandfather Atotarho."

At the mention of his name, anger filled Tila, and she could not afford the energy it required. She closed her eyes for several heartbeats to let it drain away. "My grandmother—that would be your great-great-great-grandmother—used to have a saying. She said that for every one person hacking at the roots of hatred, there were thousands swinging in its branches. She told me the only way to survive in this world was to make sure I was the one with the hatchet."

Kahn-Tineta rolled to her stomach and looked at Tila. A faint smile came to her lips. "I like that."

"I thought you might. You have a pure heart. But you're going to have to work to keep it that way. Don't swing in those branches or you'll fall and break your neck."

Brilliant sunshine flared when Pedeza pulled back the door curtain and stepped inside the Wolf Clan longhouse. She looked exhausted, her face drawn and jaw clamped. But when she saw Kahn-

Tineta she forced a smile. "Are you ready to go home? The high matron needs to sleep."

Tila gave her a grateful look—she did need to sleep—but more than anything, she longed to keep talking with this precious little girl.

Kahn-Tineta sat up. "Great-Grandmother, may I come back tomorrow?"

"You will have to ask Pedeza, but I would so love to see you."

Kahn-Tineta smiled and slid off the sleeping bench. When her moccasins struck the floor mats, she turned, leaned over Tila, and kissed her cheek. "I love you, Great-Grandmother," she said, and trotted to Pedeza's side.

Tila extended a gnarled hand to her. "I love you, too, child. Don't forget the things I told you."

Kahn-Tineta glanced up at Pedeza, then back at Tila. In a conspiratorial whisper, she said, "I won't. I promise."

Pedeza bowed. "Good day, High Matron. Sleep well."

"I'll try. Be careful going home."

"Yes, we will."

Pedeza took Kahn-Tineta's hand, and they walked away down the longhouse.

When they were out of sight, Tila curled into a tight ball and fought to keep the pain at bay. She felt like sharp fangs were ripping at her organs. If only she...

Something caught her attention. Tila focused on the door curtain. In the slender space where the curtain rested against the door frame, one eye gleamed. It was large and shone with an unearthly light. It seemed to be fixed upon Kahn-Tineta and Pedeza. Then it turned to Tila. It watched her for a time.

When the man ducked beneath the curtain and into the house, her gray brows knitted. He wore a plain buckskin cape with no clan symbols. White and black paint decorated his triangular face. "Who are you?"

He had a strange manner about him. As he searched the house, only his eyes moved. His tall body seemed to be carved of wood.

"I asked for your name."

"Yes, I heard you."

With the silence of a big cat stalking prey, he entered her chamber, walked to her side, and pulled the hides up, as though to keep her warmer. Then suddenly he pressed them over her mouth and nose and whispered, "It's me, Grandmother, your long-lost grandson."

Horror flooded Tila. She fought, thrashing about with the strength of a newborn, trying to suck air into her lungs so she could scream. She was so weak, it didn't take long.

The cold black shadow of Sodowego fell upon

her, and the darkness came like a soothing whisper...

20

20

Conversations filled the cold night, meshing oddly with the war songs that drifted lazily across the hills, moving with the dark shapes of thousands of warriors. The smoky air was sweet with the smell of squash baked in ashes.

Zateri watched War Chief Sindak rise from where he'd drawn the battle plan in the thin layer of snow on the ground and scan the seven people standing in Zateri's small circle. His gaze remained the longest on war chiefs Thona, Waswanosh, and Hiyawento, clearly judging their emotions—then his eyes flicked to matrons Gwinodje and Kwahseti, took in Chief Canassatego's expression, and finally came to rest upon Zateri.

"Does everyone understand?" Sindak propped

his hands on his hips. He'd pulled his black hair back and tied it with a cord. The lines around his deep-set eyes resembled dark chasms in the firelight. Behind him, a blanket of campfires rose and fell with the hills, stretching to the star-spotted eastern horizon.

"Oh, I think we understand perfectly," Matron Kwahseti said with a thin smile. Gray strands of hair fluttered around her oval face.

"Good. Sleep well." Sindak bowed and walked away.

Zateri crossed her arms beneath her cape, waiting before she spoke, giving herself time to digest what had just happened.

"I don't believe it," War Chief Thona said through gritted teeth. The white ridges of scars crisscrossing his indignant face resembled writhing amber-colored worms. "Does he think we will stand for this?"

Kwahseti's attention had fixed on Sindak as he made his way across the huge camp, talking to warriors, sharing jokes, occasionally slapping a man on the back. "It seems that Chief Atotarho doesn't trust us."

"It's an outrage." Thona straightened to his full height, towering over everyone else in the circle. "We should—"

"No." Kwahseti put a hand on her war chief's

muscular shoulder. "Be calm, Thona. Emotion only clouds our thoughts, and we must all think straight tonight."

Thona tried, but continued to seethe.

War Chief Waswanosh from Canassatego Village hissed, "This is unacceptable. How dare he tell us to stay out of the fight!"

"That's not what he said," Zateri softly reminded. "He said Atotarho wishes to keep our forces in reserve until we are needed."

"In reserve?" Waswanosh growled. "He ordered us to stay in camp. To remain behind when everyone else marches off to the fight! It is an insult!"

Chief Canassatego gave them a resigned smile. He had seen fifty-seven summers pass, and had once been a renowned war chief. A long gray braid snaked over his shoulder, looking like a silver snake against the black-painted hide of his cape. As his smile faded, his wrinkles rearranged into somber lines. "Well, War Chief Hiyawento, it seems you have your wish. We will not fight the Standing Stone People."

"Not fighting isn't the same as making peace. The only way we will ever be safe is if the fear of attack vanishes for both our peoples. We must end this war."

Zateri noticed that his fists were clenched at his sides, and his narrow beaked face had flushed.

Sindak's orders had surprised him, as they had everyone else.

Gwinodje said, "What shall we do about it? Are we going to obey?"

Short and slight of build, she appeared childlike, standing between Chief Canassatego and War Chief Waswanosh. In the darkness, one could have mistaken her for a frail girl. But her expression belied any such notions. Indignation actually shook the clamshell comb that held her black hair on top of her head, causing it to shimmer like a prism. Colors flashed.

Zateri said, "Each of our villages joined the Hills alliance. If we disobey, it will be viewed as a withdrawal from the alliance. Do we wish to do that?"

Kwahseti massaged her brow. "No, not yet. Our three villages could not stand alone. We would be vulnerable to anyone who wished to destroy us. Assuming Atotarho didn't beat them to it, the Mountain People would be the first to take the opportunity."

"Yes," Zateri added. "I've heard they're desperate. They've been so sick with the fever that they could not even harvest their crops. Their corn is moldering in their fields, and their sunflowers have all been plucked clean by birds. As winter deepens, they'll have no choice but to take what food they need from other nations. We—"

Hiyawento interrupted, "They shouldn't have to."

His deep voice had been so low, the others in the circle unconsciously leaned toward him to hear him better. Chief Canassatego asked, "What did you say?"

Hiyawento lifted his head. A somber emptiness had possessed him. It wrenched Zateri's souls. The loss of her daughters was like a knife slashing inside her, but duty demanded she set it aside until this was over. Then she would find a quiet place to hurt until she could bear it. The difference between them was that she *could* set it aside. He could not. All his life, he'd fought to protect his family and friends, offering his own life in their stead many times over, and his courage had always carried everyone around him to safety. Except for his baby daughters. Zateri knew that somewhere deep inside him, he blamed himself for their deaths. He must be saying, "If only I'd been vigilant, I would have known..." or "I should have killed him when I had the chance, then my girls couldn't have..."

A lump formed in Zateri's throat, making it hard to breathe. Guilt had eaten a gaping hole inside him, and he was being consumed by the darkness.

For her, the pain provoked another response. She became unnaturally focused and clear-headed —a lesson she'd learned in Gannajero's camp, where she had endured things that had killed other girls. She would single-mindedly, with the patience of a hungry wolf, hunt her father until she could destroy him, even if she had to turn the world on its head to do it. It was this pursuit that gave her the strength to face anything she had to.

"I said"—Hiyawento inhaled the smoky night air—"they shouldn't have to. If they attack us, it's our fault. By our own greed, we've forced them into desperate acts to feed their children."

Thona stiffened as though he'd been struck. "What are you saying? That because we need the food for our own children, we are somehow to blame—"

"Yes." Hiyawento's red-rimmed eyes rested on Thona without emotion. He might have been gazing far out into the distances instead of at a livid opponent. "Don't you see? If we helped each other, we would all have enough. We might not have an abundance that we could hoard and smile at in the dead of winter, but we would survive. As it is, I'm not sure any of us will make it through this."

Thona snorted. "You sound like you're repeating the words of your demented friend, Sky Messenger."

War Chief Waswanosh let out a low, disgusted laugh. "His vision is nonsense. I heard one of the Traders say he'd seen Elder Brother Sun flee into a black hole in the sky. Ridiculous."

Hiyawento's chin lifted. In a deep reverent voice, he replied, "When the Great Face shakes the World Tree, you will believe. There is a terrible storm coming. We will all be swimming in a cloud-sea when the eerie silence descends and Elder Brother Sun blackens his face with the soot of the dying world."

Zateri glanced around the circle. No one seemed to be breathing. They were hearing Sky Messenger's vision for the first time, or at least part of it, and none could turn away. Kwahseti's face had slackened, as though she felt the truth of it rising up from the dark place between her souls. Chief Canassatego was listening with his eyes closed.

"The sky will split wide open," Hiyawento continued, "and a snowy blanket of thistledown will fall. As it spreads out all over the world, the judgment will take place."

Thona uneasily shifted his weight to his other foot. Waswanosh observed him from the corner of his eye. Both men appeared chastened, half-believing, but not quite.

Awed, Gwinodje murmured, "It—it's Powerful."

Kwahseti nodded. As she brought up a hand and touched the cape over her heart, she said, "I don't know about the rest of you, but I want to believe. Very much."

"Wanting does not make it true, Matron," Thona remarked.

"No." A breath of wind fluttered her gray hair. She brushed it away. "But I plan to be ready, just in case."

"What do you mean, ready?" Gwinodje tilted her head.

Out in the forest, Elder Sister Gaha walked. The hem of her dress set the branches to swaying, and a musical shishing and clattering wafted to them. A light snow started to fall, featherlike, glittering on the branches.

"I mean that when the time comes, I will be on the right side."

"But..." Gwinodje looked around questioningly. "What is the right side?"

"I don't know yet, but when I get there, I will."

Still staring upward at the campfires of the dead, Hiyawento said, "The side of kindness. Which is, I regret, a side I have not always fought for."

No one responded, but Zateri could tell from their expressions that some of them were thinking that good war chiefs couldn't afford such weaknesses. Thona scowled. Waswanosh had a faint sneer.

Slowly, each person in the circle followed Hiyawento's gaze, looking upward into the night sky where a thin layer of Cloud People pushed southward, fuzzing the campfires of the dead, rushing away as though fleeing the supernatural storm to come.

"I'm going to find my blankets." Kwahseti lifted a hand. "A pleasant evening to you all."

"Before you go..." Hiyawento quietly said. Kwahseti turned back to face him. "If you could form an alliance with the Standing Stone nation to defeat Atotarho, would you?"

Kwahseti stared at him as though asking the question proved beyond a doubt that Hiyawento's soul was out wandering lost in the forest. But there was something else in her eyes—some hesitation that made Zateri's blood rush.

"Kwahseti," Zateri whispered, "just consider—"

Kwahseti turned her back and walked away. One by one, the others said good night and followed her, plodding across camp to their own fires.

When they stood alone, Zateri moved close to Hiyawento and slipped her arm through his, holding him. Quietly, she asked, "Are you all right?"

He blinked at the sky as though puzzled by what he saw there. His narrow face and hawkish nose reflected the flickers of firelight.

Finally, he answered, "My souls are broken, Zateri, and I cannot find a way to pull the pieces together."

"Well..." The word condensed and sparkled. "Perhaps you shouldn't try to."

"Why not?"

She squeezed his arm. "My husband, kindness does not dwell in souls that are whole."

21
SKY MESSENGER

The milky light before dawn casts a soft pearl glow over the snow-covered hills.

As I follow the trail up over the rise and look down across the valley to the south, an inexplicable dread fills me. I halt on the rocky ridge, waiting for Taya, who plods up the trail behind me.

Rose-colored mist eddies close to the ground, twining around trunks and boulders. In the distance, leafless trees rise and fall like gray waves, dipping down to where Yellowtail Village and Bur Oak Village nestle side by side, their palisades sheathed in frost. Reed Marsh curves around the western and northern edges of the villages, cupping them like a protective hand. Dark Cloud People blanket most of the morning sky, but a thin band of pale purple swaths the eastern horizon.

Movement. Down in the dense maples. Only my

gaze glides across the landscape. After ten heartbeats, I whisper to myself, "Warriors."

As the morning light brightens, my trained eyes begin to pick them out. Visible through the trees are line after line of archers. Four lines that I can see. As one line fires, the next will move up, and so on, until the first line must again face the enemy.

Taya's steps pat the soft earth behind me. She slips an arm around my waist and lets out a peaceful sigh. It surprises me a little. "I'm glad we're almost home."

She doesn't notice anything amiss, but why would she? Though I've been working hard to teach her to *see*, the skill takes time.

I drape an arm over her shoulders and softly say, "I want you to be calm. Can you do that?"

She tips her face up in confusion. "What do you mean?"

I kneel and draw the lines of archers in the thin snow, then make a crescent for Reed Marsh, and circles for the locations of the villages. "Do you see them?"

Taya lifts her gaze and scans the hills, glances back at his map, looks up again. Slowly, the joy drains from her beautiful young face. I see her eyes stop at each place where warriors are clearly visible in the forest.

"Oh, no. Grandmother must have received word

that we're about to be attacked. We have to hurry. Let's run!"

She starts to launch herself down the trail, and I catch her arm and pull her back. "The warriors are jittery, worried about their own lives and the lives of their families. Never run into a line of archers."

"But they know me! Every warrior out there has—"

"Fear creates a strange kind of blindness. Your eyes are wide open, but the only thing you see is your own weapons. Your ears hear only your heart pounding. Let's continue walking down the main trail in clear sight. They've already seen us. They'll be watching, monitoring our movements. Keep your hands open at your sides."

For the first time, she looks up at me as though I know more than Elder Brother Sun. A swallow bobs her throat. "I will."

I put a hand lightly on her shoulder to encourage her to walk at my side, and she clings to me like a shadow.

We've gone no more than one hundred paces when the trail curves, and I see an eerie sight behind us. To the west, a cloud of snow billows over the trees. But it's not falling from the sky. It rises from the ground, like summer dust, kicked by the trotting feet of warriors. Because of the way the hills fold, I doubt the Standing Stone archers see them yet. I swing around to look at the Standing Stone lines to the north of the villages, then back at what must be the enemy. I can hear them now. Beneath their pounding feet, Great-Grandmother Earth rings like a drum being struck. The thunderous roll echoes.

"What is that?" Taya turns to look over her shoulder.

"Just keep walking. We'll be home before they get here." I grip her hand to keep her from running.

She jerks around to look back at the billowing snow, and when understanding dawns, I feel her heartbeat stutter in her wrist.

"Are those...warriors?"

"Yes, but—"

"Enemy warriors?" she cries. "They're coming right at us!"

My grip on her hand tightens. "Do you see where the trail to Hills country meets the main trail that curves around the eastern side of the villages? When we hit that, we'll run. For now, just walk."

I lead her down the trail.

22

Elder Brother Sun blazed scarlet and gold into High Matron Kittle's eyes as she marched along the outermost catwalk of Bur Oak Village, speaking confidently to her warriors, judging their moods, as she made her way down to where Skenandoah stood. At regular intervals, jugs of water and cups hung from the palisade, at hand for later when thirsty warriors could not leave their posts. Beyond the palisade, thick morning mist curled and spun across the valley.

When he saw her, Skenandoah bowed. "High Matron?"

In the glistening vapor, he more closely resembled a pale-faced phantom than a war chief. Muscular and of medium height, he had seen thirty-four summers pass. Short black hair, cut in mourning for the many friends he had lost in the long war, clung damply to his square face. Red feathers, ornaments of war, fluttered at the bottom of his long war shirt. He had his bow slung over his shoulder and carried a quiver stuffed with arrows. A war club, axe, and two deerbone stilettos hung from his belt.

Kittle smiled. "What's going on out there?"

He propped an elbow on the palisade and gestured to the hazy battlefield. "Our archers are in place, but the fog is so thick in the valley bottom they won't see the enemy warriors until they emerge like fanged wolves from the gray."

"You've seen no Traders, no travelers, no messengers traveling under white arrows? Nothing?"

Skenandoah gave her a sad look, seemed to be debating with himself, then clearly decided to ignore her implication that she was waiting for a messenger from Atotarho, hoping to end this before it began. "No, High Matron. Just the two terrified sentries who ran in at dawn after sighting the approaching army."

Her heart sank. She didn't know what she'd been hoping for, perhaps that Atotarho wished to make peace, which was as unlikely as seeing summer replace the winter solstice. Had she grown so desperate she'd started believing in fantasies?

A slight breeze rustled across the marsh and swept the fog aside, driving it through the reeds and cattails like smoke from a bonfire. She watched it trail down the valley. Just as quickly, more mist rolled in to fill its place. The frosty world dazzled.

"How are our warriors holding up?"

Skenandoah gave her a firm nod. "They will do their duties, High Matron. They will stand until they cannot stand any longer."

Kittle braced her arms on the palisade beside him and stared out at the morning. As he climbed into the sky, Elder Brother Sun blazed through the mist like a ball of flame in the middle of a great cloud.

"High Matron," Skenandoah said cautiously. "I've heard the elders whispering. May I ask you something?"

"Of course."

For a moment, he appeared to regret that he'd said anything. His lips pressed into a bloodless line, and he frowned down at the warriors stationed at the base of the palisade. For her ears alone, he asked, "Is it true that the Ruling Council has already decided we will surrender at nightfall?"

Blood rose to Kittle's face. She felt lightheaded. She prayed they would not have to resort to that, but… "It is most certainly *not* true. Who told you that? No, never mind, it doesn't matter." She stabbed a finger at him. "We will fight until our last breaths. Is that clear? You tell your people that at this very moment, the council is planning a great victory celebration."

A faint smile came to his lips, as though he knew she was lying, but appreciated it just the same. "I will tell them, High Matron."

To cover her discomfort, she reached for the cup that hung from a peg on the palisade, filled it from the water jug, and drank. She felt wide awake. More alive than ever before. As she returned the cup to its place, she saw clouds of snow billowing over the western ridge, then a slither on the far side of the valley. The mist eddied and swirled as though brushed by a huge hand.

Kittle froze, staring. Elder Brother Sun climbed into a gap in the mist and seemed to explode. Brilliance surged across the valley. The land became a flowing field of diamonds, whiskered with frost-bright trees. The stone arrow points of her archers glittered as they aimed their bows.

She gripped Skenandoah's wrist so hard her nails drove into his flesh. "They're coming."

He nodded. "Yes. I saw them a long time ago."

23

Skenandoah disentangled his wrist from her fingers and dragged an arrow from his quiver. "Please find a safe place, High Matron."

Kittle inhaled a steadying breath and marched away down the catwalk. As each warrior saw the enemy, sharp calls went up, and arms flung out to point. A breathless sort of anticipation filled the cold morning air. The prayers being Sung up and down the line sounded for all the world like the sweet notes of flutes.

Just as Kittle reached the ladder and started to climb down, Skenandoah called, "High Matron! Sky Messenger and Taya just rounded the Yellowtail palisade. They're running for our gates!"

"Thank you, War Chief." Kittle descended the

ladder with forced dignity and walked to meet them.

Warriors opened the outer gates, and Sky Messenger shoved Taya through first, then backed in and spun around. "Utz, Hannock, there are two war parties less than one finger of time behind me. Bring more planks to barricade these gates!"

"Yes, Sky Messenger!" Utz ran to grab another plank from the pile inside the second palisade ring.

His voice had been commanding, that of a deputy war chief, and Utz and Hannock had obeyed him as they always had. It surprised Kittle, but if he wished to command in this current situation, she had no objections.

Sky Messenger strode for her granddaughter, and with soft urgency, said, "Taya, I must get to a high point where I can see over the fog to judge the battlefield."

"Go. I'll speak with Grandmother."

Sky Messenger touched her shoulder, a tender touch. "One last thing. Please take Gitchi with you? Make sure he stays in the longhouse. He's old. He—"

Taya nodded. "I'll take care of him, Sky Messenger. Don't worry."

Sky Messenger knelt and ruffled the fur at Gitchi's neck, then he hugged the wolf fiercely and said, "Go with Taya. Guard her. Do what she says."

Gitchi gave him an uncertain look, but loped to stand at Taya's side.

Sky Messenger trotted for the ladder that led to the catwalk.

Kittle studied her granddaughter. Taya's eyes had a gleam. Her serious expression was that of a woman far older than her fourteen summers. "Speak with me about what?"

"An alliance to end this battle and destroy Atotarho."

Kittle's laugh had a desperate ring to it. "What would you know of such things?"

Taya stared confidently into her eyes, which startled Kittle. "We just came from Coldspring Village. Many of the other Hills villages were outraged by Atotarho's attack on White Dog Village. They were not involved and would not have approved the attack if they had been. The Hills nation is on the verge of civil war over it. I believe the time is ripe to make alliances with those opposing Atotarho. If we can, we may be able to destroy the chief on this very battlefield."

Taya spoke like a leader. Pride filled Kittle. "I fear it is too late for that, my granddaughter, but I will hear you out. Come to my chamber. I must dress for the battle. No matter what else happens, if I am captured, I'm going to look splendid for my execution."

24

SKY MESSENGER

Where I stand upon the catwalk, I grip the palisade and gaze out at what is surely oblivion. Past the marsh, the ground slowly tips up, gently rolling until it collides with the rocky ridge to the west—the crest where Taya and I stood less than one hand of time ago. Despite the cloud cover and mist, the morning light grows brighter, revealing the enemy's lines. Thousands of Hills warriors, row upon row, march over the ridge and head down into the valley. The mist moves with the lines, slithering back and forth like a din of serpents. Clan flags drape uplifted spears, creating a panorama of red, blue, yellow, green, white, and black. In the shifting fog, the flags have an odd fluttering iridescence that resembles the disembodied wings of a thousand songbirds beating in unison.

Skenandoah comes to stand beside me. As his

grip tightens on his bow, his fingernails go white, but that anxiety never reaches the calm of the war chief's face. He is a tactician and probably already four or five steps into the battle that has yet to begin. The only outward sign of worry is the short black hair that has glued itself to his sweating brow.

"When you were out there, could you count them? How many do you think there are?" he asks without taking his eyes from the battlefield.

"My guess is around six thousand, but there could be more in reserve."

Skenandoah's head dips in a barely discernible nod. "That is my guess as well."

"How many warriors do we have?"

"All of the surrounding villages sent warriors. They know if we fall, it's over. We have three thousand two hundred, if we count every boy with a toy bow. But one thousand of those are inside the villages, five hundred in Yellowtail and five hundred here. So there are only a little over two thousand out there."

I can't help but glance down at the crowded plaza where warriors huddle, waiting for the time when they will be called to the palisade to replace a man or woman who's been killed or wounded. Boys and girls clump awkwardly around the warriors, their childish war clubs clutched in small fists, or plucking slack bowstrings like musical instruments. A few girls race around the plaza with dogs chasing them, laughing. Though they have endured attacks upon their villages, these children had never been called upon to help defend them. They have no idea what is coming.

But their parents do. Men and women stand before the central bonfire, their arms around each other's waists, watching their sons and daughters with glassy eyes, memorizing their faces. Huge pots of cornmeal mush bubble beside the fire, warm food for starving warriors with just enough time to gobble a few bites and race back to defend the walls. A low hum of frightened voices rides the wind.

Then...from a distance, a long, drawn-out howl. The distinctive call of the Wolf Clan.

I look back over the palisade. The enemy line breaks apart and re-forms into three lines, one to the north, one trotting east, and the other coming straight at them from the west. Those warriors will greatly regret it when they encounter the sucking mud of the marsh.

Unconsciously, I turn to the south, wondering who is out there. They must already be in place. I can't see them, just the pale glimmers of campfires sparkling amid the trees on the horizon.

Shouts go up. I turn back to look westward. Far away, I can identify the clan factions. As they run forward, the symbols on the darkest war shirts crystallize, stark against the dead grass, and I smell the salty stench of fear on the breeze.

Another wolf cry...then the long roar as every clan joins in, and the small valley rumbles. The Hills warriors outnumber the Standing Stone by at least three to one. It is an awful sight.

The Standing Stone warriors let fly. As the arrows slice through the mist, it shreds and seems to boil.

Sharp, surprised cries ring out, the yips of warriors who've just taken an arrow in the belly or chest but don't know yet that they are dead on their feet.

As the enemy runs forward, the archers who've just fired sling their bows and charge out to meet them with war clubs in their fists. A grunting, gasping bellow rises, followed by the mushy thuds of clubs smacking skulls. I've given and taken such blows often enough that I can see the expressions of the wounded right behind my eyes and feel the momentary relief of the attacker in my heart.

"Hold," Skenandoah whispers through gritted teeth. One of his hands, propped on the palisade, clenches. *"Hold."*

The Hills warriors shove them back, slowly at first. The lines surge and withdraw, as though breathing the death of the world, and it is a labored death. My lungs work with them. The wounded stagger away, trying to get back, looking toward home. Some of the Standing Stone warriors reach out to Bur Oak and Yellowtail villages, as though begging their relatives for help.

The first line breaks. As Standing Stone warriors race back, the second line of archers lets fly into the screaming horde chasing them and then they charge out to meet them. The whooping, grunting struggle begins again. The line holds long enough for the wounded to flee. A new sound grows—the sound of limbs ripping from trees, feet scrambling through deadfall, and finally, the hopeful cries of people rushing toward the gates of the villages.

Skenandoah cups a hand to his mouth and calls, "Utz, don't open the gates until the wounded are plastered against them. Do you understand?"

Utz lifts a hand and runs to press his eye to the crack between the plank gates, waiting. When the crashes of people hitting the gates drive him backward, he shouts, "Hannock, help me!"

It takes both of them to shove the locking planks aside and open the gates. The panicked group of warriors who rush through supporting their injured friends stuns me. There are so many. Blood drenches war shirts, stripes faces, clots on broken skulls. A few shove captives before them.

"Get them to the council house!" Skenandoah orders. "Bahna and Genonsgwa will care for them there!"

The arms and legs of the hardest hit dangle as their friends struggle to carry them across the plaza.

"Blessed Spirits," Skenandoah whispers. "We don't have long."

I turn back to the battlefield. The second line has broken. Warriors flee. Arrows from the third wave of archers glisten as they puncture the mist and arc downward toward their targets. Despite the number of Hills warriors that fall, the onslaught roars forward, barely slowed as it crashes through the third wave and lunges for the last line of Standing Stone archers.

"Gods," Skenandoah says. "They'll be here in less than one thousand heartbeats." He spins and calls, "Yonto, inform High Matron Kittle that our first three lines have broken, and the last is wavering. The enemy will hit the village *soon*."

The young woman warrior runs for the ladder, climbs down three rungs at a time, and dashes for the Deer longhouse.

Skenandoah faces me. "I need every experienced warrior I have. Will you serve as my deputy war chief?"

I throw out my hands as though to push him away. "I—I can't."

As Skenandoah strides toward me, he says, "Then get out of my way."

He shoves me hard against the palisade and continues down the catwalk, speaking to his warriors, probably selecting another for the job he offered me.

A numb sensation of helplessness fills me. My nerves hum. All down the catwalk, warriors stare at me. The revulsion is close to hatred. At this moment, many of my old and dear friends wish to crush my skull with their war clubs.

Their focus quickly changes when the first arrows rain down in the marsh to the west. The enemy archers can't see across the thick reeds, because they don't have the distance yet. But they get it quickly. The next arrows slam the palisade and sail over the walls, where they drop into the plaza. People shriek and scatter like a school of fish at a thrown rock, running for cover. Many do not make it. By ones and twos, they fall. People race back, trying to drag them to safety. When another barrage of arrows flickers through the fog over Bur Oak Village, there is nothing for them to do but lie flat and hold the ground. Arrows lance the plaza, thudding on longhouse roofs, sending up puffs of snow when they don't strike flesh. A dog howls. I see it struggling toward the central fire with an arrow all the way through its right hind leg.

The shouting and screams go on and on. I lose all sense of time. Arrows fall like the endless rains at the dawn of creation when the hero twins fought the monsters. Fight the monsters. Fight...

More arrows zizz as they cut the air over my head. Down the catwalk, Skenandoah walks through the mist. Unbelievable. He walks slowly, slowly along through the hail of arrows, chatting with his warriors, bending to talk to men who'd hunched down, hiding behind the wall, convincing them to stand up again, to nock their bows. To fight.

Out in the marsh, calls go up. Two men materialize from the mist, slogging through the reeds, their bows held over their heads. Then, more...and more. Hundreds. Several carry ladders. Others hold pots, probably filled with pine pitch. As the warriors on the palisade sling arrows at them, they continue coming, unconcerned, wave upon wave. An incredible sight, dreamlike.

An arrow slices the air over my left shoulder. I dive for the catwalk. More arrows clatter. I watch one skip down the catwalk before it cuts a bright furrow in the planks and snaps in two. I roll to my back and lie for a time, blinking up at the arrows as they pass overhead. They make different sounds. Depending upon how they are fletched, some whisper, others hum. I most hate the thin, breathless shrieks made by the arrows fletched with crow feathers. For the first time, I become aware of the different notes that make up the roar. It's composed of thousands of gasps, barks, war clubs cracking together, fragments of songs, the splats of war axes striking bone, and curses of the warriors trying to cross the marsh. Children sobbing. Like a great dying beast, the battle keens through the morning mist.

Several of the warriors standing near me on the palisade cry out and collapse. Two topple from the catwalk and crash to the plaza below. People dash to get to them, then carry them in their arms to the council house.

A dropped bow and quiver gleams not two paces from me. Actually gleams—the polished wood shines as though coated with liquid sunlight. Beads of mist sparkle on the red cardinal feathers tied to the bowstring. Just below my hearing, as though calling to my soul, the weapon's quiet voice urges: *Pick me up. Fight.*

As though competing for my loyalty, Shagoniyoh whispers, *"You are no longer a warrior."*

Skenandoah crouches with his back to me. Black. Unmoving. Speaking softly to a dying youth huddling against the wall. The young warrior has seen perhaps fifteen summers.

A wail erupts just before the enemy horde strikes the palisade. As though an earthquake has heaved the world sideways, the catwalk trembles. I get to my feet, leap over the bow and quiver, and run to look.

Below, Hills warriors slam ladders against the walls. In less than ten heartbeats, several have vaulted over the palisade and landed upon the catwalk. Eyes gleaming wildly, they whoop and charge. People rush by me. As they kill the invaders, they shove their bodies back over the palisade and push the ladders away. I look down. Gray shapes, boulder-like, scatter the edge of the marsh. More pile against the base of the palisade. Bodies. The snow is gone, beaten away by desperate feet. Blood soaks the earth.

In Yellowtail Village, thirty paces distant, melody lofts into the roar. Musicians play drums and flutes. A conch-shell trumpet blows. The haunting sound wavers through the death cries like fluttering ribbons.

As though I have stepped into another world, the

chaos suddenly increases, drowning out everything but my own hammering heartbeat.

Out across the misty forest, the enemy is closing in. Warriors plant the spears sporting their clan colors, claiming this territory. The flags hang limp. No wind at all now. Just shining mist and sickly sunlight.

Only the far northern line still holds. And it can't last for long.

25

"Take him away," Kittle said with an impatient wave of her hand.

"Yes, High Matron."

The two warriors spun the Hills prisoner around and shoved him through the door curtain back out into the chaos of the plaza.

Kittle looked around at the other five matrons. Their dire expressions seemed frozen. They sat so still that their white hair caught the firelight and became threads of gold. The warm air felt suddenly hot. Kittle pulled her cape open beneath her chin. "I say we do it."

Sihata, matron of the Hawk Clan, shifted on the floor mat. "You would risk your granddaughter's life on the word of a terrified prisoner?"

"Someone must do it, Grandmother!" Taya

insisted. Her young face looked older. Her jaw was set, and her eyes blazed with certainty.

Kittle rubbed a hand over her face. The captured Hills warrior had been so frightened, his teeth had chattered incessantly. He'd have told them anything he thought they wanted to hear, but she suspected he'd been telling the truth about this. "Yes."

Taya, who stood to her right behind the circle of matrons, heaved a breath. Gitchi lay at her feet, guarding her as Sky Messenger had instructed. Taya gazed fearlessly at Kittle, but she had her fists clenched, clearly annoyed the deliberations were taking so long.

She said, "Grandmother, please, if I'm going, I must go now, before they've completely surrounded the village."

Matron Dehot murmured, "She's right. Send her. At this point, what harm could she do?"

Sihata smoothed white hair from her forehead. "There is one thing." They all turned to listen. "She is the high matron's granddaughter. She would make a fine hostage."

A small tremor went through Kittle, but she didn't think anyone noticed. She looked straight at Taya. "I won't let them use you against us. Do you understand, Taya? If we do this, as of this moment, you are dead to me. No matter what they threaten, I will do nothing to save you."

"I understand, Grandmother." She gave Kittle a clear-eyed stare.

Kittle held her gaze for a long time before saying, "Promise them anything you have to. Hurry."

"Take care of Gitchi for us?"

"Yes, of course." Kittle put her hand on the wolf's soft back and stroked it. "Stay with me, Gitchi."

Taya grabbed her cape from where it rested beside the fire, rushed to the door curtain, and disappeared outside.

Kittle watched the leather curtain swing. Outside, she caught glimpses of children running, dodging falling arrows, followed by shouting warriors trying to herd them to safety.

Sihata threw another branch on the fire. As sparks rose into the smoky air of the longhouse, she tipped her wrinkled face up to watch them climb toward the smoke hole. She softly said, "I think she'll make it. She has courage for one so young."

Kittle replied, "Yes. She'll make it. She has to."

26

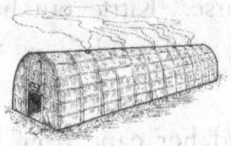

War Chief Sindak clutched his nocked bow and turned to look back. A solid line stretched out across the valley behind him, coming on fearlessly. The other war chiefs were keeping tight control of their warriors, which was not an easy thing with the enemy fleeing before them. Good men and women, every one. Despite the heavy losses they were taking, they would hold it together long enough to get into position around the villages. Then, it would become a different fight. He wiped stinging sweat from his eyes and licked his chapped lips. Each village had three rings of palisades. Breaking through them would be even more costly in blood and time. Gods, he wished he didn't have to do this. He wished it hadn't come to this. War Chief Koracoo, now Matron Jigonsaseh, was an old ally. He did not wish to kill her, and that's what would happen when they won. All of the matrons and chiefs would be lined up and their throats slit as their people watched. Atotarho had already given the order. "Leave the enemy headless. That way, when we march the captives home, they will be lost, their souls too broken to cause us problems. We'll pack their backs with every basket of food we can find, and they'll bear their burdens without a word."

Sindak frowned at where Chief Atotarho stood with his personal guards on the crest of the rocky ridge. He could just make them out in the shifting mist. The black flag of the Wolf Clan flew over his head.

Sindak turned back. A new roar and the clattering of war clubs rose when his forces cut through the third wave of archers and approached the last Standing Stone line waiting in the trees, their bows aimed, waiting. A roar went up. Elder Brother Sun, shining through the fog, cast an eerie diffuse light over the participants. Warriors' faces—some painted, some tattooed—glowed bloodred as they appeared and disappeared in the mist. His forces pushed closer, closer. One of the enemy war chiefs shouted, and the archers let fly. At that range, if they could aim at all, they couldn't miss. His stomach knotted as he watched hundreds of Hills warriors topple. They went down as though swathed by a huge flint scythe. The rest of his forces charged forward.

Most of the Standing Stone line broke and fled, but a portion of the line to the north held. Strong men and women. Good leadership to keep them in position while everyone else ran away. That wasn't Koracoo herself out there, was it? Surely they wouldn't let their new matron command, would they? No, he couldn't imagine it. Gonda? A sad warmth filled Sindak. Yes, maybe. Gonda had warred with Koracoo for many summers. He knew her tactics well.

Sindak lifted a fist and turned to yell to the war chiefs behind him, "Keep your lines tight. We will strike the last of the northern line, then push for the villages."

He yipped a shrill war cry and charged down into the battle, his warriors pounding the ground behind him.

As he ran, he gave the other war chiefs hand signals, and the whole line shifted northward, closing gaps, moving like one huge animal. It was beautifully done. Artwork. Even after the arrows began falling like a hail of stilettos, the line still moved steadily onward.

When they got closer, a few men stopped to fire back and then more stopped. Sindak shouted at their commanders. Too far. They were too far away. If they hit anything, it would be sheer luck.

Move. Keep them all moving. The terrifying sight of so many enemy warriors coming at them should send the Standing Stone warriors fleeing before they even arrived.

But they held. To his amazement. Even in the face of overwhelming odds, the remnant northern line held. They were about to be swallowed whole. But they held. Admiration filled him.

He winced when, to his right, he saw his own line breaking. Warriors too eager for blood clumped together and lunged ahead. They must have planned this, their own moment of victory. Nothing he could do about it now. They were too close. Almost upon the enemy. The northern line concentrated their fire on the men running out in front, and the heroes dropped like flies after the first hard frost.

"Come on!" Sindak shouted. "Now is the time for courage! Make your clans proud."

The Standing Stone archers tossed aside their bows, drew their war clubs, and clan cries shredded the air as they charged out to meet Sindak's forces.

27

"Stay down!" Gonda ordered.

Warriors scrambled to obey, throwing themselves to the earth, covering their heads until the endless volley slicing the air overhead ceased.

He hid behind a boulder, staring for so long at the orange circles of lichen and shiny flecks of mica in the granite that when he dared lift his head and look out across the valley at the men moving among the trees, hunched, hiding, he felt too tired to move. Many warriors had covered themselves with leaves, praying the attackers would pass them by. A bloody deer thrashed through the brush to his right, three-legged, a wrenching sight. Five paces away a man with no head lay like a torn cornhusk doll. And all around him, all around, mist eddied and roiled. Fine snow filtered down everywhere, coating faces, capes, settling into unseeing eyes. The western lines had collapsed first, followed by most of the northern line. Standing Stone warriors were fleeing for their lives, trying to reach the villages before they could be cut down. The enemy formed up behind them and let fly at their backs. A new sound. Stuttering wails. Ghostly forms staggered through shifting fog, visible one instant, gone the next.

Gonda blinked. As the enemy raced by on their way to attack the villages, he breathed out. Gradually, the air softened, and the battle sounds transformed into a distant roar.

Gonda stepped from behind the boulder for a better look.

A young boy, twelve maybe, crouched to Gonda's left, sobbing without making a sound, staring out at the rows of dead that littered the foggy vista. Gonda walked over and put a hand on his shoulder. "It's all right. It's over for now."

The boy lifted his face and gazed at him, his soft black eyes like polished jet. Stunned eyes. Uncomprehending. Gonda patted his shoulder. "Just sit here for a while. If you have any food in your belt pouch, eat. You need something in your stomach. It will help."

The boy's jaws worked, but no sound came out. Gonda patted his shoulder again and said, "You fought bravely today. No man could have done better." He moved on, stepped between two dead bodies, and headed for War Chief Deru.

Deru had just stood up thirty paces away. His massive shoulders bristled with old leaves. In profile, his face was dark and still, his caved-in cheek nothing more than an oddly misshapen shadow, a hole in his head. He clutched his war club in a bloody fist.

Warriors slowly moved among the thick brush and piles of boulders, getting to their feet. Their faces had flushed, their eyes gone blank with shock. Lips moved and tears ran down cheeks. Friends covered the dead grass, their arms and legs twisted at impossible angles. For as far as any of them could see...bodies. Hundreds. No, thousands. They filled the valley. Great swaths of blood had turned the snow the shade of fire.

Gonda walked to Deru. They stared at each other. Despite the fact that they faced each other from less than eight hands away, Gonda was having trouble focusing his eyes. He kept blinking, trying to clear them. Over Deru's shoulder, he saw the woman warrior, Wampa, standing with her feet braced, her shaking bow pulled back, guarding four wounded warriors, men with barely the strength to weep and stare up at her with utter devotion in their eyes. She had perhaps been the only thing that had stood between them and death.

From deep inside him, Koracoo's long-ago voice

whispered, *"Like stunning beauty, true bravery has no cause, no reasons or motives. It is an offering, given without a thought."*

Gonda hung his head.

Deru looked at him with a tight expression Gonda had never seen—the expression of a man bleeding to death inside. Deru said nothing, just stared. Gonda felt an eerie turning, like a mortal wound pumping the heart dry. Then he saw Deru was crying. The war chief was crying. Gonda moved closer and said sternly, "We're not finished. Not yet."

Deru lightly shook his head. "No, we are not."

"We need to form up our warriors. We'll attack the flanks. Pick off as many as we can."

Deru wiped his face on his sleeve. "How many are well enough to fight?"

Gonda looked around. He counted perhaps thirty warriors on their feet. Thirty. Thirty out of five hundred. The rest...the rest would never fight again. "Enough to hurt them."

Deru gave him a grim smile, and the gesture made his crushed cheek twitch. He called, "Gather as many dropped arrows as you can. Fill your quivers! We're heading back into the fight."

Warriors gave each other empty looks and slowly turned to collect arrows, war clubs, axes. They moved like dead men still on their feet, but just barely.

Gonda said, "What's your plan?"

Deru squinted at the thousands of Hills warriors rushing toward the villages. Though Atotarho had taken heavy losses, there had to be four thousand warriors still in the fight. Four thousand Gonda could see, which didn't count whatever the chief had in reserve waiting in the forest to the south. Deru didn't seem able to speak. He kept shaking his head, swallowing.

Gonda cast a glance at the men and women beginning to crowd around them, waiting for orders. He moved closer to Deru and whispered, "I say we swing around the western edge of the marsh. Come up from the south using the cornfields as cover. Then, decide what to do. What do you think, War Chief?"

Deru stared at the marsh for a long time, as though trying to see it in his souls. "Yes. Yes, let's do that." He turned to his warriors. "Follow me. We're going around the marsh!"

He lifted a hand, waved his warriors forward, and took off at a slow trot, heading for the dense stand of cattails wavering through the mist.

28

Zateri watched the battle with her arms folded tightly beneath her white cape. Each time she shifted, the blue wolf paw prints that encircled the bottom of the cape seemed to be running, trying to escape. She felt sick. The people standing around the fire with her seemed as stunned as she was at the swiftness of their progress. The worst part of the battle remained ahead, however. Laying siege to fortified villages was usually a waste of lives, not that her father cared. All he wanted was to destroy the Standing Stone nation.

As War Chief Sindak re-formed the Hills lines around Yellowtail and Bur Oak villages, there was a brief respite in the fighting. The shouts and war cries yielded to the low moans of the injured and dying still on the battlefield.

Zateri studied her comrades' faces. Kwahseti, Gwinodje, Hiyawento, and Chief Canassatego stood quietly, warming their hands before the flames or sipping cups of rosehip tea while they waited for the next assault to begin. Hiyawento's dark eyes had a glazed look, as though he was seeing through the battle to something far beyond, and she wondered if perhaps he was not living in the past with his daughters. Just behind Zateri's eyes, their sweet faces were always there, their arms lifted, begging to be held. Their bubbling laughter filled her ears. Hiyawento had always been able to smile Zateri out of her fears, to comfort her. She longed for the feel of his strong arms around her. But when she looked at him, she knew this man was not going to smile, or offer comfort, for his own unbearable pain had swallowed his world.

Zateri turned to see her father. He rode upon his litter with a regal tilt to his gray head. Carried by four warriors, the litter jostled and rocked as the men maneuvered it into place three hundred paces from Bur Oak Village. When he slid his crooked body off the litter, his black cape looked stark against the snow. A log bench was immediately constructed so he could sit down. From there, Atotarho would observe the final collapse of his enemies. He must be gloating, laughing. As she watched the chief's personal guards setting up his war lodge—little more than tented poles covered with deer hides—hatred seeped through Zateri's grief.

Kwahseti gestured with her chin. "There's a runner coming."

The runner slowed thirty paces away and walked the last distance to reach her fire, where he bowed deeply. "Matrons, the chief wishes you to move your forces into position south of the villages. When the cowards try to flee, he wants the leaders captured and held."

Zateri nodded. "Very well."

The runner looked around nervously. He'd seen eighteen or nineteen summers. Irregularly chopped-off black hair hung around his narrow face, which made his nose look abnormally long. "There is one other thing, Matron Zateri."

"Yes?"

He wet his lips. "The chief wishes me to inform you that he has received word that the high matron is walking the Path of Souls."

The ground seemed to fall away beneath her feet. After her mother's death, Grandmother had been the only person in the world who'd cared enough to help her heal after Gannajero. She'd nursed Zateri when she'd been sick, taught her everything about clan politics, and held her when her heart had been broken. The loss, along with that of her daughters, seemed to open a gaping black chasm in her souls. She had the uneasy sensation that she was teetering on the edge, about to fall in where she would lose herself in the icy darkness. She said, "When?"

"Four days ago."

Zateri straightened. "Thank you, warrior. When we return home, I will call the Wolf Clan—"

"That won't be necessary," the warrior interrupted as though he knew he had to get it out now, or he never would. "The chief says you should not worry about the succession. The former high matron left instructions that she wished Matron Kelek of the Bear Clan to replace her as high matron. She—"

"What!" Kwahseti lunged forward to stare with her fists clenched. The runner looked like he wanted to crawl under a log. "She would never do that! It's a betrayal of the other Wolf Clan ohwachiras!"

"Nonetheless, Matrons, the chief has already spoken with Matron Kelek. At this very moment, she is—"

"She had better not be making preparations!" Gwinodje's voice seethed. Her face had gone livid. "Our clan will not give up rulership so easily, and you can tell that to Chief Atotarho!"

"I understand." The runner bowed again, turned, and jogged away. Everyone turned to

Zateri. Their expressions were outraged. Gwinodje's thin, girlish body was shaking.

Kwahseti waved a hand. "Zateri, why didn't you say anything? You know your grandmother wished you to replace her. She said as much at the last meeting of the ohwachiras!"

A sudden frightening sensation rose and pervaded everything, stealthily closing in around her. When it settled into her chest like a frozen stone, she shivered. "He's been clever, hasn't he?"

Kwahseti frowned. "What do you mean? He just stole your inheritance. You are the rightful—"

"He's been planning this all along, and I did not guess it. Perhaps I am not fit to lead anyone."

"You no longer have the luxury of speculating, Zateri," Kwahseti said. "Will you or won't you lead the clan?"

Gwinodje was staring at her, waiting. "You must decide, Zateri. Once you accept, we can begin organizing the ohwachiras and pulling the little clan matrons together."

Zateri stared out at the battlefield. Grandmother had wanted this. In fact, the False Faces had come to her...Zateri looked down at her white cape, and a flood of certainty rushed through her. "Yes, I accept. If the ohwachiras will have me, I will lead them. Now, what do we do about Atotarho's order?"

Chief Canassatego's leathery brown face

tensed. He glanced down the hill at Atotarho, sitting hunched over on his log bench, then back at those gathered around the fire. "I, for one, refuse to accept this farce. I will not support a chief who moves without the consensus of the Ruling Council. He consulted no one, not about the high matron's position, nor about the attack on White Dog Village. Does he think he alone rules this nation?"

Gwinodje added, "I agree. Either the chief follows the will of the people, which is guaranteed by the Ruling Council's efforts to seek the consensus of the people, or our alliance crumbles."

Kwahseti stood irresolutely for a moment. Then, bracing herself as though for a fistfight, she said, "Well, what are we going to do about it? We're in the middle of a battle. We've just been given orders."

"Orders we should refuse to obey." Hiyawento seemed to have come back to himself. His voice sounded strong, confident. His dark eyes flashed. Though he'd said nothing during the exchange, his indignation was palpable. "Matron Zateri, is it your decision that I lead the Coldspring Village warriors into this fight?"

Zateri watched the mist moving through the valley below. The sky was completely overcast now. Elder Brother Sun's gleam had all but vanished, leaving the land gray and dim. The temperature was also dropping. The fog seemed to be growing thicker, filling the valley like dove-colored smoke.

"I must consult with Chief Coldspring and the other village clan matrons."

"As we all should," Kwahseti said.

"Then let us do so immediately," Gwinodje urged. "We don't have much time to get organized. You all know, don't you? If we do this, Atotarho will label us traitors and turn his forces against us. We had better be ready. In fact, we had better—"

A sharp cry rose from down the hill near last summer's cornfields. Zateri spun to look and saw two of her scouts hauling a young woman up the hill. The woman was struggling against them, fighting, and the warriors seemed to be enjoying themselves, hurting an enemy woman.

Hiyawento's eyes suddenly flared, and he shouted, "Release her, now!"

The warriors dropped her arms as though they'd turned red-hot and stared at their war chief in confusion. As soon as she was free, the young woman lifted her skirts and ran up the hill like a boy, trying to get to Hiyawento.

"Do you know her?" Zateri asked. She was beautiful, with an oval face, large dark eyes, and... "Blessed gods, that's High Matron Kittle's granddaughter, isn't it? She looks just like her."

"Yes. And Sky Messenger's betrothed. Her

name is Taya." Hiyawento ran down the hill to meet her, took her arm, and led her to the fire.

Taya was crying. Tears traced lines through the dust on her face. "I'm sorry, I—I didn't know how else to get here without being killed. I told the guards I needed to see you, that I knew you."

Gently, Hiyawento said, "That was the right thing to do. You do know me. Why are you here, Taya?"

She wiped her face with her hands, sniffed her nose, and stiffened her spine. After a few heartbeats, when she'd controlled herself, she said, "The Ruling Council of the Standing Stone nation wishes to make you an offer."

29

"You may go." Atotarho waved an impatient hand at the messenger who had just returned and gazed to the south, to the hilltop where the Wolf Clan matrons stood around a small fire. A chuckle rumbled his chest. They must be furious, plotting against him, but it didn't matter. It was almost over. After he'd destroyed the Standing Stone People, there'd be nothing to stop him from conquering every other paltry contender. Within two or three summers there would be only the People of the Hills. All other nations would have been conquered, their women and children absorbed into new Hills villages, their men killed or enslaved.

Negano's long black hair swayed wetly as he strode up to Atotarho and subtly jerked his head toward the war lodge. "While you were busy with battle..." he said cryptically.

Atotarho turned to look. The lodge stood fourteen hands tall and spread twenty hands in diameter. Painted deer hides, decorated with symbols from each of the six clans, covered the pole structure. "Thank you, Negano."

He careened to his feet, wobbled, and had to brace his walking stick to keep standing. "Inform me when the battle begins again. I need to rest."

"Yes, Chief." Negano bowed.

Atotarho slowly, painfully, made his way to his war lodge, drew back the hide over the door, and stepped into the darkness. In the rear, shapes moved. The blackness seemed to fold in upon itself, then unfold.

"So," he said as he let the door curtain drop. "You finally got here. I was beginning to wonder."

The man didn't answer. Instead, like oil oozing from a midnight ocean, Ohsinoh arose. His bluebird-feather hood had been pulled so far forward it was difficult to make out any of his features, though he'd painted his triangular face—the lower half was red, the top half white.

As Atotarho's eyes adjusted to the darkness, he saw an eight-summers-old girl on her knees in the rear. Eyes huge and wet. Tiny whimpers eddied through her gag. Though she was not struggling now, she had been. Blood caked the cords that bound her hands and feet.

Ohsinoh leaned forward. When his face was less than one hand's-breadth from Atotarho's, he whispered, "Kahn-Tineta has seen the Crow. She will be ready when the time comes." As he straightened, he began making soft cawing sounds. He danced like a demented stork around Kahn-Tineta. The girl tried to scream through her gag.

Atotarho lowered himself to the stack of hides that had been prepared for him, and replied, "Good."

30
SKY MESSENGER

When I deliver warm bowls of cornmeal mush to the exhausted warriors leaning against the palisade, they murmur soft thanks. I move on. There's no need to rush as everyone who was hungry has been fed. Every wound has been tended. I have seen to that. My cape is soaked with the tears of the dying, but they did not die alone. I thank the Spirits for the lull in the battle, but the calm is almost over. Far out in the dense fog, clan yells erupt. Orders are shouted. Deputy war chiefs are moving their people into position. War clubs smack against palms. Laughter trails away. We'll be hit again at any moment.

I have not seen Taya since just after dawn. I'm worried about her. Where is she? She must be safe. She has to be safe.

I wipe my sweating brow on my sleeve and gaze

down into the plaza. The council house was long ago filled to bursting. There is no choice now but to place the injured outside in the cold. As space is opened in the council house, the injured will be moved in. The dead rest in mounds along the walls. Loved ones refuse to leave them. They bring blankets to keep their husbands and daughters warm. They hug them and whisper in their ears. The wails are terrible.

I turn. Out to the east, thousands of feet crunch snow. Voices call. Too much fog. They are translucent ghosts swimming in a vast gray ocean, ceaselessly moving, riding waves up and down as they dip into the main trail and soar up the bank, coming on. Flat out.

An arrow slams my arm, spinning me sideways. I look down at the blood seeping from the torn muscle of my upper arm. It's nothing. Keep moving. A man sags, almost falls over the palisade, catches himself. He sinks to the catwalk with agonizing slowness. I hurry toward him. He has blood all over his chest, blood bubbling from around the arrow shaft. I kneel beside him.

"You're not dying, Idos," I say confidently as I snap off the tip of the arrow and hurl it away. "The arrow struck too high. You will get well."

He stares up at me fixedly, straining to see my face. As he slides toward the dark, I must be fading. I can't imagine what he's thinking. He gasps a breath and with difficulty says, "Tell...Tutelo I love her."

My souls go numb. I hesitate, not sure of the best course, then I grip the slick shaft and jerk it from his chest. I'm sure it struck his heart, but maybe...maybe. He writhes, cries out. When the enemy hits the palisade, the misty world shatters and becomes one long scream.

Down in the plaza, people run in all directions.

Idos stops struggling. I feel his body relax beneath my hands. He's still staring at me, but he doesn't see me now. Sodowego has leaned over him. I whisper, "I'll tell her, Idos."

I rise to my feet. The smell of pine pitch is strong, rising from the base of the palisade. Skenandoah marches along the catwalk with arrows flying all around him, giving orders, always steady. And lucky. Lucky.

I throw up an arm to shield my face and run to look over the edge. Five warriors arrived before me. They've been loosing arrows, ducking behind the palisade, loosing more arrows for ten heartbeats. A bloody tangle of bodies sprawls below, but they succeeded in setting fire to the pitch before they fell. Bright flames lick along the wall. In the mist, they resemble gauzy orange flags. Fluttering. Climbing. The warriors must have managed to splash the pitch high. Down the palisade, more fires. They've probably been set all around. That was the point of that first shuddering volley, to allow the fire teams to get in close enough. Some of the fires will burn through. Then more teams will dart in, splash the second palisade, and fire it. Finally, they will fire the third palisade...and be through. On the fabric of my souls, I can already imagine enemy warriors racing through Bur Oak Village, killing anything in their path. I remember Yellowtail Village...burning...twelve summers ago.

A cold whisper of air brushes my face. I dive for the catwalk. I'm not hit. Close, though. Right beside me, a young woman goes down with a sharp cry. I scramble toward her on my hands and knees. The arrow cut the big artery in her throat and it's pumping ferociously. She shivers, suddenly freezing. "How... how bad? Tell me the truth!"

I gently smooth black hair away from her face. I would want to know the truth. "It'll be over soon. What's your name?"

"I am...Londal." She squeezes her eyes closed for a moment, then opens them and gazes up at the sky. "Thank you, thank you...for telling me."

She seems not to hear the ululating cries of oncoming warriors or feel the palisade shudder when they hit it and their axes crack against the logs, hacking their way through the charred patches left by the fires.

I sit down and pull her head into my lap, cushioning it as I stroke her hair.

She says, "I'm feeling...weaker."

"It won't last long. Just a little while. Is there any pain?"

Her lips move. She mouths the word no. A brown autumn leaf flutters through the fog and alights on the catwalk.

She whispers, "Pretty."

I pick it up and twirl it before her eyes. "Yes, it's still veined with red."

Just beyond the palisade the world is dying, she's dying, and we're talking about leaves.

"I—I'm falling." She struggles.

"Don't be afraid. I've heard it's a long slow fall, that it comes quietly and peacefully."

"...falling."

"Yes, but you won't hit bottom. Soon you'll be walking the Path of Souls with people you once loved. Their campfires will be warm and bright."

The blood is jetting rapidly now, but there isn't much of it. Her heart is failing. It can't keep up. Then...it's over.

I rise, mindful of the hail of arrows slicing overhead. Dead bodies crowd the catwalk. Warriors trip over them, walk on their backs. Some are crying, trying to be gentle. Most of the seasoned war veterans inside the palisade are dead. Young inexperienced warriors have replaced them. Their faces are twisted into stunned masks. What happened to the two men assigned to carry the wounded and dying into the plaza?

My job now. I bend and lift the woman warrior into my arms. Walking hunched over, I see Skenandoah. He's firing one arrow after another at the base of the palisade. His war shirt has a dozen ragged holes down his arms where his cape has been clipped by arrows. His square face is hard, his brown eyes glittering.

As I struggle to move by him, to reach the ladder, Deputy War Chief Leep cries out. Four paces away, he staggers backward and falls off the palisade with an arrow through his skull. Skenandoah looks for an instant too long. The arrow strikes him squarely in the lungs. As he grabs hold of the palisade, his bow drops from his fingers and clatters on the catwalk. A strange, almost amused expression touches his face. It's a mortal wound. He must know it. He straightens to his full height, as though making a target of his broad chest, and shrilly roars a defiant war cry. Within moments three more arrows slam into his body, each knocking him back a step. He crumples like a dry blade of grass beneath tramping feet.

Every warrior on the catwalk stops. They've lost both their war chief and deputy war chief in less than twenty heartbeats. Most have seen fourteen or fifteen summers. There's no one left to lead them. I can see it in their eyes. They think it's over. There's no hope.

One youth throws down his bow and flees. Two follow him. The rest are backing away from the palisade.

I hastily lay Londal's body down and grab Skenandoah's bow. Sick helpless rage fills me. As I tug the quiver from Londal's shoulders and sling it over my own shoulder, I shout, "Get that look off your faces! There are Hills People to kill! Nock your bows!"

Young warriors suck in air. They stare at me.

"Do it now!" I shout.

As though they've been slapped from a nightmare, they scramble to obey me.

A strange madness filters through me. An old familiar madness. My practiced hands work automatically, pulling arrows from the quiver, nocking, letting fly. As I watch man after man fall to my arrows, the fever builds. I'm on fire, and the sparkling mist is so bright it hurts.

"Sky Messenger!" Yaweth cries. "They're coming through!"

I swing around and see enemy warriors flooding through two holes in the innermost palisade, streaming across the plaza. The few Standing Stone warriors run to meet them. It is a disorganized rabble. As more of the enemy floods inside, the Standing Stone warriors break and run. The enemy pursues. The sodden thuds of war clubs striking flesh rise. The victory cries of the Hills warriors are like a Spirit Plant surging through my veins.

I throw my head back and shriek a war cry. Every warrior turns to me. Aims shift. Enemy arrows stream around me.

"Yaweth!" I shout. "You're my new deputy. Pick twenty people and form teams to cover every place where they might come through the inner palisade."

"Yes, Sky Messenger. What about you?"

My eyes must be blazing. An appreciative smile crosses her face. She knows this look. We are going to win. "I'm going down to lead the warriors in the plaza. Now move! They're coming."

I charge for the ladder.

31
SKY MESSENGER

I leap off the rungs and hit the ground running. Skenandoah's bow sings in my hands. Standing Stone warriors flee around me, their faces stunned and gray, a slack-jawed mob. Most are very young, little more than terrified children. But I, above all, know what children can do when they must.

A bony girl in a torn dress has hold of an older man's arm. She is perhaps thirteen, crying, trying to drag him backward into the fight. He's seen around sixteen summers. "Please, my brother, they'll kill Mother and Father!"

He screams, "No!" shakes off her hands, and runs.

I grab the youth as he darts by and swing him around to glare full in his face. "Pull that war club from your belt! You're a Standing Stone warrior. Fight!" The man is shaking badly. "What is your name?"

"P-pato."

I release him and step into the falling arrows to shout, "I am Sky Messenger. Follow me! Now is the time to save your families from slavery and death! *Follow me!*"

I shriek another war cry and pound into the plaza battle, loosing arrows on the run. I may not know these children's names, but they know mine. I hear them coming on behind me, my army of children. Bravely following. May the ancestors protect them. I cast a glance over my shoulder. Perhaps forty. That is all the help I have to drive back the endless stream of warriors. It must be enough.

Yaweth's people race along the catwalk, getting into position. Every time Hills warriors duck through a hole in the walls, her warriors cut them to pieces. That leaves perhaps one hundred of the enemy in the plaza. Men who know the only way they'll get out is to kill every man, woman, and child in the village.

My quiver is empty. I toss it aside, scoop a war club from the ground, and lead my young warriors into the fight of their lives. My skills with a club were honed by the best: my father, Gonda, and my mother, the legendary war chief Koracoo. They taught me every nuance of the weapon.

A filthy warrior with rotten teeth charges me, roaring, his war club swinging for my shoulder. I parry the blow, shove him back, and level my club at his side. When it connects, a massive gush of air explodes from his crushed rib cage. He drops to his knees. Two more rush me.

I fight like a man possessed by an evil Earth Spirit, insanely twisting, dancing in to deliver blows, and leaping out beyond my opponents' range. They both come at me at once. I cave in the closest man's forehead and spin on one foot, ducking low, avoiding the blow that cuts the air over my head, to hammer the knees out from under my attacker. Bones crack. He falls, tries to drag himself away. He'll never walk again. But he won't have to. I crush his skull and move on.

"Sky Messenger!" someone behind me screams.

I glance back and see the youth I forced into the fight, young Pato, being beaten to the ground by a muscular Hills warrior with a triumphant grin on his face.

I'm there in three bounds. My club whispers through the mist as it slices for the man's arm. He dives, rolls, and jabs his club at me, forcing me back until he can get to his feet again.

"You pathetic worm!" the man shouts. "Do you think you can defeat the greatest warrior in the entire Hills nation? I am Ponkol of the Snipe Clan!"

When he starts to stand, there is an instant when he's off balance. I use it to rush him, hit him hard with my shoulder, and send him stumbling backward. Before he can regain his footing, young Pato slams him in the side of the head and staggers back. Pato looks dazed, stares at the dead man on the ground.

I shout, "Keep moving, Pato! Don't slow down."

As he turns to face his next opponent, an arrow rips the war shirt near my knees. I turn to...

Outside the walls, a horn trumpet blows three times. The blasts seem muffled by the fog, muted and haunting. The Hills warriors in the plaza jerk around in unison to stare. They look confused. Then there is a rush, an onslaught, dashing for the holes in the palisade. Yaweth's people kill as many as they can, but the warriors push outside.

I blink. A few are fighting a retreating action, covering their friends as they escape, but most are gone. My young warriors stagger, staring at dead friends. Disbelieving looks carve their faces.

I shout, "Stop looking at your fallen friends. We can't let anyone escape! Follow me!"

I pound toward the last four warriors who are covering their friends' escape. By the time I arrive, Yaweth's people have killed two. Two left.

With a single blow, I snap the spine of one man, then launch myself at the last Hills warrior standing in Bur Oak Village. He looks horrified. He knows what's coming. Before I can crack his skull, someone on the catwalk shoots an arrow through his belly. The man cries out in shock, throws down his bow, and charges through the charred hole in the palisade, trying to make it to his friends.

I chase after him. Just as he lurches through the last palisade, I crush his shoulder. He staggers back against the wall, calling desperately to his friends who are far out ahead, charging away. When he turns, his gaze flashes over me and fixes on something over my shoulder.

"No," the man hisses. "No. They're doing it!" He collapses to his knees. "I don't believe it!"

I turn to look toward the southern hills, following his gaze. A slight breeze has kicked up, swirling the fog into wavelike patterns that seem to ebb and flow. As it shifts, gaps open in the mist, revealing a sight that leaves me shaking my head, trying to decipher what's going on. Two sides are lining out. To the north, I see Sindak stalking down the lines, waving his war club. *Atotarho is to the north.*

I glare down at the wounded Hills warrior. "What's happening? Who is that to the south?"

He rocks back and forth, his hands clutching the arrow protruding from his belly. "Treasonous dogs! They deserve to die for this!"

"Who is that?" I draw back my war club to kill him if he doesn't answer quickly.

In a pathetic whimper, the man responds, "Chief Atotarho pulled three villages out of the battle because he thought they might refuse to fight. He ordered them to remain in camp! But they didn't. You can see that! They're marching out to face him down. The filthy traitors! Civil war is inevitable now!"

"Which villages?"

He lifted a trembling arm to point. "See there? That's War Chief Hiyawento. He's leading warriors from Coldspring, Riverbank, and Canassatego villages! Traitors!"

The wind changes. The mist blows back across the field to chill my face. The clan calls are easing off as warriors receive new orders and realign. The world goes soft and still.

My hands shake. I don't know what this has cost Hiyawento—I may never know—but the fact that he and Zateri have managed to pull the disaffected Hills villages into an alliance to fight against Atotarho...

After all my words about standing up for peace, this is where we are—locked in a death struggle.

From my right, a voice calls, "Sky Messenger!"

Father trots around the palisade with thirty or so warriors behind him. His wet cape sleeks down over his thin wiry body. His round face is haggard, his short black hair matted.

"Father! You're alive."

We throw our arms around each other in a bear hug. He laughs. "So far. Don't get your hopes up. I'm certain the Hills People would like to change that."

War Chief Deru comes to stand at my side. His eyes narrow at the sight of the wounded Hills warrior. Unceremoniously, he crushes the man's skull, then turns back to the battlefield. "What's going on out there?"

"Civil war, I think."

"They're fighting each other?" he asks in disbelief.

"Yes. So it seems."

Father's expression goes tight and sad. He says nothing for a long time, then whispers, "Warriors are asked to bear too much."

Neither Deru nor I have to ask what he means. Along with exhaustion, hunger, and the rage that leaves the heart a barren wasteland, these men and women will also have to live with the knowledge that they killed their loved ones with their own hands.

As the war fever begins to drain from muscles and sinew, my skin tingles. Those are my cherished friends out there, willing to fight their own people to save me and the entire Standing Stone nation.

My grip tightens on the bloody club in my fingers.

From out of nowhere, Gitchi glides along my leg and looks up at me with soft yellow eyes. He limps, but his tail wags, ready to follow as soon as I give the order. I don't know where he came from. One of the longhouses. Where's Taya? I turn to look, but I do not see her. High Matron Kittle must have ordered her lineage to remain within the walls of the longhouses.

I gaze down at Gitchi. "Hello, old friend. I missed you." I gently stroke his head. He leans against my hand and sighs, as though being with me is all he's ever wanted in his life.

"Well, what are we doing standing here?" Father

looks around, searching each warrior's face. "If they're fighting Atotarho, they're on our side. We should join them. War Chief, what do you think?"

Deru inhales a breath and exhales it slowly and then he nods. "It seems we have just joined a new alliance—a strange one. Us and Hills People? Who would have ever thought? But Gonda is right. If these new allies are willing to die for us, we owe them no less."

A ragged, exhausted cheer goes up from his warriors. They shake bows and clubs in the air.

Father turns to a young man. "Risto, run to Matron Jigonsaseh. Tell her we join the fight on Hiyawento's side."

The warrior bows and runs as hard as he can toward Yellowtail Village.

"All right, let's go." Deru waves his warriors forward and leads them out onto the battlefield.

Father says, "Are you coming?"

I breathe, "Yes. Soon."

He frowns, then nods, understanding there is something I must do before I can follow him. "Don't be long." He trots away.

I crouch before Gitchi. The old wolf licks my face, and his tail wags. "I know you want to go, Gitchi. You are a great warrior. But I couldn't bear it if something happened to you. I want you to stay here. Don't follow me."

Gitchi's ears droop. He drops to his haunches and whimpers as he watches me pound away into the cold swirling fog.

32

Where he stood in front of Chief Atotarho, Negano rubbed a hand over his face. In all his thirty-two summers, he had never imagined that a day like this would come. He had many cousins in Riverbank Village, men and women he'd loved his entire life. He could barely stand to watch. Blessed Spirits. He had to come to terms with this, or he would...

Atotarho vented a low laugh.

Negano turned around to stare at him. The old man had braided so many rattlesnake skins into his gray hair that it gave his skeletal face a serpentine quality. Granted, they were symbols of war victories, but this was garish.

Atotarho maneuvered his crooked body forward, carefully placing his walking stick, until he stood less than one pace from Negano. His eyes had a cold inhuman gleam. "Find a runner for me."

"Yes, my chief." Negano lifted a hand, calling, "Qonde?"

When the guard trotted over, Atotarho said, "Grab a white arrow. I wish you to deliver a message to my daughter, Matron Zateri. Tell her I wish a short truce to speak with her."

Qonde gave Negano a relieved look, bowed, and trotted away.

Negano turned to Atotarho, hopefully asking, "Will we make peace, Chief?"

"Oh," Atotarho nodded fervently, "*they* will make peace." Atotarho gripped his walking stick as though to strangle the life from it. "The arrogant fools. Did they think I would not foresee this treachery?" From within the war lodge, a deep-throated laugh rumbled.

From where he stood on the tree-covered eastern hill, Sonon could look down across the misty battlefield. He watched his brother's messenger trot toward Matron Zateri's camp, weaving through thousands of warriors, men and women preparing for the final confrontation. The fog-shrouded field echoed with their efforts: damp bowstrings whined as they were drawn back, arrows rattled in leather quivers and wooden-slat body armor clacked. The low, dreadful groan of the battlefield hung over everything like the death wails of soon-to-be-forgotten nations.

Ohsinoh laughed, and it made Sonon go still. It was like the hiss of a poisonous serpent, quiet with the promise of death. It made the skin creep.

Sonon's gaze moved to the war lodge where his brother, Atotarho, stood.

He granted himself a moment to wonder what if...

What if Atotarho's afterlife soul had not been chased from his body? What if the stream of their lives had not been broken? That boy, his brother's son, would have been a greatly beloved member of Sonon's family. Sonon would have helped raise him, would have taught him to fish and hunt, would have comforted Hehaka's tears. If he'd had the chance, Sonon would have done everything in his power to keep that boy from harm.

But Atotarho's soul had been shaken loose. The stream of their lives had been sundered. Sonon and his twin sister were sold into slavery at the age of eight, and Hehaka at the age of four. Their three lives had become a diabolical monument to Atotarho's loose soul—a soul that continued to wander shadow-like through the forests.

Sonon's soft exhale frosted and blended with the eddying fog.

Behind him, coming up the main trail, hundreds of moccasins thumped the frozen ground. Weapons jangled with their quickstep. They must have run all the way to get here, for the pungent scent of their sweat wafted on the light breeze.

He didn't turn. Soon, it would all begin again.

He wanted to look for a time longer.

Sonon kept his gaze on Atotarho's crooked, misshapen body. Strands of Atotarho's gray hair had come loose from his bun and stuck wetly to his wrinkled cheeks. The war lodge shadowed most of his expression.

Sonon cocked his head.

How strange that the most important lessons lived in shadows. To see anything clearly, a man had to be willing to stare full-face into the living darkness.

As he stared at his brother, Atotarho turned, and Sonon found his own living darkness staring back. He was looking into the black abyss that had swallowed him when he'd seen eight summers.

Someday, someday soon, he would have to confront his brother...but not today.

The warriors coming up behind him veered off the main trail and trotted toward the hilltop where

Sonon stood. Their breathing was coming hard. Their clan flags flapped as they ran.

Sonon tore his gaze from his brother and swiveled to watch their approach.

33

The mist moved as a great white ocean, waves surging and retreating, leaving lacy patterns like sea foam in their wake. Tree branches dripped incessantly. Chief Cord shivered. The damp cold ate at a man's bones.

"I don't understand this," War Chief Baji said.

Cord rubbed the back of his neck. "I doubt anyone does. Especially the warriors on that battlefield."

Where they stood upon the hilltop to the east of Bur Oak and Yellowtail villages, they could look out across the misty battlefield. The dilemma was clear. Both sides were Hills People.

"Ah. Maybe I do understand." Baji's gaze scanned the principal figures, men and women standing out in front of their forces, preparing to give orders.

"Well, explain it to me."

His adopted daughter had grown into a strong muscular woman, broad-shouldered with long legs, and the face of a Sky Spirit. Oval, with large black eyes, high cheekbones, her face would have been perfect were it not for the white knife scar that slashed across her pointed chin. She did not wear a cape, just a knee-length buckskin war shirt and high-topped black moccasins. Weapons dangled from her belt. She carried a bow and quiver over her left shoulder.

She tipped her chin. "To the south, do you see the tall man with the war axe? That's Hiyawento. The short slender woman to his right is Zateri."

Cord gave her a curious look. "We're too far away to see their faces. How could you possibly know that?"

Her gaze moved across the battlefield and seemed to fix on some far point. Her voice turned soft. "The same way I know that that's Dekanawida trotting out from Bur Oak Village. I know them, Cord. In ways I will never know any other human beings. The motions of their bodies live in my souls. Every tilt of their heads, every wave of their hands, the way each stands, is part of me. I might as well be looking at myself in a slate mirror. I know that sounds strange—"

"No. It doesn't." Cord nodded his understanding. They had gone through so much together as children it made sense that they would have a mysterious sort of connection.

He gave her a sidelong look. "Very well. Then we know a little more about what's happening. War Chief Hiyawento's forces are to the south." As he said the words, Hiyawento's archers trotted down the hillside. When they knelt with their bows aimed, waiting for the command to let fly, Cord asked, "Are you suggesting a course of action?"

She didn't answer right away. Her gaze tracked Dekanawida's progress across the field and up the hill toward Hiyawento. When the two men embraced, tears welled in Baji's eyes. Pain and longing, and something Cord didn't understand, tightened her expression. For just a moment, she seemed to be looking backward to another time, another embrace—one that had wrenched her heart.

Cord's attention shifted to the warriors to the north. Lines slithered into position. While archers trotted out and stationed themselves fifty paces in front of Hiyawento's line, men with war clubs snugged up behind them. An old man in a black cape drew Cord's attention. Where the main trail cut through the flats to the east of the villages, a single war lodge stood. The man stood outside it, surrounded by warriors, probably personal guards.

Cord said, "Is that Atotarho? Standing before the war lodge?"

Baji turned. Hatred hardened her features. "Yes. It must be."

"Then Hiyawento's forces are standing against Atotarho's?"

As though a plan was forming right behind her black eyes and she didn't wish to be disturbed, she softly replied, "Yes."

Cord noted, "Hiyawento is greatly outnumbered."

Shouts erupted. Orders. Both sides let fly.

The mist seemed to rip apart, punctured in a thousand places by streaks of silver. The warriors with the clubs charged into the fray. The line to the south wavered, ragged now—many had fallen. Frightened warriors ran, strides eating the distance to the tree cover, shorter legs falling behind, being cut down. Long gaps appeared in the lines on both sides, leaving warriors scrambling to close them. The mixed howls of victory and anguish resembled the peculiar serenade of panicked wolves.

As though Matron Jigonsaseh had been waiting for this exact moment, warriors flooded out of Yellowtail Village and flanked Atotarho's forces. Shrill war cries split the day. The low growl of hundreds of clashing war clubs rumbled. The Hills warriors had been surprised. Many ran in confusion. Others turned one way and then another, not sure who to fight first. Inexorably, the Yellowtail warriors pushed Atotarho's forces toward Hiyawento's, trapping them in the middle.

A slow smile of appreciation came to Baji's lips. "That's Koracoo."

"Where?"

She pointed. "In the red war shirt, leading the Yellowtail charge."

Cord saw her, and nodded in respect. It did not matter that she was the village matron now. She had a warrior's heart. The situation was desperate. She knew it. She would not let her warriors go into the fight without her.

"Do we join the battle, War Chief?" Cord asked. "Or bide our time and wait to see what happens?"

Baji's eyes narrowed. Her blood was up. The vein in her throat pulsed. She slid her bow from her shoulder. "We fight on Hiyawento's side."

34

Zateri watched the battle with her heart in her throat. She couldn't let herself lose sight of Hiyawento. She feared if she did, he would vanish like so many other friends had today. Keeping him in view wasn't easy. The mist was like a giant undulating beast, constantly shifting, gobbling one portion of the battlefield, then twisting to swallow up another.

Someone sobbed. She did not turn.

Wounded warriors lay on the wet ground all around their camp, dragged in by their friends, who had spoken softly to them for as long as they could before they had to charge back into the fight. Some wept inconsolably.

A monstrous disgust caused Zateri's hands to tremble. She tried to keep them hidden beneath her cape. *You can't afford to show any weakness. Not now.*

Kwahseti stood beside her in front of their fire. They had not spoken in a while, but she could hear Kwahseti's ragged breathing.

"Who is that?" Kwahseti asked, and pointed at a man running hard along the western edge of the battlefield. The blue and yellow shapes on his cape had blurred to a green smear.

"I can't tell."

"Qonde, maybe? Isn't that his cape?"

Zateri shook her head like a woman trying to get rid of a deafening ringing in her ears. The runner swerved wide around the battle, holding his white arrow over his head for all to see.

"It is Qonde. I'm sure of it. What does he want?"

Zateri pulled her gaze from Hiyawento's broad back long enough to glance at Kwahseti. The Riverbank Village matron's face had flushed. Short hair lay wetly against her forehead and curved down over her cheeks, wreathing her dark eyes like gray paint.

When Qonde finally made his way around the battle and trotted up the hill to the west, two sentries grabbed hold of his arms, searched him for weapons, and escorted him the rest of the way.

Kwahseti's jaw set. "It can't be an offer of surrender. Atotarho would never give up so easily.

His huge pride—" She stopped short, and her eyes flew open. "Who's that? Blessed ancestors, are those Flint People?"

Zateri swung around to stare, and Taya hurried forward with her long black hair swaying around her slender waist. She was so pretty. "They came! I don't believe it!"

"What do you mean?"

Taya whirled to face Zateri. "Matron Jigonsaseh went to Flint country to ask them to form an alliance with us to fight Atotarho."

Zateri breathlessly watched the tall woman in the lead. There was something... "Oh." She put a hand to her lips as tears constricted her throat. "That's Baji. Baji and Chief Cord."

As though time had mysteriously reversed, Zateri found herself sitting in a birch bark canoe twelve summers ago, with Baji's strong arms around her. The moonlit night had been quiet and cold. Mist hovered just above their heads, slithering along the course of the river. She could see it all again. War Chief Koracoo had paddled in front, and War Chief Cord in the rear of the canoe. *"I am your friend forever,"* Baji had said, and tightened her arms around Zateri. Tears had filled Zateri's eyes, for it had been the first time in moons that she'd felt truly safe.

The same feeling stole over Zateri now. It was irrational, even ludicrous, in light of everything happening on the battlefield, but she couldn't help it.

She watched as Baji dispatched a runner to Hiyawento, probably to announce herself and her intentions—so Hiyawento wouldn't mistakenly turn his forces on Baji's.

Though it wasn't necessary. Both Hiyawento and Sky Messenger were staring at Baji where she stood on the eastern hilltop. They had recognized her instantly, just as Zateri had.

When her runner returned, Baji led her forces down onto the battlefield. There had to be six or seven hundred Flint warriors. Ecstatic roars went up from Hiyawento's warriors, and on the far side of the field, Jigonsaseh's warriors whooped. They had Atotarho's forces completely surrounded.

"Chief Cord from Wild River Village?" Kwahseti asked.

"Yes," Zateri replied, and when she turned to look at Kwahseti, she noticed that Taya's young eyes had riveted on Baji.

Taya straightened. With dignity, she asked, "She's a war chief? Not just a warrior?"

"Apparently. I didn't know it myself until just now."

Taya seemed to wilt.

As the sentries shoved Qonde toward Zateri and Kwahseti, the man clutched his white arrow in both hands.

"What is it?" Kwahseti asked.

"I bring a message for Matron Zateri. Your father asks for a short truce so that he might speak with you."

"Why?" Kwahseti demanded to know.

"He did not give me that information, Matron Kwahseti."

Kwahseti turned to Zateri. "Perhaps now that he's doomed, he wants to negotiate with the rightful leader of the Wolf Clan and the nation?"

Zateri ground her teeth while she gazed across the battlefield. As the mist eddied, her father's black cape appeared and disappeared. He couldn't negotiate. He *had* to win. If he didn't, he would no longer be the chief of Atotarho Village. In fact, the clan mothers would strip him of his name. He wouldn't even be Atotarho. The name would be taken back and eventually given to someone more deserving.

Zateri said, "Tell my father there is nothing to discuss."

Qonde's heart seemed to sink. His expression sagged, but he bowed. "Very well, Matron."

As he sprinted down the hill, Kwahseti said, "Good for you. We're winning and he knows it. It will be over soon."

In a soft voice, she said, "Not soon enough," and her gaze returned to Hiyawento.

He stood in the midst of a tormented knot of

warriors that clashed not more than fifty paces from Atotarho's war lodge. The fighting was desperate. Through the blowing fog and smoke from the burning villages, the figures were somehow unreal, just floating phantoms, condemned to forever fight a battle no one could win. They were killing aunts, uncles, cousins, brothers. In a fight such as this, victory was impossible.

Hiyawento and Sky Messenger fought side by side, guarding each other's backs as they had done since they'd seen eleven summers. Slowly, inexorably, they were closing in on her father's position. When they got there...when they got there...

Zateri closed her eyes and let the darkness soothe her fear and hurt. She didn't want to see any more of this. Dear gods, *no more of this.*

35
SKY MESSENGER

There is a sudden deafening roar when the sides converge. War Chief Sindak is in front of me, blocking the path to Atotarho, who has retreated into his lodge as though the thin deer hides will protect him.

I glance to my right, where Hiyawento swings his war club. He needs no help from me. Someone yells, "Got to pull back!" Another shouts, "No, no! Can't. Nowhere to go!" The Hills warrior in front of me has wild eyes and his head shakes violently. He leaps for me with a stiletto in his fist. The sharpened white bone shines as it plunges toward my heart. I flip sideways, and he crashes by. My war club crushes his hip. Ten paces from the war lodge now. Sindak's face, the face of the man I consider to be one of my saviors, is raw and determined. He'll never let me pass, never let me get to Atotarho.

I am aware suddenly of the cold tears blurring my eyes.

As though the world has slipped sideways, from the corner of my eye, I see Atotarho step from the war lodge, hauling a little girl by the arm. She is perhaps eight or nine, gagged, but when she spies Hiyawento, she goes crazy, trying to scream, twisting to get away from Atotarho, falling to the ground kicking. Hiyawento is occupied, running down a wounded man. There's something familiar about her, but I can't place it. She looks like someone I know.

From the lodge behind her, steps a man. His cape is stunning, made of thousands of bluebird feathers. He has his hood pulled up. The blue fluttering around his hidden face and down his chest creates a sensation of movement, as though he's about to lift off the ground and fly away. When he sees me, he tilts his head like a man who has heard a blast of thunder right over the top of him. As though he can't quite hear, or is deaf and trying to understand the world through sight alone.

When people see him, a hiss erupts, the gasps like a beating of great wings.

Then...a cry. A long, shuddering, deep-throated wail.

Hiyawento lurches past me.

The next few moments happen so quickly, I can't move, can't...

Hiyawento throws himself at Sindak, and Sindak pivots and swipes Hiyawento's feet out from under him with his war club. Hiyawento lands hard. As Sindak brings his war club into position for a killing blow, there is an instant of hesitation. His eyes tense. I unthinkingly jump between Sindak and Hiyawento, my club cutting upward, crashing into Sindak's. We are eye to eye, shoving each other, trying to gain leverage, but I can see it in his face. He wishes he didn't have to do this. From the edge of my vision, Hiyawento leaps, slams Atotarho to the ground, and roars like a wounded grizzly as he grabs the old man around the throat.

"Help! Help...me!" Atotarho cries. He's choking. Struggling.

"Leave my daughter alone! Leave her alone, you—"

Negano's club takes Hiyawento squarely in the left shoulder, knocking him off Atotarho and sending him rolling.

"Hurry, my chief, get up!" Negano shouts, and drags Atotarho toward the lodge.

Hiyawento slowly crawls for the little girl. Tears are streaming down her face. She's trying to wriggle free of her bonds to get to him.

Blessed gods, that's why she's familiar. She looks like Zateri. Zateri as a child. *She's Hiyawento's daughter. His oldest daughter. Kahn-Tineta.*

"Sindak," I hiss through gritted teeth, "let the girl go."

So low no one but me can hear it, he says, "I knew nothing of this. Give me a chance."

Our eyes lock.

Negano runs back, jumps between Hiyawento and his daughter, grabs her, and suspends a stiletto over her heart.

The ragged cry that escapes Hiyawento's throat could sunder the world. Two of Atotarho's guards grab him and haul him four paces away from his daughter.

Atotarho cries, "Drop your weapons! Do it, or the girl dies!" He lifts a hand, ready to give the order to plunge the stiletto into her heart.

Negano is ready, the stiletto poised for a lethal blow.

I shove away from Sindak, pause for only a moment, and then my war club drops from my hand. Every other Standing Stone warrior follows my lead. Dull thuds sound as the weapons fall.

Atotarho turns to Hiyawento. "Order your warriors to cease fighting! Retreat!"

Without an instant's hesitation, Hiyawento turns to a warrior I do not know. "Call retreat."

"But War Chief!" the man objects.

I bellow, *"Do it now!"*

The man hesitates for a moment, then the horn trumpet blares three times. Warriors turn to stare, confused, afraid to step away from their opponent for fear their skulls will be crushed.

The words go down the line like dropped rocks—*stop, stop, retreat.*

Gradually, like a gigantic monster dying, the roars and grunts dwindle to an agonized base note of moans spiked with sobs. The battlefield seems to churn as the mist swirls around retreating men and women.

A breathless silence descends.

I am sucking air, my exhausted arms like dead weights.

Atotarho careens as he turns and sternly orders, "Bring me that child." The rattlesnake skins flash and flutter in his hair.

Negano carries her over and dumps her at Atotarho's feet. A hoarse cry explodes from Hiyawento's lips, and he struggles ferociously against the muscular arms that hold him. The little girl's sobs shred my heart. They must be tearing Hiyawento apart. His face has twisted with a mixture of rage and hate.

"Kahn-Tineta," Atotarho says in an affectionate voice. "You're such a pretty child."

I look at Sindak and find him staring at me. His eyes plead for me to wait, wait.

I know if I make one wrong move, that little girl will be the first to die.

Now that we've stopped fighting, my body is

cooling down, the sweat chilling on my skin. A rhythmic whooshing thump pounds in my ears. After several heartbeats, my vision goes strangely gray and shimmering, as though a veil of tears wavers between me and Wrass. He has not looked at me. He has eyes only for his daughter. She's reaching for him with her bound hands, her fingers flexing in a *please, please* gesture, crying against her gag.

Atotarho twines clawlike fingers into her sleeve and drags her to her feet. Holding her, he says to Hiyawento, "You dare to defy me! I should kill your daughter before your eyes! I will kill her if your forces do not surrender and pledge themselves to me."

Hiyawento's face twists with hatred. "I don't have the authority to—"

"I know that! Get it!"

Hiyawento turns to look out across the battlefield toward where Zateri and the other matrons stand on the southern hilltop. He's dying inside. I can feel his agony in my own strangling heart. He gives Kahn-Tineta a desperate smile. Nods. "Tell your forces to stand down, and I'll speak with the matrons."

Atotarho nods to Sindak.

Sindak turns. "Saponi, tell them to back away!"

Saponi trots out onto the field, and the order flies through the ranks like swallows diving. Men and women step back.

Atotarho flicks a hand at the men who hold Hiyawento, and they release his arms.

Hiyawento braces his feet, seems to be trying to resign himself to this last betrayal, and slowly trots away. He does not even look at me.

A strange crawling sensation, like icy ants, runs up my neck. My head swivels toward the war lodge. The Bluebird Witch is staring at me. When he walks toward me, it is as though he's gliding on air. His feathered cape faintly rustles as he spreads his arms like a huge bird and hops around in a bizarre dance that resembles Crow hunting mice in a field. Shrill caws rip from his throat. "I saw it, you know," he hisses. "I saw what he did to you after he dragged you into the forest."

Suddenly, I can't feel my body. Just the air cooling, growing unbearably icy. My insides are freezing into amber pools of brilliance. Images flare... *A muscular giant swaying, his eyes rolling... "You, Standing Stone boy, go with War Chief Manidos. Get up, boy!" ...Tutelo wailing in a high-pitched voice I've never heard before, "Leave my brother alone! Leave him alone!"*

I stagger backward. As though to defend myself from the memories, I thrust my hands out before me.

Manidos crushes my hand and drags me away into the forest. My heart is thundering. He's walking very fast. I keep tripping. I...

Atotarho says, "What's wrong with you? I asked you a question."

Facedown. His heavy body crushes me. A rough

hand covers my mouth. Lips against my ear. "Lie down, boy. Stop crying or I'll cut your heart out."

...Pain. Shock.

I twist my head, looking for Wrass. Watching him as he stumbles out into the warriors' camp. Dumping the bag of poison into the stew pot. If I can just...see him...I can...stand this—

Sindak's voice breaks in. "Chief, end this battle. You're asking your warriors to murder their cousins!"

I look at Sindak, at the warriors behind him, and shout, "Sindak's right. Chief, clear the battlefield so we can talk to one another. Please, just give me fifty heartbeats to—"

Atotarho laughs, the sound low and disdainful. "Clear the battlefield? You've always been a coward. I remember when you were a boy, you..."

I'm trembling all over when I turn eastward and lift my arms into the air, as though reaching out to touch the Sky World. I shout, "This war must end! We're killing Great-Grandmother Earth!"

There is a momentary hush.

A curious far-off rushing sound echoes to the east. Everyone hears it. The battlefield whispers as warriors turn, their eyes wide, asking questions. It is as though the mist has been suddenly sucked away, leaving cold sparkling sunlight behind. I squint against the brilliance. The rushing grows louder, like a tidal wave coming in, and a black wall boils over the forest canopy, swelling into the sky, rising so high it blots out Elder Brother Sun's face as it floods toward us.

"What is that?" Atotarho props his walking stick and shifts to look at it.

Sindak's dark eyes narrow. He shouts, "Get down! Everyone get down!"

A few people obey and hit the ground, but most run, trying to find cover before the leading edge of the blackness strikes. At the first opportunity, Sindak pulls a chert knife from his belt and cuts Kahn-Tineta's bonds, but orders, "Stay down!"

She flattens on the ground.

I seem to be frozen, my hands extended over my head, as though I am the first to surrender to the monstrous storm. Shocked cries erupt. A torrent of fleeing warriors floods around me, the Standing Stone warriors trying to get back to the safety of the villages, the Hills warriors just running, running with all their strength. A few dive behind boulders and others crouch near the most massive tree trunks.

I turn to the east. Into the storm. Close my eyes. Voices fill the wind—powerful, hushed, as though the ancestors have walked the Path of Souls back to earth and are riding the backs of the Cloud People, soaring straight for us. For me. The thundering of their ghostly feet pounds in my chest.

"Blessed gods," Sindak shouts. "Run!"

I open my eyes. The men who'd thrown themselves to the ground rise and flee. One carries Chief

Atotarho over his shoulder. There are only two people before the war lodge now. Two people left in the open. I kneel before Kahn-Tineta. She seems too terrified to breathe. "I'm Sky Messenger. Stay with me. You're safe with me."

Her tear-streaked face is disbelieving. She looks over my shoulder just as the trees on the eastern hills explode. Dark fragments of branches and leaves blast upward into the spinning darkness and vanish, crushed to powder.

"Please, let's go. We have to run!"

"No, don't run."

"It's coming! It's going to kill us!" Kahn-Tineta throws her arms around my neck in a stranglehold.

I clutch her tightly against me, whispering, "Just listen, Kahn-Tineta. Close your eyes and you'll hear them. Our ancestors are telling our story on the wind."

Against my cheek, I feel her squeeze her eyes closed, and I lift her into my arms and stand up to face the telling. All stories are lived between the listener and the teller, but until this moment I have never realized there is a third person in the story. The silence. Just before the ancestors enfold us in their arms, silence steps into the space between us. It is a pause in the heartbeat of the world. But I feel it like muscular arms tightening, pressing us close, encircling us with an invisible palisade of human bodies.

And perhaps that's what it is. Perhaps the souls of all the lost warriors in the palisade logs have stepped out for just a moment, just an instant in time, to defend us, as they have always defended their people.

"Hold me! Don't let go of me!" Kahn-Tineta screams.

When the blackness strikes, I crush her small body against me and close my eyes.

36

Hiyawento threw his arms around Zateri and dragged her to the ground as the blackness swept over them. All around, people in the camp shrieked, racing for whatever cover they could find.

Hiyawento never closed his eyes. He kept watching, watching Kahn-Tineta and Sky Messenger. A thin spiral of mist rose from the ground and seemed to cling to Sky Messenger's cape and then the worst of the blackness thundered down upon them, swallowed them, blackness and spinning darkness, grass and dropped arrows swirling high into the air, as though to fuel some sky war.

Then it was gone.

Passed over.

In the distance, the blackness continued to

uproot whole trees and cast them about like cornhusk dolls, but the deafening roar receded, slowly, until all that possessed the world was blinding sunlight and the silence of the grave.

In the midst of the quiet, quiet world, Sky Messenger still stood, holding Kahn-Tineta in his arms. She had her small face buried against his neck, clutching him like a frightened animal. Sky Messenger took one step toward the east, and his chin tipped up, as though he'd lifted his face to gaze straight into the brilliant eye of Elder Brother Sun.

"Are they all right? Can you see them?" Zateri squirmed beneath his heavy body, trying to turn, to look out across the battlefield.

Hiyawento softly said, "Yes, I see them. They're all right."

As he got to his feet, shocked voices erupted throughout the camp. People gasped and pointed. A few ran forward to the edge of the hill to look. Zateri staggered to her feet and grabbed his arm to steady her weak legs.

Sky Messenger set Kahn-Tineta on the ground, then took her hand and slowly started weaving through the dead bodies, now tossed here and there into tangled piles, bringing Kahn-Tineta to Hiyawento and Zateri.

Zateri threw off Hiyawento's hand and was out of camp, down the hillside, dashing across the battlefield, the fringes of her skirt slashing around her legs, running for them with her arms outstretched.

37
SKY MESSENGER

Light cold rain falls, pattering through the forest, creating a melodic symphony of plops and shishes.

I flip up my buckskin hood and lean one shoulder against a sassafras trunk. Gitchi lies at my feet with his gray head braced on his paws. I have my back turned to the hundreds of campfires where warriors sit discussing what happened today. In the branches that surround me, fire shadows flutter like dark humming-bird wings, beating at the soft awed voices. I concentrate on the sensation of cold. It helps me to block out the emotion. Every voice is saturated with it. They are watching me, and have been since this afternoon when most of Atotarho's remaining forces trotted over the hills, heading home.

"I tell you, I saw it. I was there. He told Sindak to clear the battlefield, and when Atotarho laughed..."

The warrior hesitates, as though reliving the moment. "Sky Messenger opened his hands to Elder Brother Sun, and it was as though thunder was born in the heart of the mist. The sound—the sound was like Great-Grandmother Earth being ripped apart."

"You're exaggerating, Saponi," another man accuses.

"No," Saponi murmurs with deep reverence in his voice. "I *saw* it. Sky Messenger lifted his hands for help, and Elder Brother Sun answered him. And then, just before the blackness struck, clouds formed on Sky Messenger's cape. I swear it looked like he was wearing a cape of white clouds and riding the winds of destruction. Just like the old stories say. I'm telling you, he's the human False Face."

Everyone around the campfire murmurs.

There is a brief lull and then singing rises. The notes lilt through the darkness.

I feel drained, utterly empty. Like a transparent husk, useless now. I straighten, preparing to go back...

Gitchi lifts his head, and his tail thumps the ground.

Behind me, whispering through the grass, I hear her long legs. The muscular grace of her movements, just the feline placement of her feet, is like a physical blow. I swallow. As she walks closer, I say, "I knew you'd find me."

Her moccasins shift, as though she has braced

her legs. "It wasn't hard. Every eye in the camp is upon you."

She has one of those deep female voices that seem to reach inside a man and stroke his heart.

Gitchi trots away, and I turn to see him leap up to place his big paws in the middle of her chest. She hugs him hard. His tail swipes the air as he whimpers his happiness. "I missed you, Gitchi. Are you all right?"

At the sight of her, guilt blends with a love so powerful it is impossible to explain. The air seems to glitter around her, playing in her long black hair, sculpting the muscles of her arms, flowing across her broad shoulders and pooling in the curves of her narrow waist. I know every line of her body, every hollow, even the slightest imperfection of her skin has lived beneath my fingertips. My gaze moves over her beautiful face, comparing it to my memory. Her black eyes shine. It's a look that trembles the blood in my veins.

Gitchi returns to my side, gazing up at me as though to say, "Look, she's back. Isn't it wonderful?"

I step toward her with my fists clenched. "I'll never be able to thank you enough for what you and Cord did today. When I saw you leading your warriors down the hill and into the fight...Baji...."

A bare smile turns her full lips. "I have always been on your side, Odion. I always will be."

The faintest breath of wind brushes her hair. Jet

strands flutter and seem to be suspended upon the firelight itself, pure amber silk, shimmering. They softly fall back to her shoulders.

I rush to say, "I am to be married."

"I know."

I jerk a nod. There is silence.

She smiles and walks forward. When she looks up at me, the desperate longing in her eyes is gemlike, crystal bright.

"Are you well, Baji?"

"Well enough, Dekanawida."

As though she can't help herself, she reaches up and touches my cheek. "It's all right. You did what you had to, and I did what I had to. That is how things must be."

The sensation of her fingers trailing across my skin is like the shock of the air just before lightning blinds the world.

"Baji, forgive me for what I said to you that day. I was wrong."

Her hand lowers. She closes her fingers, as though to hold onto my warmth. "I forgave you long ago. You thought the boy was better dead than a captive in an enemy village. I understood. I just disagreed."

"If only I'd had more time to think it over, I..."

A small voice calls, "Sky Messenger?"

I look over Baji's shoulder and see Taya. She stands four paces away, at the edge of the trees, watching us uncomfortably. I wonder how long she's been there. I pray not long.

"Taya." I extend a hand. "Please, come. I want to introduce you to War Chief Baji of the Turtle Clan of the Flint People."

Taya hesitantly comes forward. She wears a doeskin cape much too long for her; it drags the ground. She must have grabbed the first thing she could find. Which means she probably has a reason for being here, more than just finding me.

I move away from Baji, go to Taya, and put my arm around her, pulling her close against my side. She clings to me like a raft in a raging ocean. "Baji, this is Taya, soon to be my wife."

Taya looks at Baji from beneath her lashes, not sure what to say. She is barely a woman. Meeting the legendary Baji must be threatening.

Baji takes the initiative. She smiles genuinely. "You are High Matron Kittle's granddaughter, yes?"

"Yes." Taya nervously wets her lips and casts a glance up at me.

"I hope we will become great friends, Taya. I suspect that you and I have heard Dekanawida's vision so often we've both memorized what's coming. We will need to be friends. The road ahead is not an easy one."

Taya's face slackens. "Does that mean you've decided to join the peace alliance?"

Baji blinks in surprise. "Our Ruling Council

approved it with barely any discussion at all. Dekanawida is a hero among our people. They believe his vision."

With childlike excitement, Taya rushes to tell me, "That means we have the Flint People and Zateri's faction of Hills People. Now all we need to do is get the People of the Landing, and the Mountain People, and surely we will be able to destroy Atotarho!"

I brush black hair away from her young face. "All in good time, Taya." I let out a slow breath. "For now, let us just enjoy the night."

"We can't yet. I'm sorry. Grandmother requests that you come and tell your vision to the assembled chiefs and matrons."

Baji is watching me. I feel her gaze. It is life itself.

"I'm grateful to have the chance. Lead the way, Taya."

The three of us walk out together, with Gitchi trotting at my side, but as we proceed across the cold battlefield to find High Matron Kittle, Baji drops behind. After ten heartbeats of not hearing her steps behind me, I glance over my shoulder, looking for her. She's gone. Probably wandering among the warriors. She is war chief. She has duties. And more than that, this is as hard for her as it is for me.

"Hiyawento told me what you did today, Taya. It was very brave, and very dangerous. I don't know what possessed you—"

"I was the best choice."

"Yes," I answer. *But you knew it. No one had to tell you. No one had to convince you to risk your life. It never occurred to you that it might not be worth it.* "Someday, you will be the greatest of the matrons of the Standing Stone People."

She stops and searches my expression, as though greatly surprised, perhaps because she just saw me with Baji. She seems to be trying to determine if I am telling the truth. "Did you Dream this?"

"No. But I know it just the same."

She slips her arm around my waist, and we start climbing the southern hillside. On the crest of the hill, a large fire blazes. I see Mother sitting beside Chief Cord, smiling. Father and his wife, Pawen, nestle beneath one blanket to their right. Pawen is much stronger, getting well. Hiyawento and Zateri lean together, their shoulders touching, as though they need to know the other is close. Kahn-Tineta sleeps in Hiyawento's arms with her mouth slightly open. There are many people around the fire that I do not know. It makes me slightly uneasy. High Matron Kittle stands a short distance away, smiling a little too eagerly at Sindak, who seems to have no illusions about the game that is afoot. He smiles back.

"Has War Chief Sindak decided what he's going to do yet?" I ask Taya.

"I don't think so. After he deserted Atotarho's forces, Gonda offered to adopt him into the Standing Stone nation, but so far, Sindak has declined. The last

I heard, he said he might go off and become a Trader with his old friend, Towa."

Warmth seeps up around my souls. "I hope so. He deserves—"

"Sky Messenger," she interrupts. "Look at me."

I frown down at her.

She swallows hard, obviously preparing herself. "I...I've grown up some. I don't know if you noticed—"

"I noticed."

"Well..." She nervously licks her lips. "Among our people, marriages are matters of status and duty, not love. I know—as I did not when we started this journey—that my responsibility is to my clan, and to your vision. I will help you as much as I can, and I expect the same from you." Her expression is serious, somber. "But that is all I expect."

Above us, a great horned owl calls, *hoo, hoo-oo, hoo, hoo*. We both look up to watch it sail over the battlefield with its wings tucked.

I am so hollow I can hear my heartbeat echoing. I put my arm around her again, and as we walk, I say, "Let's take it one day at a time, Taya."

Our moccasins crunch the frost as we climb the hill. Ahead, there is firelight. I look at Zateri and Hiyawento. My muscles relax. My breathing is easier. I am not alone. Trust is no longer in exile.

Taya says, "Before we get to the fire, you need to know several people. The tiny woman sitting beside

Zateri is Matron Gwinodje of Canassatego Village. On the opposite side of the fire, the woman with gray hair is Matron Kwahseti of Riverbank Village, and beside her, the elderly man is Chief Canassatego. Kwahseti's war chief, Thona, is the heavily scarred man with the scowl on his face. He—"

"You've become quite the politician," I praise. "Thank you for helping me."

She tightens her arm around my waist. "I've been listening to Grandmother speaking with the other matrons. You're going to need a good politician. Keeping this alliance together is going to take a miracle. And *I* am going to make sure it happens."

I stop for a moment. Her eyes are filled with determination. I run my hand over her soft hair. "I believe you."

38
SKY MESSENGER

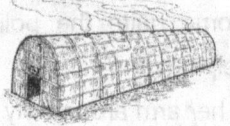

Around midnight, the Cloud People part and the campfires of the dead become a conflagration. The light is so brilliant every branch casts a shadow.

As I walk the battlefield, I unconsciously stroke Gitchi's gray muzzle. He licks my palm. Across the meadow, bright lights bob and sway. Many cluster near the villages, moving in and out of the palisades, perhaps saying goodbye to loved ones. Others roam aimlessly, confused, waiting for the deer.

There is a sound on a battlefield that's hard to define. The dead are not silent. As muscles go rigid there are thumps, whispers. Teeth grind in tightening jaws. Wings. Wings flap as night birds feed.

I study the wide cold eyes on the ground. I will keep them in the space between my souls, the place I keep all terrible things, to be taken out and contemplated when I think I cannot go on, because it's too hard, or I'm too tired, or the loneliness has become too much to bear. These men and women will remind me that the nearness of death is grace on fire, and I must learn to live the flames. I, at last, understand Bahna's words.

A warning growl rumbles Gitchi's throat.

I turn. In the trees to my right, the moonlight seems to shudder. A man stands out there, in the cold darkness, all alone.

There is a low, insidious laugh. "It's Odion, the boy who was always afraid."

His feathered cape whispers. I can't tell if he is coming toward me or just shifting positions. When I dropped my war club today, it was truly for good. I have only my words to protect me now. Words and an old wolf whose life I will not risk, not even to save my own.

"I'm still afraid, Hehaka."

"But why? You are the great man now. Elder Brother Sun obeys Sky Messenger's commands." His laughter is mocking, filled with disbelief. "Isn't that enough?"

I tilt my head. Enough? All night long—in glimpses—I've been reliving the horror of War Chief Manidos. I'm grieving, feeling wounded, and it clouds the thoughts. What is enough? I pause to consider. In a man's lifetime, is it enough to forgive just once when one did not have to? Or perhaps "enough" is only reached when a person makes forgiveness his Road of Light, and spends every day walking to the Land of the Dead, expecting nothing more.

I say, "I know where it is."

He doesn't answer at first. Then, "Where what is?"

"Her pot."

He takes a quick step forward. I see wide eyes shining in his hood. His voice replies from the midst of rustling feathers, "Which pot?"

"You know the one I mean. Her soul pot."

The witch twists his head in a birdlike manner, observing me through one eye. He must be trying to figure out why I would tell him. We have never been friends. Even when we were in agony together as children, he was never one of us. Never one of the trusted few for whom we would have willingly given our lives. And perhaps that is the reason to choose the Road of Light.

"Why do you tell me this?" he asks.

"You've been searching for it for many summers, haven't you? If I'd known, I would have told you sooner. Do you remember our last camp on the river where she ambushed us?"

His voice is soft. "I do."

"Walk due northeast about one thousand paces, and you will see a small oval clearing on a hillside surrounded by maples. There are three rocks in the middle of the clearing. That's where she died. Just before Mother found us, Zateri took the soul pot from the old woman's pack and buried it between the rocks." I turn to look at the darkness in his hood. I can't see his face at all now. "Do you want me to go with you?"

Silence, for a long time.

"No, Sky Messenger."

I nod and lift my eyes to study the star-silvered heavens. The dead ferns beneath the trees thrash. He is gone, vanished like a shadow eaten by utter darkness.

I continue my walk across the battlefield, periodically petting Gitchi's head or halting to study a frozen face before I continue on. One hand of time later, when I finally look up, I discover that my feet have taken me to a high point above the Flint camp.

As I gaze out over the sleeping warriors rolled in blankets, I try to imagine where she is. Moonlight gleams from hundreds of upturned faces.

Tomorrow, I will find her. Tomorrow, we will talk.

Somewhere ahead of me, there is a black sun and a crack like the sky splitting. Will she be there with me? I have not seen this. She isn't in any of my Dreams.

But I believe in things seen and unseen.

I pray the Spirits will show me the path.

A LOOK AT BOOK SEVEN:
PEOPLE OF THE BLACK SUN

The darkness that Dekanawida has envisioned is drawing closer, and the warring Iroquois nations have refused to listen to his message of peace and compassion. Consumed by madness, Chief Atotarho is determined to subjugate all five nations—beginning with Dekanawida's own people, the Standing Stone nation. All who stand in his way will be destroyed.

On the brink of devastation, Dekanawida gains an unexpected ally: a great storm, seemingly summoned by his call, that scatters Atotarho's forces. With this divine intervention, Dekanawida rises to the status of Prophet, but the battle is far from over. He enlists the help of his steadfast friends Baji and Hiyawento to spread his message. They must convince the hostile neighboring clans that the fall of one nation spells doom for all.

Will Dekanawida's mission of peace prevail, or will darkness consume their world? *People of the Black Sun* is an unforgettable tale of courage, friendship, and the enduring power of hope. The journey is far from over!

AVAILABLE SEPTEMBER 2024

ABOUT W. MICHAEL GEAR

W. Michael Gear is a *New York Times*, *USA Today*, and international bestselling author of sixty novels. With close to eighteen million copies of his books in print worldwide, his work has been translated into twenty-nine languages.

Gear has been inducted into the Western Writers Hall of Fame and the Colorado Authors' Hall of Fame—as well as won the Owen Wister Award, the Golden Spur Award, and the International Book Award for both Science Fiction and Action Suspense Fiction. He is also the recipient of the Frank Waters Award for lifetime contributions to Western writing.

Gear's work, inspired by anthropology and archaeology, is multilayered and has been called compelling, insidiously realistic, and masterful. Currently, he lives in northwestern Wyoming with his award-winning wife and co-author, Kathleen O'Neal Gear, and a charming sheltie named, Jake.

ABOUT KATHLEEN O'NEAL GEAR

Kathleen O'Neal Gear is a *New York Times* bestselling author of fifty-seven books and a national award-winning archaeologist. The U.S. Department of the Interior has awarded her two Special Achievement awards for outstanding management of America's cultural resources.

In 2015 the United States Congress honored her with a Certificate of Special Congressional Recognition, and the California State Legislature passed Joint Member Resolution #117 saying, "The contributions of Kathleen O'Neal Gear to the fields of history, archaeology, and writing have been invaluable…"

In 2021 she received the Owen Wister Award for lifetime contributions to western literature, and in 2023 received the Frank Waters Award for "a body of work representing excellence in writing and storytelling that embodies the spirit of the American West."

GLOSSARY

Flying Heads—Just heads with no bodies that thrash wildly through the forests. These fearsome creatures have long trailing hair and great paws like a bear's.

Gaha—The soft wind. She is spoken of as Elder Sister Gaha.

Gahai—Spectral lights that guide sorcerers as they fly through the air on their evil journeys. Sometimes, gahai lead their masters to victims, and other times to places where they can find charms.

Hadui—A violent wind.

Hanehwa—Skin-beings. Witches sometimes skin their victims, enchant their skins, and force them to do their bidding. Hanehwa warn witches of danger by giving three shouts.

Hatho—The Frost Spirit.

Haudenosaunee—The People of the Longhouse, called "Iroquois" by the French.

Ohwachira—The basic family unit. An ohwachira is a kinship group that traces its descent from a common female ancestor. The ohwachira bestows chieftainship titles and holds the names of the great people of the past. It bestows those names by raising up the souls of the dead and requickening them in the bodies of newly elected chiefs, adoptees, or other people. In the same way, if a new chief disappoints the ohwachira, after consultation with the clan, it can take back the name, remove the soul, and depose the chief. It is also the sisterhood of ohwachiras that decides when to go to war and when to make peace.

Otkon—One of the two halves of Spirit Power that inhabit the world. The other is Uki. Don't think of these as good and evil, however. Both powers share equally in light and dark. Otkon and Uki form a unified spiritual universe that must be kept in balance. Otkon has a trickster-like character. It's unpredictable and can be either beneficial or harmful to human beings. It's half of the day lasts from noon to midnight. Otkon is often associated with the Evil-Minded One, the hero twin also known as Flint.

People of the Flint—The Mohawk nation. However, the word *Mohazuk* is an Algonquian term meaning "flesh eaters." They call themselves the Kanienkahaka, or Ganienkeh, meaning "People of the Flint."

People of the Hills—The Onondaga nation. The word *Onondaga* is an anglicized version of their name for themselves, *Onundagaono,* which means "People of the Hills."

People of the Landing—The Cayuga nation. Including People of the Landing, several other possible derivations have been offered for the word *Cayuga,* including, "People of the Place Where Locusts Were Taken Out," "People of the Mucky Land," and "People of the Place Where Boats are Taken Out."

People of the Mountain—The Seneca nation. They call themselves the *On-ondowahgah*. Their name can also be translated as "People of the Great Hill."

People of the Standing Stone—The Oneida nation. The word *Oneida* may be a rather poor Anglicization of their name for themselves, *Onayoteka-ono,* meaning "Granite People," or "People of the Standing Stone."

Requickening Ceremony—The raising up of souls for the purpose of placing them in other bodies, such as those of adoptees. This concept does not exactly correspond to the Eastern religions' concept of reincarnation. For example, there's no idea of karma to be accounted for. Being reborn is neither punishment nor reward. Instead, there is a strong concept of duty to the People. Only strong souls were requickened, usually within the same maternal lineage. The ceremony was performed in the hopes of easing grief and restoring the spiritual strength of the clans, but a returning soul also had an obligation to help the People in times of crises. Many "Keepings" of the Peacemaker story say that Dekanawida was the returned soul of Tarenyawagon—also spelled as Tarachiawagon—the cultural hero also known as Sapling, the Good-Minded One, who served as the Creator. Those same traditions identify Atotarho as Sapling's troublesome younger brother, Flint—Tawiscaro/Tawiscaron)— who was called the Evil-Minded One. Jigonsaseh, similarly, was the returned soul of Sky Woman's daughter, the Lynx.

Uki—One of the two halves of Spirit Power that inhabit the world—see *Otkon*. Uki is never harmful to human beings. It's half of the day lasts from midnight to noon. Uki is often associated with the Good-Minded One, the hero twin also known as Sapling, or Tarenyawagon.

SELECTED BIBLIOGRAPHY

Bruchac, Joseph. *Iroquois Stories: Heroes and Heroines, Monsters and Magic.* Freedom, CA: The Crossing Press, 1985.

Calloway, Colin G. *The Western Abenakis of Vermont, 1600-1800.* Norman: University of Oklahoma Press, 1990.

Custer, Jay. F. *Delaware Prehistoric Archaeology. An Ecological Approach.* Cranberry, NJ: Associated University Presses, 1984.

Dye, David H. *War Paths. Peace Paths. An Archaeology of Cooperation and Conflict in Native Eastern North America.* Lanham, MD: Altamira Press, 2009.

Ellis, Chris J., and Neal Ferris, eds. *The Archaeology of Southern Ontario to A.D. 1650.* London, Ontario, Canada: Occasional Papers of the London Chapter, OAS Number 5, 1990.

Elm, Demus, and Harvey Antone. *The Oneida Creation Story.* Lincoln: University of Nebraska, 2000.

Englebrecht, William. *Iroquoia: The Development of a Native World.* Syracuse: Syracuse University Press, 2003.

Fagan, Brian M. *Ancient North America. The Archaeology of a Continent,* 4th ed. Thames and Hudson Press, London, 2005.

Fenton, William N. *The False Faces of the Iroquois.* Norman: University of Oklahoma Press, 1987.

--. *The Iroquois Eagle Dance. An Offshoot of the Calumet Dance.* Syracuse: Syracuse University Press, 1991.

--. *The Roll Call of the Iroquois Chiefs. A Study of a Pnemonic Cane from the Six Nations Reserve.* Cranbook Institute of Science, Bulletin, No. 30, 1950.

Foster, Steven and James A. Duke. *Eastern/Central Medicinal*

Plants. The Peterson Guides Series. Boston: Houghton Mifflin Company, 1990.

Hart, John P., and Christina B. Reith. *Northeast Subsistence-Settlement Change: AD 700-1300*. Albany, NY: New York State Museum Bulletin 496, 2002.

Herrick, James W. *Iroquois Medical Botany*. New York: Syracuse University Press, 1995.

Hewitt, J. N. B. "The Iroquoian Concept of the Soul." *Journal of American Folklore*, VIII (1895): 107-116.

--. "Orenda and a Definition of Religion." *American Anthropologist*, N.S., IV (1902): 33-46.

--. "Status of Woman in Iroquois Polity before 1784," in Smithsonian Institution, *Annual Report of the Board of Regents*, 1932, (Washington, D.C. 1933) 475-488.

Jemison, Pete. "Mother of Nations: The Peace Queen, a Neglected Tradition." *Akwetkon* 5 (1988): 68-70.

Jennings, Francis. *The Ambiguous Iroquois Empire*. New York: W. W. Norton, 1984.

Jennings, Francis, ed. *The History and Culture of Iroquois Diplomacy*. Syracuse: Syracuse University Press, 1995.

Johansen, Bruce Elliot, and Barbara Alice Mann. *Encyclopedia of the Haudenosaunee (Iroquois Confederacy)*. Westport, CT: Greenwood Press, 2000.

Kapches, Mima. "Intra-Longhouse Spatial Analysis." *Pennsylvania Archaeologist*, XLIX, no. 4 (December, 1979): 24-29.

Kurath, Gertrude P. *Iroquois Music and Dance: Ceremonial Arts of Two Seneca Longhouses*. Smithsonian Institution, Bureau of American Ethnology, Bulletin 187. Washington: U.S. Government Printing Office, 1964.

Levine, Mary Ann, Kenneth E. Sassaman, and Michael S. Nassaney, eds. *The Archaeological Northeast*. Westport, CT: Bergin and Garvey, 1999.

Mann, Barbara A., and Jerry L. Fields. "A Sign in the Sky. Dating the League of the Haudenosaunee." The Wampum

Chronicles, www.wampumchronicles.com/signinthesky.html.

--. *Iroquoian Women: Gantowisas of the Haudenosaunee League*. New York: Peter Lang, 2000.

Martin, Calvin, *Keepers of the Game. Indian-Animal Relationships and the Fur Trade*. Berkeley: University of California Press, 1978.

Mensforth, Robert P. "Human Trophy Taking in Eastern North America During the Archaic Period: The Relationship to Warfare and Social Complexity," chap. *The Taking and Displaying of Human Body Parts as Trophies by Amerindians*, edited by Richard J. Chacon and David Dye, New York: Springer, 2:007.

Miroff, Laurie E., and Timothy D. Knapp. *Iroquoian Archaeology and Analytic Scale*. Knoxville: University of Tennessee Press, 2009.

Morgan, Lewis Henry. *League of the Iroquois*. New York: Corinth Books, 1962.

Mullen, Grant J., and Robert D. Hoppa. "Rogers Ossuary (AgHb-131): An Early Ontario Iroquois Burial Feature from Brantford Township." *The Canadian Journal of Archaeology/ Journal Canadien d'Archeologie*, Vol. 16, (1992): 32-47.

O'Callaghan, E. B., ed. *The Documentary History of the State of New York*. 4 vols. Albany: Weed, Parsons and Co., 1849-1851.

Parker, A. C., *Iroquois Uses of Maize and Other Food Plants*. Albany: New York State Museum, Bulletin 144, 1910.

--, writing as Gawasco Wanneh. *An Analytical History of the Seneca Indians*, 1926. Researches and Transactions of the New York State Archaeological Association, Lewis H. Morgan Chapter. New York: Kraus Reprint Co., 1970.

Parker, Arthur C. *Seneca Myths and Folk Tales*. Lincoln: University of Nebraska Press, 1989.

Richter, Daniel. *The Ordeal of the Longhouse. The People of the*

Iroquois League in the Era of European Colonization. Chapel Hill: University of North Carolina Press, 1992.

Snow, Dean. *The Archaeology of New England*. New York: Academic Press, 1980.

—. *The Iroquois*, Oxford: Blackwell, 1996.

Spittal, W. G. *Iroquois Women: An Anthology*. Ontario, Canada: Iroqrafts, Ltd., 1990.

Talbot, Francis Xavier. *Saint among the Hurons. The Life of Jean De Brebeuf.* New York: Harper and Brothers, 1949.

Tooker, Elizabeth, ed. *Iroquois Culture, History, and Prehistory*. Albany: The University of the State of New York, 1967.

Trigger, Bruce. *The Children of Aataentsic: A History of the Huron People to 1660*. Montreal: McGill-Queen's University Press, 1987.

Trigger, Bruce, ed. *Handbook of North American Indians. Vol. 15: Northeast*. Washington: Smithsonian Institution Press, 1978.

Tuck, James A. *Onondaga Iroquois Prehistory. A Study in Settlement Archaeology*. New York: Syracuse University Press, 1971.

Wallace, Anthony F.C. *The Death and Rebirth of the Seneca*. New York: Vintage Books, 1972.

Walthall, John A., and Thomas E. Emerson, eds. *Calumet and Fleur-de-Lys. Archaeology of the Indian and French Contact in the Midcontinent*. Washington: Smithsonian Institution Press, 1992.

Weer, Paul. *Preliminary Notes on the Iroquoian Family*. Prehistory Research Series. Indianapolis: Indiana Historical Society, 1937.

Whitehead, Ruth Holmes. *Stories from the Six Worlds. Micmac Legends*. Halifax: Nimbus Publishing, 1988.

Williamson, Ronald F., and Susan Pfeiffer. *Bones of the Ancestors. The Archaeology and Osteobiography of the Moat-field Ossuary*. Gatineau, Quebec: Canadian Museum of Civilization, 2003.

Printed in the USA
CPSIA information can be obtained
at www.ICGtesting.com
LVHW031403230824
789088LV00016B/291